PRETTY LITTLE THING

PRETTY LITTLE THING

KIT DUFFIELD

THOMAS & MERCER

Published by Thomas & Mercer, Seattle

www.apub.com

Amazon, the Amazon logo, and Thomas & Mercer are trademarks of Amazon.com, Inc., or its affiliates.

ISBN-13: 9781662521546
eISBN: 9781662521539

Cover design by Tom Sanderson
Cover image: © Suzanne Tucker © KRIT GONNGON / Shutterstock; © Stephen Mulcahey / Arcangel

Printed in the United States of America

For Ben, my oldest friend

1998

At night, when the house is sleeping, that's when I hear the little laugh.

Thin and gurgling, like a baby's.

My eyes are open, but I cannot move. My throat is closed tight.

'Beckett?' Mumma's footsteps in the hall, at my door. 'Are you awake?'

I never know if I'm awake.

'You've disturbed your father again, Beckett.' Her shape is in the doorway. 'Making the most awful noises.'

She sits on the bed and my covers go tight. I try to talk, but all that comes out is a nasty groan.

'Shush, now. It's all in your imagination.'

Mumma's voice sounds wrong. Muffled, like she's buried in a box.

'Don't be silly, now,' she says, far away from me. 'Look at me. You're safe in your bed.'

But I'm not looking at Mumma. I'm looking past her, into the corner of my room, at the two eyes shining in the dark.

2023

1.

I've always hated being watched.

I think it's the helplessness. You're not allowed to touch some-one without their permission, are you? But looking's different. People can look all they want.

Like this guy. Drinking Red Bull, spread over three train seats. Sizing me up through slitted eyes.

'This train is for Ashton Bay. The next station is Heaviport . . .'

Ignoring him, I gaze out of the window as the train passes through an archway of craggy, rust-coloured rock. I'd forgotten all about this final stretch of railway, a meandering branch line that clings to the coast while the sea churns away beneath you. Looking down, you feel like you're floating on water. Like you're arriving at the edge of the world.

'If you see anything suspicious, please report it to a member of staff . . .'

My eyes flick right. He's still staring at me.

Silly girl, my mother would say, *it's all in your imagination,* and my father would shake his head. *Not everything's about you, Beckett.*

Well, they might've said those things, if they hadn't both died last week.

'D'I know you?'

See, Mother. Now he's talking to me.

'Hey . . . girl.'

I'm feigning fascination with my phone, but he's not playing ball. I look up.

'Don't I know you?' he repeats.

'You don't.'

'I *do* know you,' he says, bobbing his head, like a pigeon. 'From that story in the paper. Picture of you, and all.'

I crinkle my brow. The story, I was expecting. But was a picture really necessary?

'You're fitter in real life.'

'*This station is Heaviport,*' intones the train-voice, and I rise from my seat.

'Can't believe it,' he continues, as I wheel my suitcase towards the doors. The train slows to a stop. 'You're that writer, Beckett wasserface. Beckett Ryan. Is it true y— hey, wait.'

I prod the exit button and the doors hiss open.

'It's true, ain't it?' he calls, as I step out into the cold. 'You killed your parents.'

2.

Heaviport, south coast. Gateway to the English Riviera.

The wheels of my suitcase crackle on the asphalt as I drag it from the station car park and into the town square, a drab little precinct lined with ice-cream parlours and souvenir shops. A light rain is falling and the air is heavy with the funk of algae and sea salt, mingled with a hint of chip fat. Jarring music wafts from the empty games arcade. Gulls circle in the sky.

It's almost exactly as I remember, and that's a depressing thought.

'Ay, where y'off to, gurl . . . ?'

Over the road, an old man is teetering against the pebble-dashed wall of the Wreckers Arms, pint glass clutched in his skinny fingers. He points in my direction and stretches his lips into a gummy leer.

'Where ya going, ma gurl?'

He flicks his drink at me, foam sloshing over the rim, and I push onwards, increasing my pace. I'm not certain I can rely on memory for this journey, so I pull out my phone and tap in the address. Outside the public toilets, splattered graffiti welcomes me home. *Hell is empty, all the devils are here.*

The road rises steeply after the arcade, winding its way past the bank, the post office and a parade of boarded-up buildings. The pavements are quiet, but not deserted, and I sense eyes on me as I walk: a stout, moody woman with shopping bags; two crisp-eating teenagers, chatting behind cupped hands.

You killed your parents.

Let's hope that's not the party line round here.

At the crest of the hill, the shops thin out, giving way to rows of identical terraced houses. Squat and filthy, blackened by exhaust fumes, they huddle together, watching me as I veer off the main road and into the tight backstreets of Heaviport's east end, a tangled rabbit warren of council homes and industrial estates. Each street is much like the last, but some feel distantly familiar and my internal map is regenerating as I go. By the time the corner of Umber Lane creeps into view, I have closed the map and pocketed my phone.

I'm just metres from the turning when something catches my eye. A high stone archway, set back from the road, guarding a sprawl of concrete buildings and a thirsty-looking playing field. I slow to a halt.

Heaviport Secondary School.

In the centre of the arch, etched into red stone, sits the school crest: a ship's anchor, bound with ropes. *A Better Future For All*, reads the motto.

Classes are in session, so the school's perimeter fence is locked, but I could climb that fence, easy. Grab the top rung and lift myself over, dropping on to the wet tarmac. Stride towards the main entrance, but before I make it there, I swerve to the right and head for the large room on the corner, the headteacher's office, and I can see his desk through the window, and I'm plunging my fist through the glass, shrieking at the pain, and the window hangs in bloodied shards as I drag my arm back out, watching my skin peel thickly from the bo—

Jesus, Beckett.

Enough.

I force out a breath and peer across the road into the Poundpusher mini-market. Shelves of wine bottles run the entire length of the shop.

My throat begins to tingle.

10

3.

LEANNE

I've dreamt about this moment for twenty years.

Beckett Ryan, in my town. So close I can see the phone in her back pocket.

As she reaches the far side of the road, a van stops at the traffic lights, blocking my view. I slide along the bus stop seat until I find her again, opening the door to Poundpusher's and pulling her suitcase inside. The case is very small, so she can't be staying long. My chest goes tight. I thought I'd get more time.

I'll have to make the most of her while I can.

She walks through the shop, looking left and right. She's had her hair cut, probably at one of those fancy salons where they bring you champagne. It's a pixie cut, short at the back but long at the front, so her fringe almost covers one eye. She flicks it away and I imagine her at book parties in London, surrounded by fans, admirers. Dressed in a long black ballgown.

A bus engine backfires. It makes me jump, and I lose Beckett behind the shelves. When the bus pulls in, I stare at the ground, counting the chewing gum blobs on the pavement.

'You getting on today, my love?'

I shake my head but don't look up. The bus driver mumbles something and shuts the doors.

When the bus has gone, I look into the shop again. Beckett is at the till with a bottle of wine. I don't know anything about wine, but I bet she's an expert. I bet she understands the different grapes, and doesn't even look at the price tag.

Beckett Diane Ryan only drinks the very best red wine.

BECKETT

This is the cheapest bottle of wine in the shop. I know, because I checked every one.

'Nine seventy-five, altogether,' says the shopkeeper, ringing the bottle through the till and placing it next to the five packets of microwave noodles I've stacked on the counter.

'Card?'

He shakes his head. 'Ten pound minimum.'

Unclipping my purse, I fish for change while he packs my wares into a blue plastic bag. As I'm rummaging, my eyes wander to the window, pausing on an A4 poster tacked to the glass. Hairs bristle on my arms.

MONDAY 20TH NOVEMBER, 7PM, HEAVIPORT TOWN HALL

AN OPEN FORUM TO DISCUSS THE LASTING LEGACY OF MR HAROLD
BECKETT RYAN, BELOVED HEADTEACHER AT HEAVIPORT SECONDARY
AND HIGHLY VALUED MEMBER OF THE COMMUNITY . . .

'Miss?'

I swallow hard.

'. . . Miss?'

The shopkeeper is watching me, brow folded. I pull a fistful of coins from my purse, but my hand is unsteady and they spray across the counter. Coppers roll off the edge and clatter on the floor.

Outside, I set my suitcase and shopping against the wall and press my fingertips into my eyeballs.

Breathe, now.

Focus on something. That empty bus stop across the road.

The lasting legacy of Mr Harold Beckett Ryan.

Don't foul it up for me, girl.

I stare at the bus stop until my vision pinholes. Until it's the only thing I can see, as if I'm floating in space. I count to ten.

Gradually, my heartbeat settles and the world seeps back in – the shopkeeper on a murmured phone call, the squawk of a seagull. I pick up my bags. Ahead, the sign for Umber Lane is calling out to me from a hedgerow.

I can't put this off forever.

I gaze up at Charnel House, into the murk of its windows, and it stares back at me, unmoved. All the houses on Umber Lane are grander than most in this town, but my childhood home is the grandest, big enough for a family of six, standing apart from its neighbours behind a rusting iron fence. Squarish and heavy-set, like a tank, it dominates its quiet corner, a great hulk of grey masonry rearing up against the sky.

I hold tight to the handle of my suitcase, taking it all in. The broad front door, a shock of blood-red mahogany in the shadow of a columned portico. The two-hundred-year-old stonework, beginning to show its age. The trio of windows spanning the first floor, almost tall enough to display a person head to foot.

It's been over a decade since I last stood on this garden path, but up in the master bedroom there's no expectant twitch of the curtain. No face at the glass.

I reach for the front door.

Inside, the house is bitterly cold. Puffing heat into my cupped hands, I scan the gloomy hallway, shapes forming around me. An empty coat rack. A dangling chandelier. To my right, a solid-looking door hides a room I half remember (a study, perhaps?) and with a flush of curiosity I reach for the handle. Then I notice the pattern on the antique brass knob – oddly ribbed, like a beached jellyfish – and pull away again.

I grope for a light switch. The chandelier sputters to life, casting a pallid glow across the hall, and my eyebrows climb. The house is not in a fine state. Dust cakes the furniture, mould speckles on skirting boards. In one high corner, a small hole yawns over me like the mouth of a child, and I peer up at it, wondering what might be happening behind the walls.

Black damp, slowly prickling.

A piercing ringtone is hammering my ears, suddenly and awfully, like the clang of an old fire bell. Turning, I find my parents' ancient rotary dial telephone sitting on a doily-clad table. I glare at it, unsure whether to answer, as if this is a phone call from the past.

'H . . . hello?' The receiver is cold against my skin.

'Miss Ryan?' She's well-spoken, with the hint of an accent. Asian, maybe.

'Speaking.'

'This is Baroness Jhaveri, from Anchora Park.' She lets her title sink in. 'A friend of your parents.'

The sentence feels wrong in my ear. I've never really thought of my parents as the kind of people who had friends.

'I was devastated by their deaths, Miss Ryan.'

'It's . . . call me Beckett.'

'You won't remember me, Beckett, but I've known Harold and Diane – I knew them – for many years. They were wonderful people.'

I finger the rubbery phone cord. 'Can I help you with something?'

'I wanted to make sure we'll be seeing you at next Monday's town meeting. It's in your father's honour.'

'Oh . . . right. I'm afrai—'

'As chair, I'll be presenting a proposal that may be of interest to you.'

'I have to get back to London.'

A loaded silence.

She clears her throat. 'Perhaps you don't fully appreciate how much your father did for this town. His death has saddened a great many people.'

I press a fist to my mouth. 'Thing is, uh . . . Baroness . . . I'm not visiting. I only came to settle my parents' affairs.'

'This concerns their affairs.'

The line goes quiet again. She lowers her voice. 'I don't wish to be indelicate, but some rather extreme allegations are being levelled in your direction, regarding their passing. Now that you're back, it may reflect poorly on you – among the community, I mean – if you don't attend.'

I glance around. The front door is still ajar, my suitcase untouched. I haven't even taken my coat off.

'How did you know I was here?' I ask, nudging the door closed with my foot. It shuts with a rusty click.

'This is Heaviport. People talk.'

I think of the shopkeeper and his murmured phone conversation. The baroness takes a sharp breath. 'Beckett?'

'Look, can't you just . . . fill me in now?'

'Not possible, I'm afraid. I have some details to finalise over the weekend.' She pauses. I notice what sounds like a grandfather clock in the background. 'Should we expect you at the meeting?'

I drop against the wall, fingers in my hair. 'Fine. I'll be there.'

'Good,' she says, her voice softening, ever so slightly. 'Seven p.m., Monday. Town hall. Goodbye.'

The call disconnects and I stare into the receiver, listening to the insect hum of the dial tone.

4.

Standing at the foot of the staircase, I pour the last of the wine into my glass. It's nearly one in the morning, but this is the closest I've come to the first floor all night.

I couldn't face it sober.

A wet stillness is hanging in the air, and as I scan the upstairs landing, I feel pressure inching over my shoulders. I wonder if I'm really alone, or if I might see a little girl – if I might see myself – lean out from behind a doorway, crack a smile, and disappear.

I close my eyes.

My mother was right.

That imagination is nothing but trouble.

The wine burns in my throat as I climb the stairs, listening to the hiss of my fingers against the banister. I can feel it above me, the weight of the house, the metal and the mortar. The rooms I least want to remember.

When I reach the landing, I pause, waiting for my eyes to adjust to the darkness. A green chest of drawers is pressed against the wall in front of me, topped with a vase of long-dead flowers. A liver-spotted mirror reflects my shadowy form. To the left is the bathroom, with its peach-coloured tub. I knew these things, once. I remember.

And then, their bedroom.

Dim and vast, it's like a film set between takes, waiting for the actors to return. My mother's slippers are still underneath the dresser, one turned on its side. A leather belt hangs over a chair. The towering four-poster bed is unkempt, covers ruched on the mattress.

The hospital told me that was where they both died.

I'm not sleeping in there.

This house has many rooms, but at the grand old age of thirty-two, I refuse to sleep on the floor all weekend, and that leaves me only one choice.

Pivoting, I squint into my childhood bedroom. The wine is fogging my vision, so the doorframe has a ghostly mirror image on each side of it, like it's one of those riddles where you have to pick the right door, or plummet to your death. *Eeny, meeny, miny, moe.*

Inside, the dainty single bed sits neatly against the far wall, perfectly made, as if it's been waiting that way since the day I left. I press a cool palm to my forehead and squeeze my eyes shut.

It's only falling asleep, Beckett.

You've done this thousands of times before.

Eyes open.

Darkness looms above me. I'm rigid in the bed, limbs set in concrete. I feel like I haven't moved a single inch in hours.

My skull is pounding, throat dry, and when I run my tongue around my mouth, I taste metal. Rolling over, I find the offending wine glass on the bedside table, speckled with red dots, like splatter at a crime scene.

Then, through the distorted prism of the glass, I see something across the hall, in my parents' bedroom, that slows the blood in my veins.

There are shapes in the bed.

Shapes of people.

No, come on.

I'm half asleep, still a bit drunk, and I'm seeing things. Pulling in a breath, I blink a few times and grit my teeth, a memory from last night forming in my mind. *Yes, that's right.* I remember peering into the master bedroom, before I went to sleep, and finding the covers bunched up on the mattress – and now I'm seeing them again and my brain is jumping the gun. There really is no one there.

So why is there a foot moving under the duvet?

No.

'No!' I say out loud, surprising myself, a boozy cough hacking out of me. I swing my feet off the bed and sit upright. It's dumb, but if I don't do this now, I'll be awake all night.

Unfurling like a rusty droid, I pad from the bedroom and make my way along the landing, keeping my gaze low. Past the green chest of drawers, and the dead flowers. My shadow crossing the mirror.

At the threshold of the master bedroom, I stop, one hand on the wall. Pulse throbbing. *Nearly there, little Beckett. Just look up. We've been waiting for you.*

I lift my head and my shoulders relax. The bed is empty. Exactly as it has been, for almost a week.

Now that I'm closer, I can see where my mother must have lain in the hours before she died. Her small indentation is still there in the greying sheets, a sad, bean-shaped curve like a hospital kidney dish.

I hang my head.

What were you expecting, exactly?

Of course they're not in here.

How could they be, when in less than seven hours' time I'll be sitting in a room full of strangers, watching them burn?

5.

LEANNE

I pull my hair in front of one eye to see if it makes me look like her. Press it against the socket, like an eye patch.

I imagine myself on television, or at a press conference. Reporters are asking me questions. *Did you get a haircut? Are you working on a new novel?*

I frown into the mirror, blushing. This is a waste of time. My hair's too light, too boring . . . *muddy blonde*. Not dark and mysterious like Beckett's. I'm not pretty enough for her hairstyle anyway, and I couldn't answer questions at a press conference.

I'd be sick with worry. Sick all over myself.

I turn to my bed, where my black clothes are lying in a messy heap. I'm being selfish, today of all days. Beckett must be heartbroken right now, and she has no one to care for her. She's all on her own in that big house, waiting for a funeral, and I'm fussing over my hair like a schoolgirl. I smooth down the creases in my pencil skirt and take a deep breath. Maybe I can't do much to help her today, but I can try. I can be a good friend.

I think about my mum and dad, sitting on their manky old sofa, not talking. I don't much like my parents, but I'll still be sad when they die. And Beckett has to say goodbye to both of hers on the same day. I just can't imagine how she must be feeling.

BECKETT

My black Converse slap the tarmac as I hurry across the car park towards Heaviport crematorium, sweat beading at my hairline. A clock above the entrance reads 11.10.

I'm late.

I tramp through a puddle, distracted, and rainwater splatters my trousers. My head swims unpleasantly. Hungover and sleep-starved, I stumbled from the house without charging my phone and it died on the way here, leaving me lost in a labyrinth of side streets. The crematorium is all the way across town, back past the school and deep into Heaviport's west end, and I ended up half jogging most of it, tired limbs protesting every step. I'd been hoping that my late arrival would be masked by other stragglers, but on my approach to the chapel entrance there are none to be seen.

Holding a palm to the door, I shut my eyes and hear my father's voice, close and low inside my skull.

Try to behave, Beckett.

Don't make me tell you twice.

Inside, the building is packed to the rafters. Bodies are pressed against bodies, every seat filled, and yet the place is bathed in a reverent silence. As I pass down the aisle, there's a furtive sweep of eyeballs in my direction, like a field full of corn stalks leaning in the wind.

'There's the daughter,' comes a whisper from my right.

'Surprised she'd dare show her face.'

'Is she wearing jeans?'

Frowning, I scan the room for a space and find a solitary gap on a nearby row. I gesture at the lady on the end and she makes me wait for a second or two before shuffling sideways, causing a ripple effect all the way down the pew. I sink down next to her, nodding thanks, but she just stares at me. Then she turns to her husband and says something low and taut that I can't quite hear.

Unbuttoning my coat, I glance around the building, eyes skating along the rows of heads. There must be two hundred people in this room, maybe more. Tissues are being passed about, handkerchiefs unfolded, and there's a delicate tension in the air, like a held breath. At the business end of the chapel, two coffins lie side by side on a large wooden plinth, their brass fittings gleaming in the wintry sunshine. I examine them, curiously. They're always so shockingly large, aren't they, coffins? Like Viking longboats.

A memory stirs. A recurring memory; one of the very few I have from those early years at Charnel House. Sometimes, if I made enough noise during my night terrors, my mother would slip into my room and sit on the bed. But when she spoke, her voice would sound muffled, far away, as if she were buried in a box.

Shush now, Beckett. Don't be silly. It's all in your imagination.

'Miss Ryan?'

'Jesus!' I exclaim, shocked at the sudden voice in my ear. A plump lady with kind eyes is standing next to me, Bible pressed to her bosom. She rests a hand on my shoulder.

'Not quite,' she says, with a muted smile. 'More like . . . his representative.'

I blink at her, baffled.

'Reverend Worcester,' she adds. 'We spoke on the phone?'

'Yes, of course.' I pin a clammy hand to my brow. 'Sorry, Reverend.'

'Not at all. But we're about to start, so . . .' She glances left and right. 'Would you like to sit in the front row? I've reserved a spot for you.'

My gaze ricochets from one coffin to the other, and for a second I consider it. The Ryans, reunited at last.

'Don't worry,' I reply, hugging my arms to my chest. 'I'm fine here.'

With a bow of her head, the reverend peels off towards the altar, nodding at familiar faces on the way. I lean back against the hard wood of the pew, ears pinking at stares from the congregation. People are really watching me, now. Evaluating.

Then something catches my eye. Across the aisle, hemmed in among tall, sombre-looking men in grey coats, a petite woman with dirty blonde hair is giving me a sweet, sad smile. I have no idea who she is, but it's weirdly comforting.

When I return the smile, her entire face lights up.

As the reverend backs away from the altar, hugging her Bible, the coffins sink in agonising tandem. A brittle silence has been hanging over the room like a sheet of glass, but when the flower-laden caskets finally disappear from view, it's shattered by a hollow cry, then the sound of sobbing.

And not just from one person. In front of me, all around. Even the reverend looks dewy-eyed.

Part of me feels indignant. *You didn't really know them, did you? Any of you.* But maybe they have every right to feel this way. They're gathered here in this soulless building, draped in black, holding each other's hands, while two people they loved and respected are being lowered into a raging furnace.

I just wish, standing among these foreign bodies, these people who held Harold and Diane Ryan in the highest of regard, that I felt even a trace of their sadness.

'I'd like to say a few words,' comes an unexpected voice from across the chapel, and all heads swivel, bird-like, to its owner. A woman in her late forties is clutching a wad of tissues to her chest, a glum-looking child at her side. Her eyes are circled red. 'Is . . . is that OK?'

From her station by the back wall, Reverend Worcester nods, hesitantly at first, and then more emphatically. 'Um, yes . . . yes, of course, Joanne. Of course it is.'

Joanne takes a quivering breath, her gaze shooting about as she realises how large her audience is. She rubs an eye with the heel of her hand.

'I don't . . . I wasn't planning to do this, but I think I have to.' Her voice is cracking. Her young son, embarrassed and confused, buries his face in her thigh. 'My eldest, Harvey, really wanted to be here, but he can't, 'cos he's in Scotland . . . he's at uni in Edinburgh, and I couldn't afford to fly him down . . .' She looks at the floor, shakes her head. 'A-anyway, the point is, he really wanted to be here today because Mr Ryan – Harold – changed his life.'

An expectant hush. Joanne tucks a lock of hair behind her ear.

'Harvey was a difficult little boy, and when he got to Heaviport Secondary, he could barely read. Everyone had written him off, to be honest, and I couldn't— I mean, I'm a single parent, I didn't know what to do. But Harold did. He saw something in Harvey, looked out for him, worked him hard, gave up evenings and week-ends for him, and now my son—' She breaks off, tears cresting in her eyes. A friend curls an arm around her shoulder. 'Harvey's got a future now, and that never would've happened without his headteacher.' She lets out a relieved sigh, smiling through the tears. 'That's all I wanted to say.'

Murmurs of agreement percolate around me, and scattered claps snowball into applause. Joanne's son looks up at his mother and smiles.

'I've something to say an' all,' comes a different voice, croaky and loud, from behind us. Shoes squeak on the floor as everyone turns to find an old lady sitting in a wheelchair, blanket over her lap. 'We're from the old folks' home, up on the hill.' There are four of them, the old folks, flanked by two uniformed members of staff. 'I'll tell you now, that Harry Ryan—' *Harry?* '—he was a Bobby Dazzler.' Warm laughter from the congregation. The atmosphere is loosening. 'He'd come up and read to us, once a month, and we loved it. None of these "modern" writers, mind – load of rubbish, Harry said – but the classics, *Wuthering Heights* and Charles Dickens, and it was wonderful. I'd give him a knighthood if it were up to me.'

Hearty laughter, more applause. Even a tentative whoop. This funeral is beginning to feel like a chat show.

'I want to say something too.'

Heads turn left.

I feel a pang in my chest.

'My name's Simon, Simon Slater.' A young voice, this time, a teenaged boy. He's standing in one of the front rows in an ill-fitting suit. 'Some of you probably think I'm a bit of a shit—' he's smiling when he says this, and it raises pockets of laughter '—but truth is, I dunno where I'd be without Mr Ryan.' He focuses on his shoes. 'I was crap at school, and a right twat as well, always mucking around, but . . . he didn't treat me like everyone else did, like I was trouble. He reckoned I must be good at something, and I said I wanted to be a tree surgeon, and before he got ill, he got me on this apprenticeship . . . and . . . thing is—' He falters, and for a split second I think he's going to cry as well, but he sniffs it back. 'My old man left when I was a baby, so I never really had a dad, but Mr Ryan, he . . . he looked after me like I was his own kid.'

Something hits me in the gut, hard and fast, like a battering ram. I clutch at my stomach, short of breath. It's like I've been hit, but no one's touched me. No one was even looking at me.

My head spins.

Is this what grief feels like? Like you've been hit by a crossbow?

Leaning on the end of the pew, I glance back towards the chapel entrance, my vision beginning to cloud. I can't be in here anymore. I have to leave.

LEANNE

Tears are running down my face, all my tissues used up. My eyes are stinging.

I'm not crying for Harold and Diane, though. Or Joanne Withers, or Simon Slater. I'm crying for her.

'Uh . . . well, thank you for your kind words, everyone,' says the reverend, as the whole room watches Beckett push through the chapel doors. 'If you'd like to open your programmes, we'll end today's service with the hymn on page four, "Abide With Me" . . .'

The doors swing shut behind her. A sad organ starts to play.

'Excuse me . . . sorry, excuse me.' I'm squeezing past the people in my pew, forcing them back. They're whispering about me, but I don't care. I head for the doors.

I think I know where she's going.

6.

BECKETT

The sea air nips at my cheeks as I head for the coast, body bent against the wind. It's quiet up here, close to the cliffs, and I'm walking in the middle of the road, fists balled in my coat pockets.

He looked after me like I was his own kid.

I can still picture Simon Slater's boyish face, ham pink in the glare of the chapel lights. He meant every word of that monologue – they all did – but the person they were eulogising, that wasn't my father. That was some figment of the town's imagination.

Harry Ryan, Bobby Dazzler.

Always there when you needed him.

I stop to lean against a fence post, lungs billowing. Something bubbles up at the base of my throat – a scream, or a sob, I'm not sure – and I squeeze my eyes shut, pushing it down. I count in my head, shapes floating behind my eyelids, and by the time I've reached ten, the feeling has ebbed.

I wipe a cold hand across my brow and it comes away wet. The weather has turned, the mid-morning sunshine giving way to a petulant drizzle, and dark clouds are threatening, but I'm not going back to Charnel House. Not yet. After leaving the crematorium, I retraced my steps towards Umber Lane and then carried on further east, over the railway and up Shotts Lane, an old farm track, following my nose as the landscape grew wider, the air clearer. Heartfelt praise for my father ringing in my ears.

From where I'm standing now, I can just about hear the ocean, foaming and churning in the distance. The fence post I'm leaning on is attached to a stile, and my inner compass is telling me that a stomp through the swampy field beyond will take me to the precipice, to the red cliffs of Heaviport. I'm not exactly sure why I'm here, but it feels like some invisible force is dragging me, and I'm willing to let it. Anything but that house, for an hour or two, until I clear my head.

Mud splatters my sneakers as I trudge up the field, which takes a steep rise before levelling out to an exposed plain, where the wind whips and twists around me like an impatient child. I can see the vista of the English Channel now, choppy and dark, and a lighthouse stands lonesome against the bone-white sky.

As I move closer, it becomes clear that the lighthouse is out of use and has been for years. Many of its windows are smashed, and its paintwork is missing in large, rusty patches. Where there used to be a door is now only a hole, gaping like a toothless mouth.

I stare hard through the doorway, straining to make out details. I've been here before, I'm sure of it.

WARNING

Landslides on cliff edge

KEEP AWAY!

Beside the lighthouse, a metal warning sign leans at a despondent angle, as if aware of its own failure – people have been here, and recently, too, judging by the crumpled beer cans and ash rings in the grass. Taking my chances, I make my way past the sign and head for the cliff edge, the briny reek of the sea filling my nostrils. This close to the precipice, the wind is even sharper, dancing around me with a girlish moan. Goosebumps blossom on my arms.

'Hello.'

A soft voice startles me from behind. Turning, I find the petite woman from the chapel, the one with the sad smile, standing by the warning sign. My jaw levers open. 'H-hello,' I reply, although it sounds more like a question than a greeting. What on earth is she doing up here? We're over a mile from the crematorium. 'You were at the funeral.'

She tilts her head, gaze riveted on mine. It's her turn to speak, but she doesn't seem to realise.

'I'm Beckett,' I add, and she nods.

'Beckett Diane Ryan.'

I feel the urge to step back, but I'm dangerously close to the edge. 'What was your name?'

She wrinkles her nose at this, as if I've said something funny. 'Leanne.'

I paw my damp fringe from my face, studying her. Her straggly, cappuccino-coloured hair frames doe eyes and elfin features, and her delicate skin is freckled, like a child's. She's pretty, but she doesn't know it.

I cast a look over her shoulder. 'You could've stayed if you wanted. There's a wake at the cricket club.'

'I know,' she says, stepping forward. 'I wanted to make sure you were OK.'

That's kind of sweet, I think, at first. But she seems to have appeared from the direction of the lighthouse, as if she were here before me. As if she knew I was coming this way. 'How did you know I'd be here?' I ask, trying to sound conversational but failing.

Leanne's cheeks redden. 'Oh, it's . . . well . . . it's sort of a long story.'

'Try me. I like stories.'

'I know, I've read all your books.'

I side-eye her, lifting my shoulders against the cold. 'I'm sorry, have we me—'

'Met?' she pre-empts, unable to quell a smile. Then she closes the gap between us, lowering her voice as if sharing a deep, dark secret. 'Of course we've met, Beckett. I'm your best friend.'

7.

LEANNE

'You're . . . sorry, what?'

Beckett looks shocked. I've said the wrong thing, already. 'W-wait, no.' I scrunch my fists. 'That probably sounds crazy.'

She doesn't reply.

'What I mean is: I *was* your best friend. When we were little.'

Her eyebrows jump up. 'Right, right.' She laughs. 'Sorry . . . I thought you might be a maniac.'

I know she doesn't mean that, but it hurts. 'We were at school together,' I say, pulling my hair behind my ears. 'We sat next to each other every day.'

I wait. She's silent.

'W-we played games at break time, and you shared your packed lunch with me. We said we'd always stick together, even if . . .' I trail off. She's making a face. 'Don't you remember?'

'It's nothing personal, honestly. I only have a handful of memories from before I was sent away.'

I try not to panic. She'll remember again. She just needs time.

'So, listen—' Beckett is waving a hand at the abandoned lighthouse '—this long story you mentioned. You knew I'd come up here, after the funeral?'

'Uh-huh.'

'That's pretty fucking spooky, Leanne.'

I start to smile. I know it's not a good idea, but I can't help it.

'I'm not joking,' she says, and my smile drops.

'N-no, sorry . . . I . . .' I can feel my knee jiggling. I'm really messing this up. 'It's nothing like that.' I point to the lighthouse. 'This was our secret den, when we were kids. We used to come here all the time.'

She looks around, frowning. 'My parents let us play up here?'

'We told them we were at my house. And my mum and dad . . . well, they didn't care where I was.'

Beckett thinks for a while, watching me. 'So this place was, what . . . our clubhouse?'

I beam at her. 'Yes! *Our clubhouse.* Where we escaped to.' I look up at the lighthouse again. 'If you climb to the top of the building, to the old control room, there's a hatch you can lock from the top, so no one can get to you. That was our hideaway.'

Beckett narrows her eyes, like she's trying to remember.

I look across the water. 'Then, if we were ever angry or sad about something, we'd run down here and scream off the cliff edge. We thought if we shouted things loud enough, the wind would steal them away and throw them in the sea, and they'd be gone forever.'

A bird shoots into the black water, chasing a fish. I wait for it to come out again.

'Did it work?'

'Huh?' I turn back to Beckett. She's half smiling at me.

'Our little ritual. Did it work?'

'Oh . . . I don't know. Sometimes.'

She picks up a stone from the grass, rubs it with a thumb. 'Wonder if it'd do the trick for grown-ups,' she says to herself, throwing the stone over the edge.

I watch it fall. 'What do you mean?'

'No, nothing.' She shakes her head. 'You don't need to hear my problems.'

'Please. I want to.'

She almost starts to talk, but stops herself. She pushes a hand through her hair. 'Come on, Leanne, you're not a therapist. We're basically strangers.'

'Not . . . strangers,' I say, flicking at a thumbnail. My heart twists in my chest. *We're not strangers.*

'I'm tired, that's all. I can't sleep in that creepy old house.'

'Oh, really? I always thought it was beautiful.'

I used to love going to play at Charnel House. The big, echoey rooms. All the places to hide.

'I suppose it was, once. But when my father got ill, they let it go to seed. It's quite rundown.' She rubs her eyes. 'It needs a ton of work before it goes on the market, and I can't afford that.'

I crunch my forehead. 'What about all the money from your novels?'

Beckett goes very still. She glances towards town. 'I should be going,' she says, and I bite down on my tongue. I've done it again.

'I'm sorry, I didn't mean to pry—'

'No, it's fine. I just . . . I have some papers to go through back at the house. Dead parent stuff, you know.'

The rain is getting heavier. A fat droplet lands on my neck and rolls down my back. Beckett buttons her coat.

'Thanks, though,' she says, looking up. 'For coming to find me. I appreciate it.'

'That's OK. I don't mind.'

I'd do anything for you.

'Now—' she looks over my shoulder '—I wonder what the quickest route home is. Back the way I came . . . ?'

I've stolen something from you, Beckett.

'. . . Can't be, no. I went all the way up Shotts Lane on the walk here, which has to . . .'

I took something from you, when we were little, and I never gave it back.

'. . . then there's that old farm in the way, and you end up walking round it . . .'

One day, soon, I'll tell you about it. But not yet.

I need you to trust me first.

'Turn left after the stile,' I say, pointing, 'and you can take the main road straight to the railway bridge. You'll be home in twenty minutes.'

'Thanks.' She nods down the hill. 'You coming?'

I'm desperate to go with her. All I want is to be around her, but I have to be careful. I've already annoyed her with stupid questions, already embarrassed myself. If I want us to be friends, I have to act cool, like she does.

'Um, no. I might stay here a while . . . look at the birds.'

She gives me a curious look and flicks up her coat collar. 'Fair enough. See you around, then?'

'Sure,' I say, watching her as she passes. 'I'll see you around.'

8.

BECKETT

I am sprawled on the floor of my father's high-ceilinged, wood-panelled study, legs forked in front of me like an overgrown toddler. The bottom drawer of the filing cabinet is jutting open beside me, ageing bank statements fanning out across the floorboards. A sticky bottle of rum, pilfered from my parents' liquor cabinet, is nestled at my thigh.

I lift the bottle, rum sloshing thickly. I suspect I wasn't allowed in this room as a child, but I must have snuck in from time to time, because it feels familiar. The mottled green leather of the pedestal desk; the smoky scent of timber. The slight gap between the floor and the bottom of the door, just wide enough to betray a person stealing by.

I swig at the rum, and wince.

If you could see me now, Pops. Drinking your booze, snooping through your finances. That'd warrant a quick twist of my little arm, wouldn't you say? Just to crimson the skin. A warning shot.

My phone pings from beneath the pile of papers.

Zadie
Hope today wasn't too horrific. Thinking of you. Z x

Edging sideways, I lean against the filing cabinet and smile at the screen. I left London less than two days ago, but it already feels like a week.

Beckett
I've been to worse double-funerals. Though it has driven me to rum.

I gulp another sugary mouthful while Zade types her reply.

Zadie
How's the ol' hometown? They wicker-manned you yet?

Beckett
Not yet, but you should know . . . you've got competition.

Zadie
Don't tell me you've met someone else who can name all ten members of Blazin' Squad.

Beckett
As if. But you do have a rival in the best friend department.

Zadie
EXPLAIN.

I squirm against the sharp corner of the cabinet, thinking of my cliffside encounter with Leanne. The way she stood so still, waiting for me to speak. Her angelic face in the rain.

Beckett

She followed me after the funeral and told me we were bosom buddies at primary school. Knows my middle name and everything. I have zero memory of her.

Zadie

Sounds like a catch.

Beckett

She's definitely . . . unique. Possible stalker vibes. This is what happens when you never leave Heaviport.

I crane my neck to peer out of the bay window into the street, where parked cars are frosting over for the night. This town is unnervingly quiet after dark.

My screen lights up again.

Zadie

Do make sure she doesn't murder you. I mean, I don't care or anything, but I am TOO OLD to find another drinking buddy.

Beckett

I'm 70% sure she won't murder me.

Zadie

I'll take those odds. Night darl x

Beckett

Night x

I lock my phone and toss it back into the mess of bank statements. As it skims over a credit card bill, I'm reminded of why I'm sitting in this room in the first place. My situation is bad – I've known that for months – but an hour sifting through the Ryan finances has proved it to be even worse than I'd imagined.

Harold and Diane were hard-working, God-fearing people. They looked after their money, for the most part; kept within their means, nurtured their savings. But what wasn't spent on my father's in-home dementia care was donated early last week to a domestic abuse charity in Exeter, and though the will states that, as soon as practically possible, Charnel House is to be sold, the first £350,000 in proceeds will go straight to Heaviport Secondary School for the construction of a brand-new, state-of-the-art science department.

Then, and only then, will provision be made for Miss Beckett Diane Ryan, sole progeny of the deceased.

I think of the damp I've seen speckling the walls, the creaking and sighs I hear at night. This is a cold, neglected house. I don't know much about the property market, but Heaviport is hardly a boom town, and while this place is big, everything in it is decades out of date. Without a major facelift, will it ever fetch more than the cost of a new science lab?

Swivelling clumsily on my rear, I pick up a dog-eared sheet of paper from the pile and force myself to read it again. This one isn't my father's. This one I brought with me. A thick red bar throbs at the top of the page.

** MORTGAGE ARREARS ** MORTGAGE ARREARS **
Ref: Beckett Ryan, 108 Waldorf Rise, London W11 3VP

> Since September 2022, you have consistently failed to meet your mortgage repayments and your arrears have reached unacceptable levels. As

per the terms of the loan, we are now entitled to take action and therefore require a prompt and full settlement of the outstanding balance.

Failure to make this payment with immediate effect will leave us with no alternative but to repossess the property.

Seven years ago I signed my biggest book deal, a six-figure contract for the fantasy trilogy *Halloween Skies*. I even sold the film rights. Finding myself flush for the first time in my adult life, I bought a flat in Notting Hill – a tiny bolthole, far from glamorous, but expensive and desirable, a stone's throw from the Portobello Road. I had money and prospects at the time, and assumed that would never change. Until it did.

So when Charnel House is valued on Monday, I'll find out, one way or another, just how lost at sea I am. Just how many thousands of pounds I'll need to raise to save my boxy little home in London's flashiest borough. *Other people have real problems*, I hear my mother say, and she's right.

You always are, Mother.

I lift the rum again, shivering in the chilly air, and frown at the pirate on the label. She wouldn't approve of this, either. Spirits are unbecoming of a woman. I stopper the bottle.

If I want to stay warm tonight, I'll have to start a fire.

Standing on the bare stone floor of the utility room, I'm hugging my arms to my chest, squinting at my parents' decrepit gas boiler. Countless years old, it's like a prop from a steampunk theme park, a jumble of limescale-crusted pipes, furred vents and confusing dials.

I scan the frontage, face folded.

CALL THIS NUMBER FOR ASSISTANCE (OFFICE HOURS ONLY).

Looking up, I feel a tiny prick of joy at the sight of a small paper booklet – the instruction manual? – peeking out over the top. I reach up to grab it but, teetering on my tiptoes, fumble the corner and knock the booklet off into a narrow gap between the boiler and the wall. Snaking my arm into the space, I push through a mesh of spiky detritus, grimacing as it crackles around my fingers like old crisps. What am I touching here, I wonder? Cobweb nests, dead flies? Flakes of human skin?

Once I'm armpit deep, my fingertips brush the edge of the booklet. But as I shift my weight to pull it out, I make an alarming discovery.

Somehow, I'm stuck.

For some reason, this makes me laugh. I mean, it is kind of ridiculous. *Help me, Mumma.* But then someone else laughs too, and it stops being funny.

I whip my head around. 'Hello?'

That wasn't an adult laugh. It was a child's.

My arm still anchored to the boiler, I strain my eyes in the darkness, scanning for movement. The pale hint of flesh.

And then I feel something. Little chilly fingers, stroking mine.

'No!' I exclaim, panicking, yanking my arm free and grating my hand horribly against the jagged wall. Stumbling back and landing on my bum, I press my injured arm to my chest and let out a yelp as a family of insects swarm up my flank and hurry across my stomach. 'Get off . . . get *off.*' I bat them away with my good hand and they scatter into the darkness.

Pain fattens beneath my skin. I watch the blood bead up through the graze, like hatching tadpoles.

Eyes open.

Am I at home?

No.

This place is darker, cavern black. And it's *so cold*.

I try to sweep my arms outwards, to feel the sides of the mattress, but they don't move. I try to curl my toes, turn my ankles, but they're locked in – and that's when I remember. I'm in my childhood bed, upstairs at Charnel House. Panic pinches at my heart.

I shouldn't be in this bed. I shouldn't be here at all.

Around me, the watching house stirs, creaking like a moored boat. It knows I'm here, palsied, and it likes that. It shows me things.

Packets of flour in the pantry.

A crouched spider in a wastepipe.

You have to wake up, Beckett. You're not awake yet. None of this is real.

The angry red rock of the Heaviport cliffs, waves foaming over mucusy seaweed. A rusting anchor. The little girl who killed her parents.

You're dreaming, you're dreaming, you're dreaming.

My breathing quickens into a desperate, ragged pant, and I can taste blood on my tongue, feel clumps of food in my gut. I need to wake up. I need someone to wake me up.

Mumma?

A weight settles at my feet. The mattress bows and I feel that familiar tug on the covers as she sits, softly, to watch over me. I wait for her to speak. To tell me, in her muffled, distant voice: *Shush, now. It's all in your imagination.*

You're safe in your bed.

But her voice doesn't come.

Groaning hard, through my teeth, I force my head up to meet her gaze and find a hunched black form, perched on the edge of my bed. It has no eyes, no mouth. No hair. It watches me, faceless, and the groans die in my throat.

Silence cloaks the room.

The thing tilts its head, like a curious animal, and its neck crackles – the sound of someone stepping on dry firewood. The sound gets louder, closer, filling the room, and I can't breathe, I can't move. I can't scream. The creature's neck is bent at a ghastly angle, an impossible angle, and just as it seems like its skin is going to pop, it collapses on to the bed like a dropped sheet.

Free to move, suddenly, as if released from handcuffs, I desperately search the mattress, bracing for contact with another body. But there's nothing there at all. I'm completely alone in this house.

There was never anything there.

9.

It's Monday evening, four days after my arrival in Heaviport, and the town hall is bustling. Voices bark off the walls, spoons clink in drinks. Leanne and I have found a discreet place to sit – in the corner, near the back – but my presence hasn't gone unnoticed. Every twenty seconds or so, someone will zone out of their conversation and steal a secret look at me, veiled by the steam from their tea cup.

'Good evening, all, good evening,' comes a voice from the stage, over the frothing chatter. A tall, striking woman is standing at a lectern, surveying the crowd. 'I think we're ready to start, are we?'

The din fades.

I keep my eyes low.

'Welcome to the town hall, and tonight's open forum. For those who don't know me, I'm Baroness Jhaveri, and this meeting is a chance to remember the wonderful Harold Ryan, who sadly passed away earlier this month at his home on Umber Lane . . .'

Her voice is sonorous, commanding, but I'm struggling to concentrate. My head feels muddled and soupy. I barely slept again last night, and it wasn't just the rum.

I'm seeing things in the dark.

'. . . As you may have heard, in an act of extraordinary generosity, Harold pledged a substantial sum from his estate towards the construction of a new science department at Heaviport Secondary.'

Warm, gentle applause. 'The proposed development will transform the school, which has long suffered from outdated equipment and insufficient teaching space, and the benefits will be felt for generations. In honour of this, a plaque on the building will pay tribute not only to Harold but to his father, Wallace, and grandfather Beckett, all of whom served as headteachers at the school and were celebrated in the area for their volunteer work and social activism.'

At the mention of my namesake, Great-grandfather Beckett, I sense a faint shuffling of bodies around me. The name seems to hover in the air above my head.

'But beyond that,' continues the baroness, 'I'd like to discuss how we, the people, might best honour Harold's commitment to the town. The Ryan family are in Heaviport's DNA and it is our duty to ensure this legacy endures, just as Harold and his beloved wife, Diane, would have wanted.'

Beloved wife.

'So thank you all for coming.'

I turn to Leanne, sitting beside me with hands folded in her lap. I catch her eye and she smiles.

'I'll open the floor to your thoughts in just a moment, but I'm going to start with a proposal of my own that I believe may go some way to achieving our aims here.' The baroness raises a level palm to her forehead, shielding her eyes. 'Ken, could you dim the lights?'

The invisible Ken does his duty, and the hall fades into half-light.

'Take a look at this photograph.' On a screen at the back of the stage, a fuzzy image appears. My father, his shirt and tie loosened, is kicking a football around a field with a gaggle of excited-looking children. Behind him, there's bunting and what looks like a cake stall. 'Some of you may remember that day – July, nineteen-ninety . . . nine, I believe it was? This picture was taken during one of a number of fundraising events Harold organised to raise money for a local children's charity, and you can see, from the look on his face, just how much this kind of philanthropic work meant to him . . .'

July, 1999

'Mumma, why isn't Daddy here?'

I'm at the kitchen table, eating breakfast.

'I told you, he'll be at the school all day.' Mumma is standing at the sink. I can hear her voice through her back.

'But it's a Saturday.'

The new story I've made is on the table, next to my cereal bowl. It took me four weeks to write, and I've drawn a cover on it, so it looks like a real book. 'I want him to read my story.' I chase a soggy cornflake around the bowl with my spoon. 'Will he read it when he gets home?'

'He'll be too tired.'

'He's *always* too tired.'

Mumma goes very still. Then she takes off her yellow washing-up gloves and turns around.

'Do you know what your father's doing today?' she says, pointing down the hallway towards the front door. I shake my head. 'He's at that school, on his day off, running a fundraiser for a charity. A charity that helps little children in need. Not children like you, who live in big houses and have everything they want, but children who are poor, and lonely, and have nothing. Do you understand?'

I nod, staring at the lines in the table.

'And actually, Beckett . . . about your stories.' Mumma lets out a long breath, like she's sad. 'We have to talk.'

I look up, blinking. Mumma folds her gloves and puts them by the sink.

'Your father thi— we think you should stop writing them.'

45

I scrunch my eyebrows. 'Why?'

'We just think, all the witches and pixies—'

'*Trolls*, Mumma.'

'Whatever they are, that's what's giving you nightmares.'

They don't know anything. They don't know anything about my nightmares.

'That's bullcrap.'

'I beg your pardon?' Mumma's back goes all straight. 'Where did you hear that word?'

'I don't get nightmares because of my *stories*. They make me feel better.'

'Your father says—'

'How would he know anything?' I shout, crashing my fist into my cereal bowl, making it flip over and spill. 'He's never read my stories. He wouldn't know because *he's never read them!*'

I try not to cry, because I'm supposed to be grown-up now, but I can feel my eyes getting wet.

Mumma is breathing very quickly.

Milk is dripping off the table, and it makes me think of sick.

Brrrnnnngg.

Someone's phone is going off.

'Can we have phones on silent, please?' says the baroness, from the stage. 'I'd like to think we can survive forty-five minutes without *Candy Crush*.'

Patches of laughter. Another *brrrnnnngg*.

People are throwing glances in my direction, so I press a hand against my pocket and wince. 'Sorry. Sorry . . .'

I slide the phone out. It's my agent. Declining the call, I switch it to silent. Moments later, a text appears.

'I'm sorry, but I really can't take any more of this.' A man has stood up, a few rows in front of us, his hands raised in the air.

'I haven't actually opened the floor yet, Joseph,' says the baroness. Joseph flexes his jaw.

'I know that, and I'm sorry, but I have to say something before we go any further.' He rotates round and his eyes settle on me. 'I think we should all stop pretending she isn't here.'

The people of Heaviport follow Joseph's lead, and soon I'm the centre of attention. A roomful of blinking faces, twisted towards me.

'Joseph . . .' The baroness steps away from her lectern. 'I'm not sure this is the time or the pl—'

'If you don't know me, I'm Joseph Arnold; my wife and I run the coffee shop on the seafront. I also write for the local paper and, well, many of you will have read my article this month.' A few people clap, and some cheers of approval vault through the air. Joseph turns to me again. 'Miss Ryan, this might seem strange to you, but your parents' sudden passing has affected every last person in this room. We are all grieving. And while I don't wish to be vindictive, you really ought to know . . .' He folds his hands at his belt. 'You should know that we hold you responsible.'

A hum of consensus sweeps the hall. I fire a glance at the baroness, but she's retreated to the side of the stage, hand over her mouth.

I take a deep breath.

'Your father was wasting away with dementia for, what – four years?' continues Joseph, eliciting jeers from all around. 'And as far as I can tell, you didn't visit him once.' The hum is building to a clamour, and people are beginning to throw taunts at me. 'Worse, when Harold died and your mother was left alone in the world, even then you refused to come, only turning up a week too late, after the grief had driven her to suicide. Your parents cared profoundly for this town, and you had a responsibility to care for *them*, but clearly, you never have. Sure, you deigned to take time out of your no doubt busy writing schedule to turn up to their funeral, but you didn't even stay for the wake.' He pushes a hand through his hair. 'If you ask me, she's only back for one reason. To cash in on the house.'

This sparks a baying cacophony, voices echoing off the high ceiling, and I sense a hive-like movement towards me, a shrinking of my personal space.

I rise to my feet. 'Look, I get that you're all angry, and I can tell my father meant a lot to you, but—'

'You swan back here, thinking you're too good for us, but you don't know anything about this town.' This is a new person now. Could be anyone, to be honest. I'm surrounded. 'Maybe if you'd spent less time at poncey media parties and more time with your own flesh and blood, they'd still be alive today . . .'

'Why don't you go back to London?'

I try to speak, to form words, but nothing comes. My jaw feels wired shut. Because maybe these people are right. My father's death certificate may list a stroke, my mother's suicide, but that's only half the story. It's been more than ten years since I came home to visit.

And loneliness kills.

'Don't you have anything to say?'

'They're dead because of you . . .'

After that, the insults descend into shapeless noise, people yelling, shoes squeaking on varnished wood. I push my fingers into my temples, pressure building inside my head, and images skitter across my mind like a broken movie reel. The Heaviport anchor, dripping and green. A puddle of spoiling milk. The black shapes of my parents in bed, writhing and thrusting.

Two burning coffins, a muffled voice beneath the flames.

This is what you get, you little cunt.

'Shut up, shut up, shut up!'

A woman's loud voice, right on the edge of a shriek, cuts through the noise. Disoriented, I look ahead, towards the stage. That can't be the baroness, surely?

Then the voice comes again. 'Shut up, all of you!'

Beside me, Leanne is standing on her chair, fists clenched. She has stunned the hall into silence. 'You're all . . .' Her chest heaves with the effort, her face dappled red. 'You're all being unfair.'

Her balled hands are trembling.

A solitary cough breaks the hush.

'Y-you don't know anything about Beckett,' she continues, stammering, looking very small, despite her high perch. 'You've got no right to judge her. Just . . . leave her alone. Leave her alone.'

An odd stillness has settled over the room. Fists still bunched, Leanne glares downwards, unblinking, and for a passing moment I think of a gargoyle watching over a crumbling stately home.

'Can we move on, please?' suggests the baroness, from the stage. She has returned to her lectern. 'This is a town meeting, not a slanging match.'

She directs this comment at Joseph, who is sitting straight-backed in his chair, eyes dark pinpricks.

'As I was saying . . .'

When Leanne is settled in her seat, I reach over and lay a hand on her thigh. 'Thank you,' I whisper, unsteadily, and she stares in wonder at my hand on her leg, as if it were a precious bird that had landed there.

'. . . said was entirely helpful, Joseph did mention the potential sale of Charnel House, Harold and Diane's home, and that's actually what I wanted to speak to you all about this evening.'

As calm blankets the hall, my lungs pump like bellows behind my chest. No one's watching me anymore, but I can still hear whispers, hissing off the walls.

'Currently, Charnel House remains in the ownership of the family, as it has done for generations. But plans are afoot to put the property on the market, as per Harold's wishes, and with this in mind, I have a proposal that I hope will benefit a great many people for years to come.'

A murmur or two trickles through the audience; people fidget in their seats. Headlights from a passing car sweep the room.

'We know that Harold was deeply troubled by the plight of disadvantaged children in Heaviport, and that he found the provision of council protection for those children to be severely lacking.' The baroness tracks her gaze across the hall, taking in each and every person. She raises a finger. 'I believe that, as a community, we can change that. We have a unique opportunity here to honour the legacy of a remarkable man while also investing in the future of this town, and of its youth.' Her hands curl around the edges of the lectern. 'Friends, I propose that, should it suit Miss Ryan's wishes, we acquire the property and work together to open a brand-new institution – the Heaviport Care Home For Children and Young People, situated in the former residence of one of the town's proudest inhabitants.'

Approval ripples through the building, heads nodding, people leaning in close to share thoughts.

The baroness raises her voice. 'Of course, many of you may wonder where the capital for this venture will come from, given the poor health of the local coffers. So to allay any fears, I am pledging to fund the project myself, at least in the early stages.'

The noise swells, then breaks into clapping, and the baroness allows herself a modest nod.

I stare up into the lofty, vaulted ceiling.

A children's home.

'Thank you,' says the baroness, over the continuing applause, 'thank you for your enthusiasm.'

My ears ringing with the sound, I think about the fundamental flaw in Baroness Jhaveri's plan, and what she'll say when she finds out.

'I'm delighted to have your support. It really will make all the difference . . .'

I had the house valued this morning. The agent plodded the floorboards, sniffing at mould patches, twisting taps, his mouth turned down at the corners. He tossed me a figure at the end, with all the enthusiasm of a fast-food cashier, and my shoulders slumped.

Five thousand *under* Harold's science wing threshold.

'I'll have more details soon, and of course there'll be regulations to meet, health and safety and so on, but I'm confident we can weather those storms . . .'

Whatever happens now, I will lose my flat. Which means I can either be homeless in London, or I can stay here, imprisoned in Charnel House, the sole impediment to Heaviport's much-needed children's home. My neck heats up like an element.

'Any questions?'

Hands shoot skyward, and the baroness fields all kinds of queries about planning permission, safeguarding and environmental surveys. I can't focus, though, and barely register the answers.

Eventually, the meeting draws to a close.

'Once again, I'm extremely grateful to you all for attending tonight, and please, don't hesitate to contact me over the coming weeks with any ideas, questions or feedback. I do hope we can make this happen. Good night, all. Night.'

Hovering at the back of the room, I decide to wait for the rest of the congregation to file out before making my escape. Their eyes rake my face as they leave, lips tight.

When the hall is empty, I pull on my coat and turn to Leanne. 'Hey, thank y—'

'What happened to your hand?'

She's pointing at the nasty-looking scrape from last night.

'Oh, nothing. I had a fight with a domestic appliance.'

She pitches her head. 'I don't understand.'

'The boi— never mind.' I slip my hands into my pockets. 'Thanks again for sticking up for me tonight.'

'You don't need to thank me,' she says, looking at the floor.

I duck down to catch her eye. 'I do, actually. You saved my skin back there.' She allows herself a timid smile, and I hitch my handbag over my shoulder. 'It's been a relief to have someone on my side, these past few days. If I wasn't leaving tomorrow, I'd suggest we hang out.'

Her face opens, sadly. Those big, pretty eyes, like a helpless fawn. 'But wh—'

'Beckett.' A confident voice interrupts us from behind. We both turn.

'Can we talk?' says the baroness.

10.

The hot water urn is burbling at us, impatiently. The baroness lifts a cup and saucer from the table. 'Tea?'

I fight a yawn. 'Don't suppose there's coffee going, is there?'

'Of course you're a coffee drinker,' she replies, with a sly smile. 'You're an artiste.'

'Hardly. Just knackered.'

She sets down the tea cup. 'Wait here. I have a better idea.'

Sweeping across the hall, she pushes through a set of double doors into a kitchen and I am left alone in the large, empty space. I glance around at the rows of vacant chairs, the velvet-curtained stage and the rejected tea urn, and think about Leanne, looking over her shoulder at me before disappearing into the night. She seemed crestfallen that our brief courtship was over. But we exchanged numbers, and she said she'd call if she ever came to London, in that way people do. *I've always wanted to visit London.*

I'll probably never see her again.

'I knew there was something special in that back room . . .' The baroness's voice carries through from the kitchen as the doors swing open and she re-emerges, carrying a bottle of whisky. 'This was left over from the rotary club raffle.' She peels the foil from the neck. 'Are you a whisky girl?'

My throat tingles. 'Uh . . . sure. Why not.'

Pulling the cork with a soft pop, she slides a couple of tumblers across the table and pours two generous shots. We sit.

'To your good health, Beckett,' she says, lifting her glass.

'Thanks, uh—' *chink* '. . . I'm sorry, what do I call you, exactly? Is it "m'lady"?'

She laughs, warmly, and shakes her head. 'Just Nadia. Let's not stand on ceremony.'

'Nadia. Cheers.'

She leans back in her chair, considering me. 'So what did you think of my proposal?'

I'm halfway through a sip of whisky, and it sticks in my throat. I cough, pressing a fist to my mouth. 'It . . . well, it sounded great, it really did. And believe me, I do not want to come between the people of Heaviport and their philanthropy.'

'But?'

I set my drink on the table. 'It's not whether I *want* to sell the house. It's whether I can afford to.'

'Ah.'

I run my tongue around my teeth, catching the sharp taste of the whisky. Nadia watches me, expectantly.

'I've been having some . . . tough times, money-wise.' I let this fact hang for a moment, but her expression doesn't change. 'Truth is, my flat's about to be repossessed. I was hoping the sale of the house would get me out of that hole, but that'll only happen if it goes for a decent price.'

'And?'

'I had the house valued this morning, and to reach that price it'll need major renovation, which I can't afford.'

'I know.'

My brow crumples. 'You know . . . what?'

'I know you had the house valued, and I know what it's worth.'

'But I haven't tol—' I drop my head back, spilling a rueful laugh. 'Wait, don't tell me. This is Heaviport.'

She lifts her eyebrows. 'You're catching on.'

I pick up my drink. 'So, you see, I'm stuck. I either go back to London and sofa surf, or move into Charnel House and wait until I can afford to renovate it. Which would put the kibosh on your foster home.'

'You're on the horns of a dilemma.'

I nod, chewing my cheek. She crosses her legs.

'Do you mind if I tell you a story?' she asks, and I shake my head. She rests her tumbler on her knee. 'My parents arrived in England in the early fifties, off a boat from India. They ended up in Birmingham, but never much cared for it there. Too dirty, too noisy. Baba was a shrewd businessman, though, and before long he had a thriving food shop, and some money set aside.' Her face softens into a smile. 'He had this idea that he wanted to live by the seaside – the English Riviera, he called it – and everyone thought he was crazy, because in those days, Indian immigrants all lived together in big cities. London, Brum, and so on. But he'd always been the type to forge his own path, so he moved to Heaviport, opened a curry house and started a family. And this was where I grew up. It wasn't always easy, and there was a lot of racism, but we stuck it out, and enough people were kind to us that it began to feel like home.

'In the eighties, I married Andrew, a dashing helicopter pilot who, yes, also happened to be a baron, living on the Anchora Park estate, just outside town. It was somewhat scandalous at the time, although I shouldn't imagine such a thing would turn many heads these days.' She exhales. 'We were very happy, but he died, rather young, before we could have children, and I've never remarried.'

'I'm sorry to hear that.'

She tips her head, shrugs a shoulder. 'Well, thank you. But here, you see, we come to the reason I'm telling you this.' She holds a finger in the air, that distinctive gesture of hers. 'I'd come into considerable wealth, and it didn't sit so easy with me. My father arrived on Britain's shores with nothing, and built himself up from there. He instilled the same drive in me, and I studied hard and became an immigration lawyer, on a good salary, and had little need for the money myself. My father used to say to me that, before he came to England, he imagined everyone here had a good life, with enough to eat, a decent roof above their heads, but he found that not to be the case. He saw terrible poverty in this town, and it shocked him. He always said that if I ever had a chance to help the poorest in my community, I should.'

She pauses, moistening her lips.

'Beckett, I will take Charnel House off your hands for ten per cent above the asking price. I won't haggle, I won't make demands, I won't hound you about plumbing or dry rot or the square footage of the second bedroom.' I move forward to speak, but she holds up that finger again. 'I'll take care of all the renovations, to the highest standard. I know people in this area, good people, and I'll arrange everything. All you have to do is grant me the sale.'

I can feel my pulse in my throat. My mouth falls open.

'On one condition,' she adds, her forehead sinking. 'You have to appreciate that what happened here tonight really upset me. I was upset for *you*, because my gut tells me you don't deserve it, but I was upset for them, too. They're hurting, and they're angry, and I understand why. I want to fix that, if I can.'

I tug my hair from my face. 'What exactly are y—'

'I'd like you to stay in Heaviport, regardless. For a week or two, maybe three.'

My eyebrows knit together. 'You actually think that would . . . help?'

She nods.

I suck in a sharp breath, then puff it out again. 'Look, you're being very good to me, Nadia, and you have no obligation to . . . but I've had a few run-ins with the locals now, and you saw them tonight. They despise me. They near enough accused me of murder.'

'Consider it from their perspective,' replies Nadia, leaning back in her seat. 'Your family's roots run deep in this town. Over the years that school has sheltered vulnerable children, fed the needy, housed flood victims. Legend even has it that your great-great-grandfather was among the team of labourers who converted it from an old textile mill, back in the eighteen-eighties.' She unfurls a palm. 'Then, over a century later, teenage Beckett, heir to this illustrious legacy, does something no Ryan ever has and leaves Heaviport for good. You rejected the place your ancestors helped to build.'

'I never meant it as a rejection.'

'Of course you didn't. But they felt it that way.'

Talking to this woman is like boxing with your own reflection. She always has a comeback.

'So you're suggesting . . . what, exactly?'

'Walk in their shoes for a while. Try and remember what it's like to live in a place like this.'

I glower into my whisky. 'I was sent away to boarding school when I was nine. I barely remember anything.'

'Those memories will return, if you let them. Did you ever keep a diary, or a journal, as a child?'

'I was the journal kind, I suppose. But there's nothing like that at the house.'

She waves it off. 'Never mind. You're back here now. Show your face on the streets, hang out in the pubs, the cafes. I'm certain it'll make a difference.' She props an elbow on her knee. 'These people may not know you, but they feel like they do. In you, they see how the rest of the country looks at them – as if they're narrow-minded, parochial.'

'I don't actually think that.'

'Are you sure?'

I draw my head back in surprise.

She raises a hand. 'I'm not getting at you personally, but London is a bubble, and when you're in that bubble, it's easy to forget that the rest of the country exists.' She looks at the wall, as if seeing through it. 'Communities like ours, they feel forgotten, and that's one of the reasons people like your father make such a difference. A lot of the kids around here, boys especially, they grow up with this feeling of hopelessness, like life has nothing to offer them, but then they'd go to your father's school and come out the other end strong, resilient, aspirational. Not all of them, sure, but many. And their parents are grateful for that.' She sits back in her chair, rocking her whisky glass. 'Harold was a symbol of hope, and we don't have much of that in Heaviport.'

I picture some of the things I've seen since the day I stepped off the train from London – the graffiti, the neglected streets, the gawking drunk outside the pub – and can't help but wonder whether it's any different from what you'd walk past on an average Saturday night in the inner city.

'Is it really so bad?' I ask.

Nadia purses her lips. 'Have you ever been up to the abandoned lighthouse?'

My shoulders tense, like a guilty teenager in the headteacher's office. I decide to lie. 'Um, no . . . I don't think so.'

'Past Barnard's farm, off Shotts Lane . . . ? Anyhow, the cliff edge there is unstable. Has been for years. The council refuse to do anything about it, so we've put up a sign warning people of landslides, telling them there's a danger of death. And so far, it's worked.'

I think of the crushed beer cans and ash rings in the grass. *I wouldn't be so confident of that, m'lady.*

'But one of these days,' she continues, 'a young kid, or a local drunk, or just someone who isn't in their right mind will walk past that sign and the ground will give way, and they'll be tossed into the sea. And not until that happens will the council bother to fix it. That's how they feel about Heaviport in general. They won't spend money until people start dying.'

My eyes flit down to her manicured hands, her trio of diamond rings. I shift in my seat. 'If you have spare cash, couldn't you pay to have the rock stabilised, or something? Isn't that what your father was talking about?'

She lifts her brow, nodding. 'I can see why you'd ask, but it would be like pouring water into a bucket full of holes. I'd repair one thing, and more problems would come up.' She anchors her strong, dark eyes on mine. 'But a children's home? I put my money into that, and I'm fixing something for generations. That's real change, change that'll last far longer than I do, and not just one random task ticked off a list.'

She sips slowly at her whisky, and I press fingers to my mouth, thinking. I'm a figure of hate in this town, and I doubt I can fix that, whatever Nadia says. But she's a smart woman. She knows I'm backed into a corner.

'So, that's my plan, in broad terms,' she concludes, brushing dust from her skirt. 'Question is: what's yours?'

There's the message from my agent, too. I haven't got another book in me, not yet, but I have to start writing again, or I might lose it forever, the way tissue paper disintegrates underwater. Could I do that here, while I ride out the storm? Time on my hands, space to think, no one to distract me in that big, old, creaking house . . .

I swallow the last of my drink. 'OK.'

Nadia cocks her head. 'OK . . . what?'

'You have a deal.'

She balls a fist, shakes it triumphantly. 'Well done, Beckett. You're making the right decision.'

'I doubt the locals would agree.'

Her mouth curls up at the side. 'Give it time, my dear. Heaviporters are cuddlier than you think.'

'I'll have to take your word for it.'

She leans back in her chair. 'You've heard the cliché about towns where people don't lock their front doors? That's actually true here, or at least it used to be. People get to know their neighbours. They trust each other.'

I peer into my last finger of whisky, trying to imagine leaving my home in London unlocked, or knocking at the downstairs flat for a natter and a cup of tea. I could barely pick my neighbours out of a line-up.

'They'll trust you too, if you let them,' Nadia adds, and I hear a woody squeak. Looking up, I find her holding the cork in one hand, bottle in the other. 'One for the road?'

I proffer my glass.

'You remind me of Harold, you know,' she says, charging our drinks. 'You have his resilience. And his eyes.' She slides the bottle on to the table. 'Something tells me that doesn't please you.'

I pause, tumbler at my lips. I could tell her everything, if I wanted. About how the esteemed humanitarian she so keenly admires used to beat his own daughter. How I don't remember much from before boarding school, but I do remember that: the sight of him above me, towering like an ogre. Angry scabs on my thighs.

But she doesn't want to hear it, and neither does anyone else. *Our dreadful little secret.*

'We weren't close,' I say, taking a slug of my drink, and Nadia looks away, a pulse on her jaw. We fall silent for a while, listening to the distant ebb of the sea. It can be faint or loud, depending on where you are, but in this town, it's always there.

She sits up straight. 'How about we meet again at the end of the week, see how you're getting on? You can come to Anchora Park, if you like. I have a top-of-the-range coffee machine there, and a chef who doubles as a barista.'

'Ah, you see, that's where you're going wrong. Back in London I have a French chef and an *Italian* barista, because real aficionados don't compromise.'

She gives me a knowing smile. 'Sunday?'

'It's a date.'

'Excellent.' She rises from her chair. 'Now, if you'll excuse me . . .'

As she makes her way to the ladies' room, humming something classical, I unlock my phone and scroll through my contacts. If I really am going to stay for a while, I should make an effort to be sociable.

And aside from the baroness, I only have one friend in this place.

Change of plans. I'm staying for a bit. Fancy hanging out sometime? B x

She'll like that, Leanne. I can still picture her face when I told her I was leaving: so lost, so woebegone. As if she'd been waiting years for my return.

I'm actually looking forward to seeing her again.

Zade may be my one true partner-in-crime, but our nights out invariably spiral into drunken shenanigans, and something tells me that spending time with Leanne won't be like that. She'll want to talk, go on nice walks. Savour the coastal air.

Maybe staying here will be OK. Maybe it'll be good for me.

The townsfolk won't be happy about it, but I really want to trust Nadia. To believe that people can change. After all, the locals may talk a big game, but there's no one here who actually wants to hurt me, right?

11.

Leanne

I run my finger along the letters of her name. *B-e-c-k-e-t-t*.

I can't believe she's leaving. I might never hear from her again. And I can't even follow her on social media, because she's not on it. I have my memories from the last few days, but I need more. I need to see her.

I press my hand against the cover of her notebook.

THE SECRET DIARY OF BECKETT DIANE RYAN,
AGED ~~8~~ 9
TOP SECRET!! KEEP OUT!!!!

Stealing is wrong, I know that. But is it wrong to steal because of sadness, or love? It can't be.

My phone buzzes with a text. I gasp out loud.

Beckett Diane Ryan
Change of plans. I'm staying for a bit. Fancy hanging out sometime? B x

She's staying. She's staying! Oh, this is wonderful. And she wants to see me. I feel dizzy. I need to think of something cool to do.

She could come to the pub, on Friday. It would be nice to have company. But would she even want to? She must go to trendy places in London all the time, and this won't be trendy. It's just Heaviport, it's nothing.

And what if they fall for each other? What if she falls in love with him?

No. I have to stop thinking like that. She won't want to be my friend if I'm panicking all the time.

My hands are shaking as I reply.

I'm so pleased!! :) :) So so pleased. I have an idea – my boyfriend is playing a gig at the Wreckers Arms on Friday. Would you like to come? L x

I chew the inside of my cheek. Is that too much? Did I reply too soon?

The flickering dots. She's writing back.

Sign me up.

I press a hand to my heart, laughing. I think she really wants to come. I think she really wants to see me.

Then I remember the diary. I look down at my lap, at her handwriting on the cover. I shouldn't have stolen it from her, I know that. I shouldn't have stolen any of the things that I have, but I can't help it. It's in my blood.

This is different, though. This is the worst thing I've ever taken, because it was *hers*. When it's just a packet of crisps or a lipstick from the chemist's, that doesn't matter . . . but Beckett was everything. She was my only friend, and I betrayed her.

I know how much the diary meant to her. How much it would mean to her now. Before they sent her away, she looked for it for days. We even looked for it together, and I had to pretend the whole time.

She'd want to know where it's been.

But I have to wait.

It was right there in her text message – we're friends now. Proper friends. And if she finds out I stole from her, that might all go away.

If I do this right, it could go back to how it was. Nothing would come between us.

12.

BECKETT

She has a boyfriend?

I wasn't expecting that. She struck me as single.

I stare at her name on my phone screen, picturing her freckled face, those trusting eyes. *My best friend, Leanne Wilding.* And then, as if watching a photo negative bloom under water, I see a memory form. A school desk, at lunchtime. Little stacks of sandwiches, an acid-green apple. Packet of Hula Hoops. Two open lunchboxes, one yellow, one grey. Crumbs on the laminate.

'Right, Beckett,' says Nadia, crossing the room. She picks up her drink. 'Where were we?'

I look up, lost in the memory.

Her face pinches. 'You OK?'

I can see the apple, almost *smell* it. Sharp and sweet. 'Do you mind if I go?'

Her eyes widen with surprise. I redden.

'Sorry—' I'm already gathering my things '—this seems really rude, but I think I need to head back to Charnel House and . . . write.'

Her faces melts into a smile. 'Not at all,' she says, perching on the table. 'You go follow your muse.'

I empty my drink and shove my arms into my coat. 'This has been . . . you've been . . . just – thank you. Call me about the house, OK?'

'I will.' She raises her glass. 'See you in a week.'

I throw her a backwards wave as I head for the door.

◆　◆　◆

Back at the house, hunched over the small desk in my bedroom, I open a blank document on my laptop and fill it, feverishly, with words.

Writing is never easy, but tonight it has a flow. A flow that I dimly remember from my glory days; from a time when I wrote because my heart was full, and if I didn't empty myself out, it felt like I might explode.

It hasn't been this way in years.

> 'I'm alone in this house, but I don't feel it. There
> are noises in the walls, shapes in the dark. My
> mother, my father. The little girl who slept in this
> bed . . .'

These words won't ever 'be' anything; this isn't a manuscript. But that's not the point. I don't even plan to read it back. I just need to get it out of me.

> 'At first, Charnel House was the last place in the
> world I wanted to be. But cell by cell, I'm disap-
> pearing back inside it—'

My phone pings, wrenching me from my thoughts.

Howard

You're alive! This is wonderful news. It's so much easier for me to wine and dine my clients when they haven't died.

On my way back from the town hall, I finally gave in and replied to my agent. This may be an interruption, but it makes me smile.

Beckett

When have you ever wined and dined me?

Howard

There was that one time, in Piccadilly, after you won the Waterstones Book Prize.

Beckett

The publisher paid for that.

Howard

Well, I was there, wasn't I? I ate a great deal of potted shrimp, as I recall.

I glance at my laptop screen. The cursor flashes at me.

Beckett

I can't sit around chatting all night, you know. I'm [casual yawn] very busy writing.

It's almost as if I can hear him sitting up in his chair.

Howard

I knew you'd come round eventually! Bravo. I'll leave you to it.

I think for a moment, then send another text.

Beckett

To be clear, it's just stream of consciousness. This isn't a book. x

Howard

I'll be the judge of that. Winky face. H x

I switch my phone to airplane mode, lock it and throw it on the bed.

Silence.

Fingers hovering above the keyboard, I cast a look around the bedroom, at the strange patterns in the wallpaper, the cracks in the skirting. My watchful mirror image in the window.

This house, as oppressive as it is, it's helping me. It wants me to write.

I'm starting to remember.

1999

Mumma says I'm too old for nightmares now, but that doesn't stop them coming.

'Will you tuck me in tight?' I ask, at bedtime.

'I told you,' says Mumma, 'you're not a baby anymore. You're too old for all that.'

'But I'm only eight.'

'That's right. You're eight, you're not a baby.'

I pull the covers up high, so they're under my chin. 'You can only see my head now. It's like my head's been chopped off.'

Mumma clicks her tongue. 'Don't be silly.'

'I'm just a head, in the bed.'

'Enough.'

'Eight is not too old to be tucked in.'

'*What would you know?*' she snaps, her voice tight and hard, like a drum. I look into her eyes and they seem angry and sad at the same time. She sighs. 'Look – Beckett, for heaven's sake. I'm tired, and you're always . . . talking. Enough, now. Go to sleep.'

Then she turns out the light and goes downstairs, and I'm alone. I stare at the ceiling, counting in my head. Thinking about the insects behind the walls. I get to one thousand.

Some time goes past, but I'm not sure how much. Maybe five minutes or five hours.

The house is very quiet.

'I'm not too old to be tucked in,' I whisper to myself, still holding the covers up high, by my chin.

And then I feel a tug.

What was that?

Another tug. Hard, quick, on the covers.

I squeeze my eyes shut.

It's not real.

I'm sleeping, like Mumma said, and this is a dream.

But all around me, the sheets are getting tighter. They're pressing against my skin. I try to wriggle out of bed, but I can't. They're pressing down on me, on my legs, on my shoulders.

On my neck.

I can't breathe.

I'm going to choke.

It's not real it's not real it's not real.

'Will you tuck me in tight, Mumma?'

Who said that? It wasn't my voice. It sounded horrible and scrapy, like lots of voices squashed together.

'*Will you tuck me in TIGHT, MUMMA?*'

I want to call for help. Why can't I call for help?

I can't breathe.

Please, stop hurting me.

I want to wake up. I want to wake up. I'm going to suffoc—

And suddenly I'm awake, curled on the floor, staring up at my bed. I'm hot and sweaty and the covers are twisted round me and my face is stinging with tears, and I need her to hold me. I need her to hold me until I'm better.

I look out through the crack in my door, along the landing. The world is sideways. Their room is closed.

Mumma says I'm too old for nightmares now.

2023

13.

The bartender narrows her eyes at me. 'You're that stuck-up writer from London, aren't you?' she says, pushing a damp cloth along the bar. I give her an uneasy smile.

'That's me.' My phone glows with a text. Leanne's on her way. 'Large glass of red, please.'

'Like to see the wine list, madam?'

I glance up. 'Oh . . . sure. Do you maybe have a house Malbec, or—'

She's smirking at me, eyebrows raised.

I lock my phone. 'I'll take whatever.'

As she sploshes my drink into a glass, I scan the pub. Despite promising Nadia that I'd make an effort to show my face around town, since Monday night this is the first time I've strayed beyond the corner shop. I've been keeping busy with odd jobs, filling a skip with junk and slinking guiltily around Charnel House with the curtains drawn, telling myself that I'm only here to ready the building for sale. But that wasn't the deal, and I know it, so tonight I embrace the Heaviport nightlife. I blend in with the locals.

The Wreckers Arms is about half full and simmering with chatter, the first flush of a busy Friday evening. A woman in a leather tank top is vaping with a friend; a cluster of underage boys are gathered around pints of lager, sniggering at their phones. A generic rock song thuds in the background.

In a far corner, beneath a flat-screen TV, a battered amplifier is set up on a chair next to a microphone stand. Sliding my change off the bar, I make my way to a nearby table and sit down, cradling my wine and staring into the rusty head of the microphone. Nothing about this place screams *performing arts* to me. I hope Leanne's boyfriend has a thick skin.

'Beckett!'

I turn to the doorway, where Leanne has appeared, collapsing an umbrella. She is standing next to an arrestingly beautiful man with a guitar on his back.

'So sorry we're late,' she garbles, even though they're not, as they thread through the tables. 'It's drizzling, and . . . anyway, sorry. This is Kai.'

I stand up to greet them and Kai reaches out a hand. His fingers close around mine.

'You must be Beckett,' he says, with a musical, Scottish lilt.

I'm caught off guard, and words stick in my throat. 'Uh . . . yeah, hi.'

Our hands separate.

'Lovely to meet you.' His voice is soft and soothing, with a faint gravel edge. I don't know much about the geography of Scottish accents, but it feels coastal, almost old world.

'So, are you . . . excited for tonight?' I ask, lamely, trying not to stare too hard. His eyes are dark, verging on coal dark, like mine.

'Oh, aye. It's only a wee pub gig, but we'll see how it goes.' He slips his guitar from his shoulder. 'Hey, listen, Beckett. I was sorry to hear about your folks.'

I start to shrug, but something about the way he said it – so genuine, so gentle – hits me in the pit of my stomach, and when I speak, my voice is thick. 'Thank you.'

'I'm afraid I was away for the funeral.'

A knot rises in my throat, and I'm suddenly terrified that I'm going to tear up. I clutch at my neck. 'Oh, don't worry about that. I missed half of it myself.'

His eyes widen with surprise. My toes curl in my shoes.

'Can I . . . get you another drink?' he asks, saving me, and I look down. My glass is still two-thirds full.

'Sure, why not.'

'Wine, love?'

I'm about to embarrass myself by responding when I notice Leanne giving him a mousy nod. I'd almost forgotten she was there.

While Kai orders our round and chats with the bartender, I sit with Leanne, in silence, tapping a fingernail against my drink. Every few seconds, she steals a brief, flustered look at me, as if I'm her date to the school disco.

'So . . .' I angle my head towards the bar. 'Your boyfriend's a babe.'

She sits up in her chair. 'What?'

She looks almost alarmed. I push a hand through my hair. 'He . . . seems nice, I mean.'

Across the pub, a table of lads explode into laughter, and I take a quick glug of wine. Leanne worries at her sleeve. 'He is. I'm very lu—'

'Here you go,' comes Kai's voice, over her shoulder. He sets our drinks on the table, then leans over and kisses the top of Leanne's head. 'What are you two gassing about?'

I make a non-committal sound. 'Politics.'

He stifles a smile. 'I'll bet.' Lifting his guitar, he gestures at the makeshift stage. 'I'd love to join you, but I have to plug in and get playing. Wish me luck.'

'Good luck,' we reply, at the same time, and Leanne braves a glance at me.

'Jinx,' she says, to herself.

◆ ◆ ◆

Ten minutes later, Kai starts to play. He isn't introduced or acknowl-edged by the bar staff, and almost everyone in the pub ignores him, raising their voices as if to drown him out. Beer taps squirt and hiss over the gentle sound of guitar strings.

But as he begins to sing, the hairs on my neck stand up.

'Wow,' I whisper to Leanne, wine paused halfway to my lips. 'He's really good.'

Kai's fingers dance along the neck of his electric guitar, the sound clean and shimmering, like spring water. Eyes closed, he sings dark, intriguing lyrics, the words rounded and resonant in his melancholy accent.

I remember Christmas in the rain
I remember telling you that everything would be much better
When we grew up and moved away
Now I don't see you at all'

'Did he write this?'

Leanne nods, and I shake my head, ashamed. I feel bad for being surprised.

I think of the first time I heard Jeff Buckley's album *Grace*, when I was about fourteen. I remember gripping the CD in both hands, staring at the cover, astonished that a person could sing that way, could make that sound with the same throat, the same muscles that I had. It seemed impossible.

Kai's talent feels out of place here, like he's from another world. He's using his voice as an instrument, fluttering from deep, husky tones to a fragile falsetto, almost hymnal, like a choirboy on the brink of manhood. As he reaches the end of the song, I blink a few times and realise my eyes are wet with tears.

I turn away from Leanne, dabbing them dry. I haven't cried in years.

'Thank you,' says Kai, modestly, into the microphone, over the chime of his closing chord. We clap and cheer. No one else does.

The rest of the set goes much the same way. Kai performs a string of thoughtful, delicate songs – mostly originals, a few covers – and as each one ends, Leanne and I applaud enthusiastically, inspiring curious glances from around the pub, as if we were clapping at nothing. Forty minutes in, as I'm watching Kai tune his guitar, I reach for my drink and my elbow is knocked hard from behind, hard enough that the glass topples with a sharp crack, launching a tide of red wine across the table. I swivel in my chair. A few metres away, a small, sinewy man is sliding into a tatty booth by the toilets, carrying four cider bottles, two in each hand. His friends are talking noisily at each other, their table dotted with empty pints.

He drops into his seat and catches my eye. 'Shit. Did I spill your drink?'

I raise both arms, astonished. 'Yes. You did.'

There's a clang of strings. Onstage, Kai has unstrapped his guitar. 'You should buy her another one, then,' he says, across the room.

The man scoffs. 'Fag.'

My jaw falls open. 'What did you say?'

The man turns back to face me and, one by one, his friends abandon their conversations. 'What's it to you?' he grunts, bottle at his lips. He takes a long, lazy swig, and I shake my head.

'Don't answer my question with a question. What did you say?'

'I said . . . *fag*.'

I sit up in my chair. Kai raises a palm. 'Beckett—'

'Thing is, I'm not quite clear whether you want to borrow a cigarette,' I continue, leaning forward, 'or you're just a bigot.'

The pub has gone quiet. The man's gaze is rooted on mine. 'Your mate sings like a girl.'

'And?'

This throws him, and his nostrils flare. His friend leans over to say something in his ear, and he smirks at me. 'He sings like a girl . . . and I don't like it.'

I fold my arms. 'Well, you look like a mole rat, and I don't like that much, but such is life.'

He bristles. Kai rises to his feet.

'I know who you are,' says the man, weaving out from behind his table, pointing at me. 'I know who your dad was, and all.'

He's crossing the pub now, brushing past tables and bumping the backs of his fellow drinkers, who shuffle obediently out of the way. I stand up to meet him.

'What do you want?' I counter, heart punching my ribs.

He stops centimetres from me, a mirthless grin on his face. 'Why don't you suck my dick?'

I lean into him until I can smell the crisps on his breath. *Why don't you suck mine?*

There's the sound of shattering glass, and at first I can't tell where it's come from, but then I look down to find the severed neck of a cider bottle in his hand. He's bobbing it, left to right.

I look up again and Kai is glaring at me, urgently, from over the man's shoulder.

'Run!' he shouts, and I do.

14.

In a rush of feet and toppling glasses, a throng of people are suddenly crashing through the pub towards the exit. I can sense Leanne at my side, and I'm guessing Kai's behind us, but there's no time to check. The men from the booth are in pursuit, and there are others, too; gawpers, smelling a fight. The air fizzes with anticipation.

I hear the bartender shout something as we pass, which is either 'get help' or 'give 'em hell', but it makes no difference.

All we can do is run.

Cold rain pricks my face as I emerge on to the empty street, picking a random direction to flee in. 'Run for the hills!' comes a mocking cry from behind, and guttural cries slice the air, howls from a pack of werewolves.

As I'm pounding the pavement, I feel Leanne's small hand grasping for mine.

Wmmph.

There's a sound like someone dropping a sack of potatoes on concrete, followed by a fresh volley of taunts, and I twist round, dropping my pace. They've thrown Kai face first against a wall. Stopping, I squeeze Leanne's hand and look straight into her eyes. 'Stay here. Don't move.'

Letting go, I rush back towards Kai, watching as two of the men spin him round and a third – my old friend, the ringleader – shifts his weight from one foot to the other, jigging his arms like a boxer before the bell. He's still holding the jagged tube of glass from his cider bottle, and as he braces himself to throw a punch, I get a flash, a premonition, of the serrated bottleneck plunging into Kai's belly, tearing his flesh and sending a curtain of blood gushing to the pavement.

I tear towards them, shouting, but at the last minute the man drops the bottleneck and drives his bare fist into Kai's stomach. Kai cries out in pain and folds like a wellington boot, and I career into the ringleader, taking him by surprise. We crash to the ground, writhing on the wet tarmac.

We've been on the floor less than three seconds before he's overwhelmed me with his taut, wiry arms. Dragging me to my feet, he presses me against the wall with a forearm and bares his teeth, eagerly.

My gaze darts left and right, sweeping over watching eyes. We've drawn quite the crowd.

'This is the part . . . where you hit me . . . is it?' I manage to force out, lungs heaving inside of me, vision speckled. The man breathes through his nose.

'Only cowards hit women,' he says, with a sniff, and I can sense his fist flexing at his hip.

I look him hard in the eye. 'Then what are you waiting for?'

He eyes me back, frowning, shaking his head minutely as if having a conversation with himself. He presses his forearm harder into my collarbone, then releases.

'Go on, fuck off,' he spits, before tipping a nod to his henchmen. They saunter back towards the pub and the crowd disperses around them, young men murmuring their disappointment, bloodlust unsated. One of them gives the discarded bottleneck a petulant kick and it skitters along the pavement, pinging off a bin.

'Jesus, Beckett. Are you OK?' Kai is hobbling towards me, a nasty bruise blooming on his cheekbone. Leanne is hurrying over too, wet hair plastered to her forehead.

'Uh . . . yeah,' I reply, straightening my clothes. 'Average night out for m—'

'Hey!' We all look up. The man is shouting at us from a distance, through the hardening rain, pointing a rigid finger. 'I don't want to see you in this pub again. Any of you.'

I throw a look at the Wreckers Arms, with its beer-stained front steps and flag of St George dangling over the entrance, and think to myself: *I reckon I can live with that.*

15.

LEANNE

We're walking Kai along my street. He's limping. Beckett's on one side, I'm on the other. They've been talking the whole way home.

'Do all your gigs end like that, then, Kai?'

Kai's house is way out east on the other side of the railway, so I knew we'd come back to mine after the pub, if the evening wasn't over. I spent hours tidying this morning, making sure everything looked perfect, just in case. The special wine is ready in the kitchen cupboard.

'Aye, the best ones do.'

I'll ask if she wants a drink, but just casual.

Fancy a wine? Or: *I'd like a wine. Anyone else?*

'You could always say you got the bruise from stage-diving.'

She can have the crystal wine glass.

'Do I look like the stage-diving type to you?'

'This is me,' I say, when we reach my garden gate. I push it open with my leg and we wobble through. Kai and Beckett get their legs tangled and start laughing. I try and laugh too, but it sounds fake.

'Would you stop kicking me?' says Beckett, with a snort.

Kai scoffs at her. 'Me, kicking *you*? You're like Lionel Messi over there, pal.'

Who's Lionel Messi?

This isn't how it was supposed to go.

◆ ◆ ◆

Upstairs in the flat, Kai is sitting on the sofa with his leg up. Beckett is on the arm beside him.

'Cool place, Leanne.' She looks around the room. 'Very bijou.'

I wrinkle my nose. 'Bee shoe?'

'Bijou,' she says, again, and Kai smiles at her. A secret smile. I point to the bathroom.

'I'll get the TCP,' I say, cheeks burning.

'I didn't get a chance to tell you earlier,' begins Beckett, as I open the bathroom door, 'but your voice is *incredible* . . .'

Closing the door behind me, I sit on the loo and press my palms into my eyes. 'Calm down,' I hiss at myself. 'Stop fussing.'

I can hear their voices through the wall.

They're not going to fall in love. They're just talking.

'. . . I really thought you were gonna belt the guy,' Kai is saying, all excited, when I'm back in the living room. 'It was like having my own bodyguard.'

Beckett shrugs. 'Well, I felt kind of responsible. Though in my defence, that pub is a terrible match for your sensitive, Jeff Buckley vibes.'

'You comparing me to Jeff Buckley?' Kai's eyes have gone wide. Jeff Buckley is one of his heroes.

'You got *that* from what I said? Settle down, rock star.'

They're flirting. I knew it.

This was a mistake.

'I found the antiseptic,' I say, holding it in the air, and they turn to look at me at the same time. They're both so beautiful. Such dark eyes.

They're not going to fall in love.

'My point is this,' Beckett is saying, moments later, as I'm dabbing at Kai's face with a cotton ball. 'Cider-fuelled maniacs are not your crowd. It's asking for trouble.'

I press the ball into Kai's skin. He winces. 'Sorry,' I say, pulling away.

'It's OK, love. Look . . .' He lifts a hand at Beckett. 'I take your point, but where else would you have me play? Heaviport Coliseum?'

She smiles. 'Fair point. And I guess everyone suffers for their art. Though I doubt Buckley ever took an actual thumping.'

I pat at Kai's wound again. He sucks his teeth. 'Hey – *ow* – no, it's fine, keep going. Beck, listen: I grew up on a farm in Shetland, with a bunch of older brothers. I've been beaten up *a lot*.'

The way he shortened her name to Beck, as if they were best friends already. I'm not sure I like that.

'Shetland? Wow.' Beckett looks out of the window. 'Isn't Heaviport a bit ordinary after that?'

'Not at all. It reminds me of home.'

I drop the cotton ball into my lap and screw the lid back on the antiseptic bottle. 'I think I'm done. Is that any better?'

Kai tries to smile. 'Loads. Thank you.' He sighs. 'But I should hit the hay, if that's OK. Try and doze off the pain.'

Beckett leans over to look through my bedroom door. 'You two live here together, then?'

Kai catches my eye but I break away. I don't want to get into all that again.

'No, I just . . . crash here sometimes,' he says, trying to stand, and I help him to his feet. Beckett watches us over his shoulder.

'Thanks for playing nurse, love,' Kai whispers to me. 'Promise I'll stay out of playground fights tomorrow. Night, all.'

He hobbles into the bedroom and shuts the door, and the flat goes quiet. I try to remember the line I rehearsed, about the wine.

Beckett yawns. 'I should probably get g—'

'Don't you want a drink?' I blurt out, and she gives me a funny smile. I take a breath. 'I mean . . . would you like a drink?'

She rubs her neck. *She's going to say no.*

'Yeah, sure. Why not.'

I clench my jaw to stop myself smiling. 'I'll be right back.'

In the kitchen, I open the cupboard and lift out the special bottle of wine. *Châteauneuf-du-Pape*, says the label, in squiggly writing. I don't know if this is good wine, but it cost me twenty-one pounds, and that's more than I've ever spent on wine before. Three times more.

I pour it into two glasses. Normal glass for me, crystal for Beckett. I catch a whiff as it's pouring and my throat goes tight. I can't stand red wine, but that's what she likes, so I need to learn.

I pick up the glasses. Should I bring the bottle in? I could give her more wine when she needs it, so she's never waiting. But if I've bought bad wine, she'll know right away. She might leave.

My knee jiggles.

I leave it in the kitchen.

'Ooh, thanks,' says Beckett, as I hand over her drink. She snuggles in among the sofa cushions. 'What a fancy glass. I feel like the queen.'

I sit down next to her and raise my wine. 'To you,' I say, but she holds up a finger.

'No, to you. For making me feel welcome, in a town where everyone hates me.'

We touch glasses.

'They don't know you, that's the problem,' I say, sniffing the wine again. My stomach rolls. 'If they actually knew you, like I do—'

'Blimey,' interrupts Beckett, smacking her lips. 'This is fantastic red. I had no idea you were a connoisseur.'

'Oh, I'm not. It's just Chattonerve de Pap.'

She chokes on her drink. 'Bloody hell, Leanne. Don't waste the good stuff on me.'

'But I want to.'

She laughs to herself. 'Bottoms up, then.'

She takes another drink and settles back into the sofa. I try a tiny sip, concentrating hard not to make a face. It's so heavy.

'I hope Kai's all right,' says Beckett, gazing at my bedroom door. 'That was some night out.'

'Thanks for sticking up for him. You're really brave.'

'Stupid, actually.'

'I could never have done that.'

'Quite right, too. You're only small. You're not built for hand-to-hand combat.'

I stare into my drink, thinking about the sticky red liquid slipping down my throat. It nearly makes me gag. 'I'm sorry I was quiet in the pub,' I say, licking my teeth. They taste like metal. 'The truth is, I'm kind of . . . intimidated by you.'

'What? Why?'

'You've done so many amazing things with your life, but I just work in a boring old office, filing papers. You've written books, you've won awards. People look up to you.'

Beckett puts her glass on the coffee table. 'I think those days are behind me.'

'But even before that, when we were little, I thought you were amazing. I idolised you . . .' I cover my mouth to stop a hiccup. I shouldn't say this, but the wine is going to my head. 'I sort of wanted to *be* you.'

She looks at me with her head tilted.

I drink some more. 'You were like a dream to me, honestly. Your eyes, your clothes, your long hair. I had this horrible blonde bob, and we couldn't afford a hairdresser so Mum cut it herself, and . . . I'm babbling.'

'No, you babble away. And I'm flattered, but—' she picks up her drink '—you shouldn't think of me that way. My life is kind of sad.'

'You just lost both your parents. Of course you're sad.'

'That's not really what I meant.'

I lift the glass to my lips again. I think I might have been wrong about this wine. It's making me buzz all over. 'You're not sad about your parents?' I ask, and Beckett's face goes tight.

'It's complicated.'

'Is that why you didn't . . . I mean . . . you didn't come dow—'

'That's why I didn't visit, yeah. We weren't in the habit of week-ending together, the Ryans.' She looks past me, like she's remembering something. 'My mother did come up to London once – seven, eight years back – but it was awkward. We didn't know how to be with each other. We ended up just wandering around museums, in silence.'

Maybe I could visit Beckett in London, one day. We could go to the museums and Madame Tussauds and ride on a boat. We'd have the *best* time.

'I do get it, though. What people are saying.' Beckett stares at the floor. Her eyes seem almost black. 'Only a monster would refuse to visit her dying father.'

'What about after he passed?' I ask, trying not to sound excited. We're really talking, now. Like old friends.

'What about it?'

'Well, your mum was all on her own, so . . .'

She turns those dark eyes on mine, and my body goes tense. I've made her angry. I've gone too far, like I *knew* I would. It's the alcohol. 'This is none of my business. I'm sorry—'

'No, come on,' she says, holding up a hand. 'It's fine. Everyone in town is thinking it.'

She blinks a few times. Kai coughs in the bedroom.

'There was just . . . my mother and I . . . something happened . . .' She taps a fist against the arm of the sofa. 'Let's just say that I *was* planning to come and see her. The train I took to Heaviport last week, I booked that before she died. It was going to be a grand reunion.' She frowns. 'But how was I supposed to know that she was so tied to my father, so shackled to his fucking . . . *spirit*, that he dies and then – Jesus – five days later, she overdoses on sleeping pills. I just didn't see it coming.' Her cheeks go pink. 'She died alone, and it was my fault.'

I move sideways on the sofa and touch her arm. 'It wasn't your fault.'

She stares at my hand.

'Th-they're difficult, though, mums,' I say, lifting it away. 'Mine steals things. She has an addiction.'

Beckett pulls a face. 'Oh, dear.'

I think about the plastic bag full of lipsticks under my bed. I'll never use them, or even open them. And the box of frozen mice I took from the pet shop today. It's hidden right underneath us.

'I steal, too. I learned it from her.' Mum's eyes used to light up when she emptied her handbag on to the bed at the end of the day. Necklaces, chocolate bars. Drawing pins. 'Anyway, what I'm trying to say is . . . you had everything I wanted, back then. You were clever and pretty, and you had this big house and proper parents. You had a perfect life.'

Beckett rubs a thumb against her empty glass. Maybe she can't see it, but at the time, her life really did seem perfect.

I point to the kitchen. 'More wine?'

Back in the kitchen, I pour us two more servings, big ones. My heart is slamming. *This is going so well.* Staring into the blackness of the wine, I think about what I'm going to tell her when I get back in there. Something no one else knows. A best-friends-only secret.

I glug a mouthful of wine from the bottle.

'You really have no memories from before you were sent away, then . . . ?'

I'm back on the sofa again, next to Beckett. The wine bottle is on the coffee table. Rain is making little taps at the window.

'A handful, if that.'

I swallow a burp, feeling drunk. 'How strange.'

'Is it?' she says, scrunching her face. 'I'm not sure people remember that much from before the age of eight or so, do they? And bits *are* coming back to me, just nothing concrete. I know I had a lot of nightmares.'

'Do you remember your imaginary friend?'

Her eyebrow lifts up. 'I had an imaginary friend?'

'Mm-hmm,' I say, my foot tapping on the carpet. I knew she'd forgotten. 'A little girl.'

'Why don't I remember that? Did she have a name?'

'Yes . . . *Beckett.*'

She looks confused. 'What?'

'She was . . .' I point at her. 'She was you.'

We're staring right at each other. Beckett opens her mouth very slowly. 'I don't understand,' she says, and I can't help smiling. I like being the storyteller.

'Weird, right? I never understood it either, but that's what you told me.'

I remember how confusing it was, even at the time. Why would someone invent an imaginary friend who looked exactly like them?

I hush my voice. 'I know it sounds strange, but she had your face, your hair, your clothes. She was you, but nasty.'

Beckett laughs. 'You're saying I imagined . . . an evil version of myself?'

I nod. 'You used to wake up in the middle of the night and see her, standing in the corner of your bedroom.'

'That's horrible.' She's staring into the wall. Her eyes jump back to me. 'And, she just, what . . . watched me sleep?'

'Other things, too. You said she lived under the bed. Some nights she tugged on the covers.'

Her mouth pulls back at the corners, like she's smelt something bad. 'Creepy.' She tips her head to the side. 'Though it explains a lot. I slept terribly as a kid. I have a feeling they even shipped me off to a sleep doctor once.' Her eyes go narrow. 'How on earth do you know this stuff? You must have a cast-iron memory.'

My memory's OK. But that's not the reason.

'. . . I mean, here I am, brain like a sieve, and you've got this deep insight into the workings of my nine-year-old psyche . . .'

I know all this because I stole your diary from under your bed, over twenty years ago. You wrote about your nightmares in it, and your imaginary friend, and things that happened at school, and the fights you had with your parents. Everything.

'. . . and the scary thing is, the nightmares are coming back . . .'

And now that diary is in this room, right behind you. I'm looking at it on my bookshelf.

'. . . just being in that house has, I don't know, awoken something . . .'

It gives me a thrill to see the red spine behind your head, when you have no idea it's there.

I feel bad, too. But it's a *thrill*.

'. . . even so, it's frustrating only remembering fragments. And I've always written, so you'd think I'd have kept some kind of journal, right? But I can't find anything in my bedroom. Maybe I was too young.'

'That's a shame,' I say, like a robot.

'Or I did keep one, and I lost it.'

I glug more wine, washing away the guilt. I almost want to confess, but I'm not ready. We're getting closer. She's letting me in.

'D'you know what,' says Beckett, suddenly standing. She looks around the room like she's searching for something. 'I have to go.'

I pick up the wine bottle. 'Don't leave,' I say, but she's already throwing on her coat.

'Sorry, I just . . . I have to get back to the house. Search the other rooms. There must be something in that place that'll help me remember.'

I watch her fastening buttons, the wine turning sour in my mouth. What if she never comes back?

'Thanks again for the Châteauneuf.' She moves towards the door. 'But next time, just serve me Spanish plonk. Don't waste your pennies on me. I'll catch you soon.'

Downstairs, I stand in the doorway as she walks along the garden path, waving back at me. When she's gone, I climb the staircase, feeling wobbly and strange, sweating all over. My stomach turns. I'm going to be sick.

Starting to run, I crash into the flat and push through the bathroom door, dropping to my knees at the toilet. Vomit splatters into the bowl, red and thick and lumpy. It looks like I'm coughing up blood.

But I don't care, because I'm still thinking about what Beckett said before she left. *Next time, just serve me Spanish plonk.*

I smile, and red saliva drops into the bowl.

Next time.

16.

Beckett

I pull open the top drawer.

Empty.

The middle drawer.

Empty.

The bottom drawer sticks, so I give it two impatient wiggles and it yields. Inside is a peaked landscape of random bric-a-brac: nine-volt batteries, rusting keys, a shoebox full of golf balls. And at the back, hidden under a crinkled chamois leather, a pile of letters.

I scoop them out and rest them on my lap. The pile is satisfyingly heavy, bound by chalky elastic bands, and I can tell from the curly indentations on the paper that the letters are handwritten. Eagerly, I tug off the bands, flinching as one snaps in my fingers, and fan out the letters across my thighs.

This is my first real find of the night. The kitchen drawers were barren, as were the living room cabinets, and while I got briefly excited about a cardboard box I found in the pantry, it turned out to be stuffed with old copies of the *Heaviport Gazette*.

But this could actually be something. Love letters, medical records. School reports.

My father clearly felt the need to stow them away here, secretly, in the back of a drawer, in his private study. I wonder why.

And then I recognise the handwriting.

Battle For Emerald Bridge.

The cursive is oversized, imperfect. A child's hand. And these aren't letters, they're stories.

A fantasy tale by Beckett D. Ryan, aged eight and a half.

Maybe he did read them, after all.

Flicking through the sheets, I scan the prose hungrily, heart swelling as I take in names I haven't thought about in years. *Terrabine Castle*, *Dragonia*, even *Towers Of Morth*, a story that, amazingly, contained the seeds for what would later become *Halloween Skies*, my biggest hit.

I pause, almost smiling.

He kept my stories. Hidden, sure, but kept all the same. The few memories I've dredged up this week had convinced me that he'd ignored them, hoping I'd eventually grow out of it, but perhaps I was wrong. Perhaps, in his own buttoned-up sort of way, he was proud. Proud enough to bind them together and store them somewhere safe.

But then I notice something. One of the stories – only one – has been frenziedly annotated, up and down the page, in the margins. Angry flashes of red, some of them underlined, as if it's been marked by a teacher. Like homework.

I glance at the title and my throat turns oily. *Me & My Imaginary Friend – She Comes At Night.* I remember writing this now. I remember giving it to him.

Perverse, says one double-underlined comment, in my father's rigid script. *Deviant.*

Learn to spell, says another.

I remember him protesting at my interruption, then falling strangely silent after glancing at the title. Pulling me in here and making me watch as he scored furious marks beside my carefully handwritten paragraphs, the scritch of his pen like the sound of a rat clawing a wall.

My eyes travel the page, stopping on comment after comment.

Clearly enthralled by violence.

Inappropriate.

I feel nausea climbing inside me, but I can't stop reading. It's as if he's talking right to me.

Overly sexualised.

Crude vocab.

Ridiculous!

Disgusting.

Poor grammar here.

Nonsensical.

DISGUSTING.

I rise from the chair, stumbling, and the papers whoosh freely across the floor. My chest is thundering. Finding this story, in this room, graffitied with his vitriol, is bringing something else back. Something I'd buried even deeper than the memory of his red-pen recriminations.

This is how they started.

The beatings.

My father was endlessly dismissive of my fantasy stories. He refused to read them, typically point blank, claiming he was too busy with school, with real life. With important, grown-up things that I wouldn't understand. But this one was different. This one caught his attention, and it pushed him over the edge.

And that was why his study seemed so familiar, when I could have sworn I wasn't allowed in here as a child.

This was where it happened. Where it *always* happened.

Fractured memories carousel in my mind and I bury my hands in my hair, tugging at it, as if I might tear them from my skull. The sight of his leather shoes, black and pristinely polished, on the floor beside me. The way he'd slap my side, quick and sharp, before the real games began. Never leaving a mark anywhere that showed.

The things he'd say to me afterwards, in a low, seething voice.

If you tell a soul, you'll be sorry.

Now shut your little mouth . . .

The bottle of rum from the other night is still standing, sentry-like, on the pedestal desk, and I snatch it up, pulling the stopper. I take a long glug, cringing at the burn.

There's a nervous rage building inside me, simmering, and I begin to pace the room in circles. I think of the funeral, the town meeting, the way people spoke so adoringly of Harry Ryan, the toast of Heaviport. I think of the Wreckers Arms and the serrated bottle top; the bruise on Kai's face; the baying crowd in the rain. This place is poison, it's a tomb. It twists people.

I swipe my phone from the desk and open FaceTime.

'Bee, what's happening?'

Zadie's big grin and bouquet of black curls fill the screen. I'm pacing again.

'I need to hit something, that's what's happening.'

She sits up on her sofa, eyes popping. 'Calm down, soldier. You look frantic.'

I slow to a stop. 'Sorry, it's just . . . this town. This house. It's starting to get to me.'

'Weren't you supposed to be home by now?'

Zade may present as a party girl, but she's the most dependable friend I've ever had. She listens. And she remembers everything I tell her.

'Long, boring story. But, yes, I'm staying. For maybe a couple of weeks.'

'Jeez. I'll send emergency grappa, then.'

I manage a limp smile. She mutes her TV show.

'Zade, you remember . . .' I clear my throat. 'You remember what I told you, in the Cock & Bottle? About my father.'

It was an ordinary night in the pub, a couple of years back. We'd had too much to drink, which wasn't unusual, but that evening, something about the combination of ale and gin made me open up. She's the only person I've ever told.

'Sure.' She nods at the screen. 'I remember.'

I lower my voice, even though I'm alone in the house. 'No one here knows, and they never will.' *If you tell a soul, you'll be sorry.* 'But now he's dead, they've turned him into some kind of saint, and I can't escape it. He's everywhere.'

Zadie's mouth puckers up. 'Do you have someone there you can hang out with, take your mind off it?'

'Well, there's my stalker,' I reply, and she smirks at me. 'We actually went to the pub tonight, did some bonding. But there's something off about her. I can't . . . I can't quite . . .'

I replay my evening with Leanne, sitting in her funny little flat, sipping from that crystal glass. The way she forced herself to drink the wine, even though she obviously hated it. How she kept looking over my head when we were talking. She's hiding something from me, I can feel it.

I swig at the rum again, finding it empty.

'Some people are just quirky, Bee. I wouldn't worry.' Zadie stands up and pads around her flat. 'How was the pub? I'm guessing England flags and fruities.'

I slump into my father's swivel chair, letting the bottle drop from my hand. It hits the floor with a glassy clunk. 'I may have started a small fight.'

She barks out a laugh. 'Is it wrong to be slightly proud of you for that?' she says, but I'm no longer looking at the screen. Something on the floor has caught my eye. 'Bee?'

Between my feet, tooth-yellow against the oak, is an envelope marked 'Confidential'.

'Hey, dickhead.'

I whip my head up. 'Sorry, Zade. I have to go. I just found a thing.' I press a hand to my chest. 'But thanks, doll. I feel better.'

'S'what I'm here for.'

I hang up the call.

Squinting at the envelope, I reach down to pick it up. This must have come from the pile, too, but it's not one of my stories. The address is typewritten.

I flip it open, breathing heavily in the chilly silence. Inside is a letter.

The GoodRest Sleep Clinic

FEEDBACK FROM PATIENT CONSULTATION
Beckett Diane Ryan, aged 9

25th January 2000
Dear Mr & Mrs Ryan . . .

I look up, blinking at the wall. The sleep doctor.
I was right.

JANUARY, 2000

'We're here to help you, Beckett, OK? I promise we'll find a way to fix this.'

Daddy and Mumma have brought me to something called a Sleep Clinic, where doctors and scientists are going to try and stop my nightmares. A man with square glasses is sitting behind his desk, pretending to smile. I am swinging my legs under the chair, knocking them against each other.

'We'll talk for a while, first, you and me, and then hopefully, you'll come back next week for a sleepover in one of our special rooms, and we'll watch you through the glass.'

The doctor is trying to make that sound fun, but I know it's not. I don't like being watched.

'Tell me about your nightmares.'

I look up at Mumma, and she nods. 'Go on, Beckett.'

'Well . . . Mumma says they're only nightmares, but they feel real to me.'

The doctor puts his elbows on his desk. 'What happens?'

'I . . . wake up, and I can see my bedroom, and my toys. But I can't move.'

'Your body feels . . . paralysed, does it? Frozen.'

There's an old plaster wrapped around my finger, and I tug at the end, which is starting to peel off. It's pink and dotty, like a cat's tongue. 'Mm-hmm.' I pull the plaster away from my finger, watching it cling, all sticky, like I'm peeling off my own skin.

'Beckett,' says Mumma, patting my hand. 'Stop it.'

'What happens next?' asks the doctor.

I drop my hands into my lap. 'I see things.'

'What sort of things?'

'Like my imaginary friend,' I say, and it makes my cheeks go prickly.

The doctor writes something on his paper pad. 'And who is your imaginary friend?'

'She's me.'

The doctor leans back in his chair and kind of bounces on it. There is a funny look on his face. 'What do you mean?' he says.

'A nasty me. She's evil.'

He pokes at the corner of his glasses. 'Are you scared of her, Beckett?'

I stare at my legs and bite my lip until it hurts. 'Mm-hmm.' I look up at him, bubbles of anger shooting through me. '*I hate her.*'

'That's interesting,' says the doctor, quietly, like he's talking to himself. 'Unusual . . .'

Tears are stinging my eyes.

The doctor is writing on his pad again. '. . . imaginary . . . friend . . .'

The room feels red around me now, and blurry. The tears squeeze out of my eyes and make my face wet.

'So, Beckett.' The doctor puts down his pen. 'What sort of things does your imagin—'

'I don't want to talk anymore!' I shout, coughing on my tears, and the doctor stands up, waving his hands at me.

'It's OK, Beckett, it's fine. I'll speak with your mummy and daddy now instead. It's all right. Want to come outside?'

Because I got upset and shouted, I get to sit in the waiting room for a while, on my own. There is a big, shiny plant in the corner and a pile of Lego bricks on the floor. Other children are sitting on chairs nearby, next to grown-ups.

The doctor points at the table beside me. 'We won't be long, Beckett. There are comics for you here, if you like.'

He does the pretend smile again and goes back into the room. I watch one of the other children, a boy with messy hair and dark rings under his eyes, reading a book. He looks up and stares at me, and I turn away. I pick up a comic, but I'm not going to read it.

'Mr and Mrs Ryan . . .'

I sit up straight in the chair. I can still hear the doctor's voice.

'. . . I appreciate you both coming in today. I know it's a long drive.'

I twist round. The doctor's door is peeking open.

'Not at all, Dr Lawes.' That's Daddy talking. 'Thank you for seeing us at short notice.'

'Please, call me Neil. And don't mention it. My brother lives in Heaviport, as you know, and speaks very highly of your school. His twin sons are in year nine.'

'Ah, yes. Robert and Luke. Though I can hardly take the credit; they have wonderful teachers. Smart boys, too. It must run in the family.'

The doctor laughs, and so does Daddy.

It goes quiet for a bit.

'So, Neil. Do you have a sense of what's . . . troubling our daughter?'

Trub-ling. What is *trub-ling* me.

'Have, uh . . . have you ever heard of hypnagogic hallucinations?' He waits. No one says anything. 'They're very common, and really, nothing to worry about, but they can be rather . . . vivid.'

Next to the boy with tired eyes, a man who must be his daddy is sitting all hunched, with his head in his hands. Looking at them together makes me feel sad.

'Essentially, hypnagogia is the transitional state between waking and sleep. As Beckett falls asleep at night, her body begins to shut down, and she hovers on the threshold of consciousness – but during this period, she may still be able to experience select elements of the real world. She can see her bedroom walls, feel her duvet against her skin. These sights, sounds and textures may be as real to her as when she's fully awake.'

I look at the cover of the comic. Dennis The Menace is standing next to his dog, Gnasher, and they both have bright green faces, like they're going to puke.

'However, the onset of sleep also opens up Beckett's brain to hallucination, early-stage dreaming, and this can lead to the layering of fantastical, dream-like visions *over the top* of a real world setting. If these visions are dark or unsettling, it can be extremely distressing. To the child, it feels, quite literally, like a living nightmare.'

I wrinkle my nose at Dennis's big green face. I don't understand all the words the doctor is saying, but I don't like the sound of 'living nightmare'. I don't like that one bit.

'Oh, dear.' Mumma's voice. 'Oh, that's horrible.'

'Is there anything we can do?' asks Daddy.

'Hypnagogia has no cure, as such. It may be caused by any manner of triggers – things Beckett experiences in her daily life, her thoughts and feelings, hopes and fears. And there's a good chance it'll go away of its own accord, eventually. Which brings me to her imaginary friend.'

'Yes, of course,' says Daddy. 'She's a touch old for that kind of thing, wouldn't you say?'

'Actually, they're quite common up to the age of twelve, or so. And, again, young people conjure them up for all kinds of reasons. Loneliness, anxiety. Boredom.'

I slide the comic from my lap and drop it back on the pile. I'm not bored. I never get bored.

'This isn't an exact science, but it's my belief that your daughter is suffering from extremely low self-esteem. Possibly even self-hatred. And this imaginary friend of hers, this dark projection of herself, is a manifestation of her self-image. It's what she thinks about herself, inside.'

I still don't really understand what the doctor is saying, but it makes my stomach feel twisted. It makes it burn and hurt.

'Mr and Mrs Ryan, is Beckett . . . happy at home?'

The doctor has made his voice softer. I can only just hear him.

'Uh . . . yes.' Daddy again. 'Very happy.'

'Because – and, trust me, I'm not implying anything here – but children are complicated, as I'm sure you're aware, and if they feel . . . I don't know . . . ignored or neglected . . .'

I look over my shoulder at the door. The doctor didn't finish what he was saying, but he stopped talking anyway. Daddy is making a coughing sound in his throat, the way he does sometimes on the phone.

'Do you know, Neil, this has been extremely valuable, but I think we may need to make a move. Beckett will be getting hungry.'

I'm not hungry. Mumma gave me beans before we left.

'Are you sure? We have twenty minutes on the clock . . .'

There are noises inside the room. Chairs banging and keys jingling. I hear footsteps, and then the door opens and I quickly look down, pretending to be interested in the comics on the table.

'. . . and we haven't set a date for Beckett's observation. Would next week be—'

'Thank you again, for everything.' Daddy is shaking the doctor's hand. 'We just need to go home and think about it first, as a family. I hope you understand.'

Mumma gives me my jacket.

'Right . . . OK,' says the doctor, but he sounds confused. I stick my arms through the sleeve holes.

'Come on, sweetheart,' says Daddy, taking my hand. 'Let's go home, get you a pizza or something.'

I look at my fingers, all crumpled in his fist. Daddy never holds my hand.

'We'll be in touch, Neil. Have a lovely evening.'

We walk around the Lego bricks and past the shiny plant, towards the doors. The boy with the tired eyes sticks his tongue out at me.

◆ ◆ ◆

'Harold, talk to me.'

Later on, when I'm supposed to be asleep, I sit on the landing, next to the green chest of drawers, listening. The house creaks around me, like it always does when it's windy.

'I'm busy, Diane. I missed a vital governors' meeting tonight.'

'They can survive without you for one evening, surely?'

'That's hardly the point. I ask you to do one thing – to deal with this . . . situation – and instead, you drag me into it, wasting my time.'

'Drag you into it? She's your daughter.'

There's a smacking sound, which might be Daddy slamming down his pen.

'Am I supposed to feel guilty for doing my job, now?'

'No . . . not at all. But we have to talk about—' her voice goes quieter, like she's afraid I'll hear '—we have to talk about Beckett. About what the doctor said.'

'That man was nothing more than a trumped-up quack who never got the grades to become a proper doctor. And his nephews are bone idle.'

'But Harold, if she is unhappy, maybe we should think about . . . I don't know, why that is.'

Daddy makes a groaning sound. 'Fine, let's talk. Why is Beckett unhappy?'

Mumma doesn't say anything at first. The wind goes *tap-tap-rattle* at the windows. 'Well . . . you . . . you can be rather hard on her, sometimes.'

'So this is my fault, is it?'

'I didn't say that, but . . . I do think Beckett feels, now and again, that you—' she makes her voice quiet again '—that you spend more time worrying about the children at your school than you do about her.'

I can hear the scrape of a chair as Daddy stands up. 'My father was headteacher at Heaviport Secondary for twenty-five years. My grandfather before him. My great-grandfather helped *build* the damn place with his bare hands, for heaven's sake. This is what our family *does*, Diane. We are leaders, educators, and as a Ryan it is my duty to not only uphold those principles, but to pass them down the generations.'

Daddy's daddy is called Grandpa Wallace. He doesn't smile like my other grandpa.

'But that girl, up there, she will never lead this community. Not in a million years. She's too selfish, too caught up in herself. She's obsessed with her stories, with this ludicrous imaginary friend. She needs to live in the real world.'

'It's only a little make-believe, Harold.'

'Do you think make-believe built that school, or this house? Daydreaming will get her nowhere in life.' I hear Mumma start to say something, but he talks over her. 'I read that bizarre essay she wrote, by the way, on her night-time companion. It's . . . perverted, it's rotting her brain. Feeding her sick imagination. No wonder she doesn't sleep, her head's full of nonsense.'

Pur . . . vur . . . tid. I wonder what that means.

'Do you really want to know what I think?' says Daddy.

'Of course. Of course I do.'

'We should send her away. To boarding school. Somewhere on the other side of the country. It's the only way to force some sense into her.'

'Harold . . . no . . .' Mumma starts to cry. 'No, I won't let you, she's all I ha—'

I can hear Daddy walking across the kitchen. It feels like he's close to her now. In her face.

'She's all you have, is that what you were going to say?'

'I didn't m— I just . . . please don't do that. Not for me, for her.'

'I've made my decision. I'll place some calls in the morning.'

I stare down through the wooden railings at the telephone in the hallway. They're going to send me away? To boarding school? I should probably feel sad about that, but I don't. I want to go. I hate this place.

'You blame me, don't you?' That's Mumma's voice again.

'Blame you for what?' asks Daddy.

When Mumma talks, her voice is all broken, from crying. 'For not being able to have more children. For not . . . giving you a boy.'

It goes quiet again for a long, long time. But it's not nice quiet. It's the kind of quiet where bad things happen.

Then Daddy talks. 'Why shouldn't I blame you, Diane?' he says, and his voice sounds horrid and empty. 'It's your womb.'

2023

17.

The baroness glides, cat-like, down the steps of her magnificent Georgian mansion, wrapped in a luxurious grey scarf. She gives me a look. 'Good morning, Beckett.'

'You're upset with me, aren't you?' I say, as she crunches over the gravel, passing a tall, lichen-clad statue of an ancient stone warrior. 'But in my defence—'

'It's all right,' she interrupts, slowing to a stop. 'I understand. I do. I can't pretend to be delighted about Friday night's – scuffle, shall we call it? – but I happen to have met the man in question, and he seemed rather unsavoury.'

'Unsavoury?' I shove my hands in my coat pockets. 'That's not the word I'd use.'

She tries hard not to smile. 'I'm sure it isn't. Coffee?'

Five minutes later, we're standing on a paved veranda overlooking Anchora Park's expansive grounds, coffee cups in hand, enjoying the unusually brilliant winter sun. Nadia's estate sits high above Heaviport on the north side, affording views of almost the entire town, swathes of rolling countryside, even the black strip of the English Channel. From this height, she must feel as if she's in control of everything. Queen of the castle.

'I like your house,' I say, sipping my coffee. 'It's roomy.'

'Twenty-six rooms, to be precise.'

I twist around, looking again at the drawing room that we walked through to get here. High, gilded ceiling, grand piano. Ancestral portraits on the walls.

I wonder if she ever gets lonely. If she ever passes a painting in the night, and catches it glancing at her.

'Far too big for me, of course,' she says, as if reading my thoughts, 'but I'm very fond of it.'

I turn back to face the gardens. In the centre of the immaculate, manicured lawn, a stone fountain babbles contentedly, water shimmering in the sunlight. A trio of anchors are carved into its base.

'Whoever built the place was really into nautical imagery,' I say, pointing.

Nadia sips her drink. 'There's several inside the house, too. Hence the name.'

'Oh . . . oh, yeah.' I swallow a yawn. 'Call myself a writer.'

'Anchora is the old Latin word,' explains Nadia, gesturing across the hills, towards town. 'If you keep your eyes peeled, you'll notice them all over Heaviport. In our coat of arms, the school crest, and so on.'

'What's that about, then, apart from the obvious?'

'The anchor is a symbol of hope, especially in Christian ideology. Hope, and salvation.'

I'm reminded of something Nadia told me the first time we met. *Harold was a symbol of hope, and we don't have much of that in Heaviport.* Angling away from her, I gaze out across the garden towards a hedge-planted maze in the near distance, thinking about the Heaviport school crest. About how I felt last week when I walked past it again, for the first time.

When I see an anchor, I don't think of hope. I think of something heavy and rusting, weighing you down. Holding you underwater until you drown in your own terror.

'By the way,' Nadia continues, behind me, 'I spoke with my estate agent on Friday, and everything's moving forward with the sale.'

Thick, deep-water slime, bleeding off ruined steel.

'Oh . . . uh, right. Great. Thanks.'

'And plans for the children's home are coming along swimmingly, too. I've been in touch with all the necessary contractors, so once the sale is finalised, we'll have that old house fixed up in no time.'

Little Beckett, nine years old, peeking out from my father's study.

Bulging white eyes, too large for my face.

Like a spider.

I can't sleep in the dark. Can you?

'Beckett?' Nadia lays a hand on my arm, jolting me back to reality. 'Are you all right?'

I shake my head quickly, like a dog. 'Yes . . . yes. I'm fine. Just . . . admiring your maze.'

'Fabulous, isn't it?' She draws in a breath. 'Over the years, I've learned to live with not becoming a mother, but I have a recurring fantasy about running around in there with a brace of little ones, all of us laughing our heads off.'

I pitch my head back, casting my eye along the row of tall, ornate windows running the length of the first floor. 'Didn't you ever think of opening your foster home here?' I ask, shielding my eyes against the sun. 'You could house half the population of Heaviport.'

'Briefly, yes. But Charnel House is a much better size for what I have in mind. And your place has a certain charm, don't you think?'

I gaze into my coffee, picturing the house.

Sitting on its corner, softly rotting.

'I suppose.'

'Besides, before he died, Andrew asked that I make provisions to open Anchora to visitors one day. Turn it into a tourist attraction.'

'Will you?'

'Eventually, yes. One project at a time, though.' She leans her head to one side. 'Speaking of which, how are you doing?'

I let out a nervy laugh. 'Am I one of your projects, now?'

'You could say that,' she replies, with a warm, almost maternal smile. 'So, spill the beans. How's it going?'

'You mean apart from traumatising the locals and getting into fights?'

She raises her eyebrows in mock reproach. 'I *mean* . . . settling into Heaviport life, spending time in your family home. Is it stirring any fresh memories of living here?'

'It is, actually.' I think of the papers I found in the study, and my father's bitter red scrawlings. The imaginary friend that drove him to violence. 'They're not happy ones, though. Not so far.'

She considers this for a moment. 'Are you done?'

'Done?'

She indicates my coffee cup.

'Oh . . . yes. Thank you.'

She takes my cup, sets it down on a nearby bench and gestures into the house. 'Come back inside,' she says, her eyes sparkling. 'I have something to show you.'

◆ ◆ ◆

Nadia takes me on a serpentine tour of the ground floor, past store rooms and pantries, spiral stone staircases that wind away into nothing, and through antique-stuffed reception rooms, their windows offering sweeping views of Anchora's grounds. As we pad along the richly carpeted corridors, our journey is observed by a cavalcade of bronze busts – her late husband's forebears, presumably – who watch solemnly over us through unmoving eyes. Decapitated night-watchmen, guarding their precious riches.

Eventually, we arrive in what looks like a small library, or reading room. Nadia crosses to a bookcase on the wall, reaches up and presses her palm against one of the chunkier spines.

'You're not about to reveal a secret underground lair, are you?' I ask.

She glances back at me, eyes narrowed. 'Not quite.'

She gives the book a gentle nudge and a long, slender chink of light appears down the side of the shelving unit. I watch in fascination as she straightens her arm, and the chink grows wider.

My jaw drops. 'No . . .'

The entire bookshelf rotates with a velvety swish, and Nadia invites me inside. I steal past her, like Alice melting through the looking glass, and find myself in a small, low-ceilinged cube of a room with mellow lighting, plush leather chairs and a wall-mounted screen at one end.

'You've got a home cinema. You sly dog.'

She wobbles her head at this, that famous Indian gesture that can mean a hundred things, and my mouth curls into a smile. It's the first time I've seen her do it.

'Actually, I just call it the film room.'

I run a slow hand along the upholstered wall, enjoying the soft material under the pads of my fingers. The space is cosy and tranquil, filled with a rich silence, and it's easy to imagine a person squirrelling themselves away here for days, cut off from the outside world.

In the far corner, underneath the projector screen, sits a quaint, two-wheeled contraption – a glass cabinet with a saucepan inside it, hanging above a metal grate. 'You've got a popcorn machine,'

I exclaim, with a laugh. 'This is one hundred per cent a home cinema.'

Nadia closes the revolving door, and shrugs. 'If you say so.'

'What did this room used to be, then, back in the day? Fancy wine cellar? Oubliette?'

'Nothing remotely that interesting, I'm afraid.' She's at the back of the room now, typing on a laptop. 'It was a coal bunker. When I had it converted, I asked the builders to add the dummy bookshelf, because . . . well, why not?' She stops typing and turns round. 'My guilty pleasure is slinking in here on Sunday nights with a bottle of wine and a slab of dark chocolate and watching old movies from my youth. Bollywood classics, and the like.'

'That sounds fabulous.'

'It is,' she says, with another head wobble.

She must feel at ease in here.

'You know,' I reply, peering inside the popcorn machine, 'when I signed my movie deal with Paramount, I did some quite embarrassing daydreaming about what I'd spend my money on if the franchise took off. A home cinema was number one on the list.' I straighten up. 'Mine would've had a hot tub in it, of course.'

'You'd have had terrible problems with moisture,' says Nadia, bent over the laptop again.

'True, true.'

I cross the room and slump into one of the chairs. It's like sinking into a giant marshmallow.

'What happened to those daydreams, Beckett?'

'Huh?'

Nadia appears from behind my seat. 'Your dreams of a hot tub cinema. What happened?'

'Oh . . . well . . .' I push myself up in the chair. 'The film fell through, the book deals dried up and now my career's in the toilet. Still, best not to dwell on the past, eh?'

'Something tells me you're not done with the daydreams,' she says, her eyes searching mine, and I feel a strange heat under my skin. I gesture hastily at the screen.

'What exactly are we doing in here, then?' I ask, breaking her gaze. 'I'm guessing you didn't bring me in for an afternoon of Bollywood musicals.'

'Right, yes. Let me just . . .' She points a small remote control at the screen, and it flickers on. A blurry still fills the frame. 'I present to you, today's feature presentation: The School Fête.'

Slinking away again, she hits a key on the laptop and the film starts to play. It appears to be a home video, but the old-fashioned kind, where the date and time are displayed in the bottom left-hand corner. *PM 3.27, JUL 12 1997*. Shaky camera work frames a sun-drenched playing field, children buzzing around goal posts and a watching crowd of adults, chatting and clapping the action. There's no sound yet, which gives the whole thing an unreal sheen, and as I sit there, listening to the soft hum from the projector, an uneasy feeling pools in my bones.

'Wh— where did you get this?'

Nadia lowers herself into the seat next to mine, while above our heads the audio bleeds in. Children shrieking, parents cheering. A football being booted about.

Then my father passes into the frame.

'It's from one of the weekend fundraisers Harold organised, back in the nineties,' she replies. 'Friend of mine, Kenneth Allman – he used to run the old photography shop, behind the arcade – he sent it to me after the town meeting. He thought I might be able to use it in some way, for the children's home.' She caresses her jaw with long, elegant fingers. 'We could perhaps turn it into a promotional video, use it on the website. Give people a sense of the man who inspired us to open the place.' She turns towards me. 'I wanted you to see it.'

The ball rolls to my father. He stops it with his toe, then punts it away again.

My whole body is rigid as I stare at the screen.

'*Give us a wave, Harry,*' says the man behind the camera, presumably the aforementioned Kenneth. There's that jarring nickname again. Harry. '*Who's winning?*'

'*Absolutely not me,*' says my father, with a laugh, while a small boy bundles affectionately into his legs. My father drops an arm, absent-mindedly, around his shoulders.

'*I'm gonna score!*' announces the boy, dashing off, and my father makes chase.

'*Not if I catch you first . . .*'

I can sense Nadia checking in on me, furtively, and I know what she's thinking. She's waiting for these wholesome scenes to trigger happy memories in my brain, to remind me of the halcyon days I spent with my father, laughing and playing in the golden summer sun.

'*Hey, Harry! Come here a moment,*' calls Kenneth, from behind the camera. Swivelling round, my father walks towards the screen, a wide smile illuminating his face. It's a smile of which I have no memory.

His shirtsleeves are rolled up, his collar unbuttoned, and his hair is tousled from running. He looks relaxed, utterly content.

'*Give us a few words, Harry, about today. For anyone watching in the future.*'

My father is out of breath, his cheeks rosy. He pushes his fringe back from his forehead. '*Well . . . where do I start? Today's been wonderful, and I'd like to thank everyone who's been a part of it. Hundreds of pounds have been raised for worthy local causes, and as far as I can tell—*' He breaks off, momentarily, as the boy from earlier jostles into him again. '*Hello, Ralph. Have you had a fun day?*'

'*Best . . . ever!*' declares Ralph, before careening out of frame. My father turns back to the screen.

'*Well, as you can see, the children approve,*' he says, laughing. '*But, uh . . . as I was saying, thanks to everyone who made this happen. Without—*'

'*Come on, Harry. You made this happen. Take the credit for once.*'

My father waves a modest hand. '*It's a team effort, Ken. A team eff—*'

'Can we turn this off, please?'

My eyes are on my lap, heart juddering like a wind-up toy. Nadia jumps up from her chair.

'Sorry, Beckett,' she says, disappearing to the back of the room. She taps the laptop and the video freezes. 'I didn't mean to upset you.'

'No, it's fine . . . it's just . . . that's not him. Not to me, anyway.'

The Harold in that video, he's not the man who terrorised me, or the man who broke my mother's spirit, slowly, over an agonising forty years. I may not remember much from those early days, but the fragments coming back to me paint a very different picture from the one I've just seen. It's as if, somehow, he found a way to split himself in two. One fine, upstanding Harry for the people of Heaviport; one nasty, bitter Harold for us.

Nadia's film room is warm and snug, but there's a chill on my skin as I stare, tight-jawed, at the ghostly still of my father. Suddenly, my alter-ego imaginary friend makes perfect sense. One normal, ordinary Beckett for the daytime; one evil, twisted Beckett for the darkness.

I must have learned it from him.

'Should I not have shown you that?' asks Nadia, perched on the arm of her seat, her face pinched. I feel a stab of guilt for being so thin-skinned.

'No . . . don't worry. You're only trying to help.' I squirm against the pillowy headrest. 'You know, the last time I ever talked to him,' I say, staring at my hands, 'was his sixtieth birthday. We hadn't spoken in years, but that morning, I decided to make a change. Build a bridge.' I think back to that day, remembering the tinny sound of his voice, almost foreign to me, in my ear. 'We were civil, at first, but it didn't last long. He goaded me into a pointless argument; I lost my temper and called him a bitter old man. He fought back, telling me that the Ryans had always been a proud family, a family of leaders, but I'd destroyed it all. I would never amount to anything, he said, and I shouldn't call him again.' I worry a thumb against my palm. 'My third novel had just debuted at number two in the *Sunday Times* bestseller list.'

Nadia lets out a quiet sigh. 'Did he know that?'

'Probably not.'

'You didn't think to tell him?'

'It wouldn't have made any difference.' I close my eyes. 'And now . . . Christ, now, I have no idea how to grieve for him, and I don't even know if I want to.' I turn to her. 'But if I don't face up to his death, what then? It screws me up forever, presumably?'

Nadia blinks back at me, lost in thought.

'I have a confession to make, Beckett,' she says, abruptly. There's a spot of colour on both her cheeks. 'I haven't been entirely honest with you.'

'About what?'

She weighs the remote in her hand, running a finger over the raised buttons. 'Do you remember the story I told you about my father's journey to England? How we ended up in Heaviport, his restaurant and so on?'

'Uh-huh.'

'I told you his concern for the poor was what inspired me to open the children's home, and . . . well, that was true. But it's not the whole truth.'

Intrigued, I pull myself up in my seat.

Nadia repositions a lock of hair behind her ear. 'My relationship with my father was complex. He was extremely caring, and poverty troubled him deeply, but he was also obsessed with status. Hardly surprising, perhaps, for a man who grew up under the caste system and came to this country with nothing. When I married Andrew and became a baroness, Baba was, understandably, thrilled that I had risen so spectacularly through the ranks, when only decades earlier we had been dirt poor in Mumbai.

'He used to say to me, "Nady, you are one of the elite now. Play your cards right and you could reach the very top." His dream was for me to be on the Queen's honours list; an MBE, or even higher. I thought it was all rather pompous, to tell you the truth, but an unshakable part of me – the part that is forever him – felt otherwise. The pull of that kind of prestige, of being recognised by royalty, it took hold of me. And I'd be lying if I said it hadn't crossed my mind that building this refuge might lead to . . . well . . .'

'Letters after your name?'

She makes a pained expression. 'Precisely.' She emits a short, uncomfortable laugh. 'Shameful, really.'

I shake my head. 'I wouldn't say so. You're changing this town for the better.'

She gives me a wonky smile. 'That's good of you, Beckett, but in my heart, I know my intentions aren't the purest. It's for Heaviport, of course, but it's for me, too. And Baba.' She braces her jaw, and for a moment I wonder if she's going to well up. But she fills her lungs, breathes it out. 'He died twelve years ago, but I still feel him, somehow, watching me. Does that make sense?'

I nod, a prickle on my spine at the idea of being watched by my father. Of his presence, hovering in the shadows at Charnel House.

'Listen to the two of us,' I say, forcing out a laugh. 'Haunted by our fathers. Freud would have a field day.'

Nadia lifts her brow. 'Well, as a great philosopher once said . . . grief is a fearsome, unknowable thing.'

My face opens up. 'Wait, is that—'

'From *Halloween Skies*?' She nods.

'You read my book?'

'I read the whole set, this past week. You're extremely talented. I'm not surprised you've had such success.'

'"Had" being the operative word.'

She gives me a long, lingering stare, then lifts the remote control and kills the screen. 'Enough cinema time for today, I think,' she says, moving for the door. She nudges it open and I heave myself out of the soft chair. 'It's far too beautiful a day to be cooped up inside. Why don't you head to the beach, enjoy the sun while it lasts?'

Following her to the exit, I glance one last time at the big blank screen. I can't quite picture Heaviport beach. I'm sure we went all the time when I was small, but those memories must have perished.

'That's not a bad idea. Fresh air, and all.'

'And while you're there, do me a favour. Pop into the Seafront Cafe, the one on the pier. That place is a real community hub, and they serve a mean carrot cake.'

We're back in the study now, crisp sunlight pouring through the window. I give her a nod. 'I might just do that. Fancy joining?'

'I'm afraid I have architectural plans to look over, for the home.' She closes the dummy bookshelf. 'But you must've made a friend or two while you've been here, no? Someone you could share a slice of carrot cake with?'

I think of Leanne, and an idea drops into my head.

I shouldn't do this.

I shouldn't, but I'm going to anyway.

18.

Heaviport beach has a stark, windswept beauty to it in the cut-glass winter sun, diamonds dancing on the waves where the cold light hits the water. The long stretch of pebble and shingly sand is almost deserted, save one or two trussed-up walkers and the occasional scampering dog, and I find myself feeling strangely sentimental as I tramp along it, kicking at the odd stone, or washed-up shell.

A sharp scent is coming off the water, seaweed and salty brine. It's a smell that sits in there, somewhere, at the back of my brain, close to familiar, though I haven't set foot on this beach in years.

When my cheeks begin to sting from the cold, I struggle up the dunes and head for the Seafront Cafe, which sits at the far end of the pier. A crumbling relic from a bygone era, Heaviport Pier is a cankered, skeletal structure that juts out across the water like an underfed cat, waiting to die. Like the beach, it's ghostly quiet, as most of the amusements and food stalls have closed for the winter. As I meander along the boardwalk, I stare at my feet, watching the gnashing waves through the slits between the planks.

I seem to recall doing this, as a kid, in the summertime. Plodding down the boardwalk in purple jelly shoes, gazing in fascination at the whorling water beneath me. Imagining what would happen if the cracks opened up, and I dropped into the murky depths with a quiet plop.

Glancing up again, I notice something curious in the near distance, hunched back against the railings. It's a glass cabinet, roughly head height, sitting atop a battered metal base and sheltered by a wooden gazebo. The top half of a costumed mannequin is trapped inside, and a caption on the front reads: *What Will Grandma Say? Your answer awaits.*

I slow to a stop. This is one of those vintage fortune-telling machines, the kind where you drop money into a slot and the soothsayer reveals your future. Moving closer, I peer into the mannequin's face and my mouth sinks. Grandma has seen better days. One eye is rolled backwards in her head, the other half lidded in a kind of dumb ecstasy, and her dry, chipped mouth is stuck slightly open. The bolts in her jaw are sticky with dust.

I stare harder, feeling a gathering in my stomach.

I think I remember her.

Did Leanne and I used to come here, maybe? Challenging each other to feed money into the machine, to bring the queer old lady to life? That feels right, in a way. Like it could be a genuine memory. But when I picture myself standing here, tiptoed so I can see into the cabinet, I'm on my own.

There's no Leanne.

ONLY 50p TO PLAY, says the sign. **IF YOU DARE!!!**

I nudge a coin into the slot and push it down the well. It clatters its way to the bottom, then falls quiet.

Two seconds pass. Five.

And then, *clunk. Clnnnk.*

Cla-dnnnk.

The machine sputters into life.

A tune starts to play, flat and circusy in the background, and with a snap, Grandma's mouth drops open. Her head judders to the left, and then to the right, the whirling music swelling louder and louder, until finally she turns to face me and her mouth begins to flap.

But what comes out of it isn't speech. It's a sharp, nasal whine, like a mewling baby.

That can't be right.

Abruptly, the whining changes, mutates, into a series of rapid vowel sounds, like machine-gun fire. Like something deep inside her is jammed.

'Ah-ah-ah-ah-ah . . . ah-ah . . . ah-ah-ah . . .'

'What is wrong with you, lady?'

'Ah-ah-ah-ah . . . eh-eh-eh . . . ah-uh . . . eh-eh-eh . . .'

I give the machine a discreet thump, hoping to jolt Grandma back into life, but she continues to sputter and stammer. And as she wags her jaw at me, uselessly, like a dying fish, I feel the skin on my calves go tight.

Something is easing, slowly, out of her mouth. Something dark and shiny.

I watch, in fascinated horror, as a thick strip of leather excretes from between her yellow teeth, like a tongue. A fat, black tongue.

'It don't work, Miss.'

I clutch a fist to my heart, blood singing with the shock. A girl of around ten has appeared at my side, pointing at the machine.

'What?' I reply, in a strangled voice, over the awful, capering music.

'She don't talk anymore. She's broke.'

I look back at Grandma and she's gone completely silent, her mouth stuck open in pantomime terror. There's nothing hanging from her mouth.

There never was.

It was only in *her sick imagination, Diane.*

'That was my last fifty pee,' I say, sulkily. 'Do you think she'll give it back?'

The girl shakes her head. 'Nuh-uh.'

I glare through the glass, eyes narrowing. 'You old witch,' I mutter at her, low and cool. 'You owe me a fortune.'

Grandma gawks back at me through her skewed eyes, and I can almost imagine her voice, sick and papery, leaking out from inside that long, painted throat.

I'll come for you in the night, girl. When that house is inky black. Slip my fingers in your wet little mouth.

'She's been broke ever since Lee Mason kicked her in, summer 'fore last,' says the young girl, matter-of-factly. 'You won't hear her talk, Miss.'

I slide my hands into my back pockets. 'Maybe that's just as well.'

The girl wanders off, singing to herself, and I watch her go, picturing little Beckett at about the same age, tramping along in my jelly shoes, swinging a bucket. She veers towards the railings, drawn by a perched seagull with a chip in its mouth, and I move down the boardwalk to the Seafront Cafe.

'Hi. Could I get a flat white, please?'

The woman behind the counter wipes her hands on her apron and crosses to the till. It's on the tip of my tongue to ask for oat milk, but I don't want to be that person. That obnoxious Londoner.

'Absolutely,' she says, inputting my order on the touch screen. 'Anything else?'

I throw a look inside the confectionery counter, scanning the range of glazed treats and sugar-dusted pastries. Then I remember Nadia's tip. 'Oh, wait – a slice of your carrot cake, please. I've heard it's the business.'

She smiles. 'You've heard right.' She leans back and addresses a young girl cleaning the surfaces behind her. 'Flat white, please, Ems.'

I cast an eye around the room. The cafe is surprisingly busy, given how empty the pier was, and there's a pleasant, talkative buzz in the air. Families with small children sprawl at tables, kids colouring in while the adults cradle hot drinks; twenty-somethings sit at laptops; senior citizens sip from steaming tea cups, stopping occasionally to nibble at a sandwich or a buttered crumpet.

'That'll be four ninety-five,' says the server.

'Do you take cards?'

'We certainly do.'

She lifts the machine off its dock and presents it to me. As I wave my card at the screen and it blips, her eyes flick up to mine. 'You're Beckett Ryan, aren't you?'

I pause, debit card halfway into my purse. 'I . . . am, yes.' I try to read her expression. 'Why do you ask?'

She slips the machine back into the dock. 'I'm Juliet. My husband, Joseph, led the charge on you at the town meeting.'

'Oh.' My cheeks blaze. 'Am I about to be thrown out?'

'God, no. No. Look, to be honest, I thought Joe's piece in the *Gazette* was a bit insensitive. I told him so, too.'

I drop my purse into my handbag. 'Thanks. Thank you.'

She scoops a discarded bottle top off the counter and tosses it in the bin. 'I just feel there must be more to the story than the rest of us know. There always is.' She dusts off her hands. 'And when you're used to being pre-judged by an entire community, you should really think twice before throwing a stranger to the wolves.'

'What do you mean?'

She steals a glance over her shoulder. 'We know what it's like to be outsiders round here.'

I scan the cafe again, creasing my brow. Juliet's business is clearly thriving, and was recommended to me by one of Heaviport's most celebrated residents. 'You do?' I ask, and she raises her eyebrows, as if I'm missing something incredibly obvious.

'You try being the first black-owned business in a British sea-side town, in the late nineties, and you ask me that question again.'

She says this with a mild smile on her face, but behind it, there's bite. I redden again.

'That can't have been easy.'

The barista places my drink, carefully, at Juliet's side, and drifts away again.

'Thanks, love,' says Juliet, over her shoulder. She picks up a dishcloth and runs it in a crescent across the counter. 'We had a couple of bricks through the window, graffiti on the walls. We thought about leaving, for a while.'

'That sounds awful.'

She plants the cloth against her hip. 'It was, but we stood our ground. And it's all in the past now, pretty much. Here's your cof-fee.' She presents my flat white. A series of ocean waves have been designed into the foam.

'Thanks, Juliet.'

'Pleasure. I'll bring your carrot cake over in a second.'

I start scouring the room for a table.

'Oh, and Beckett?'

'Yup?'

'Give them time. The locals.' She gestures at the exit, dishcloth dangling from her hand. 'And don't base your opinion of Heaviport on that clown from the Wreckers. He's well known around here, for all the wrong reasons.'

'Understood.'

Her expression changes. 'I think someone's trying to catch your attention,' she says, peering behind me. I spin round, and a smile lifts my cheeks.

My date has arrived.

19.

LEANNE

She's smiling.

I don't like that. I don't like that at all.

And now she's walking over, lifting her arms for a hug. He's doing it too.

I can see it all from here, through the cafe window. They won't see me, because I'm hiding behind the old fortune-telling machine, but I can see them. I can see everything. Kai opening his arms and smiling, Beckett pressing her body against his, like she owns him.

My boyfriend and my best friend, having a secret date.

And I've got to watch them do it, watch them chat and laugh and share their secrets and fall in love. Talking about me behind my back, making fun of crazy Leanne. Just waiting until the sun goes down and the cafe closes so they can go home together and fuck.

I wish I didn't have to see it, but I can't leave now. I have to stay here and take it. I have to know.

I suppose this is what I get for spying on his Facebook messages.

'So, when's Leanne getting here?' asks Kai, as we break apart.

I rub my neck. 'She's . . . not.'

He cocks his head, confused.

'I mean, I didn't invite her.'

He gives me a slow, open-mouthed nod. 'It's . . . just us?'

'Sorry. Is that weird?'

A beat.

'No, not weird. Not . . . at all. I just – nothing.' He pulls his wallet from his back pocket. 'You need a drink?'

I extend a palm, like a traffic cop. 'This round's on me.'

'You don't have t—'

'I want to. I didn't get a chance to return the favour at the pub, remember? On account of accidentally setting that crazed lunatic on you.'

He laughs, touching two fingers to his purple-green bruise. 'That wasn't your fault.'

I screw my face up. 'Kind of was though, eh?'

'Either way,' he says, pocketing his wallet, 'I appreciate it. Flat white, please, oat milk.'

'Ah, nuts.'

He gives me a bemused look. 'Y'all right?'

'I didn't realise oat milk had made it out this far.'

'We're not all knuckle-dragging hicks outside the M25, you know,' he says, with a warm smile, and I hang my head, laughing.

'I deserved that. Carrot cake?'

'Aye, grand. It's dead good in here. I'll grab us a table.'

A few minutes later, we're sitting opposite each other in a busy corner of the cafe, our table replete with steaming coffees and fat triangles of cake. Kai checks his phone, then places it face down by his drink.

'I hope you didn't mind me randomly Facebooking you,' I say, breaking off the tip of my carrot cake with the side of a fork. 'I just thought it would be nice to, I don't know . . . hang out.'

'Course,' he replies, lifting his coffee cup. He looks at me over the foam, those dark, searching eyes settling on mine. 'How you getting on, after Friday night? I believe that's what they call a baptism of fire.'

I pop a morsel of cake in my mouth. 'Well, I haven't got into any more scraps, so on reflection, not bad.' The cake starts to dissolve on my tongue. 'Christ, that's better than sex.'

Kai nods, knowingly, and sets down his cup. 'It's all about the secret ingredient.'

'And what would that be?' I reply, through a half-mouthful.

He leans in closer, lowering his voice to a soft, Highlands whisper. 'Pineapple.'

'Shut up.'

He shakes his head. 'I will not.'

'And how do you know this, exactly?'

'I make a fine carrot cake myself,' he says, leaning back in his chair. 'Pineapple's a winner. And if you want it extra moist, brown sugar and a spoonful of Greek yoghurt.'

Extra moist. Is he flirting with me?

I skewer another blob of cake. 'You cook, you sing – you're a regular fifties housewife. Is there anything you can't do, Kai Cunningham?'

'Defend myself, apparently,' he says, pointing at his war wound.

I set my fork down with a light *tink*. 'Well, you're a lover, not a fighter,' I reply, and he swallows a grin.

'Neat line. You should be a writer.'

I wipe my mouth with a napkin. 'You're funny.'

'Nah, I'm just playing.' He rotates his cup in its saucer. 'You write beautifully, Beck.'

'I – what? How do you know?'

'The usual way. I've read your books.' He gives me a sideways look. 'You seem surprised.'

'I *am* surprised.'

'Leanne talks about you non-stop. I wanted to see what all the fuss was about.'

We fall quiet, our eyes locking, and I find myself thinking about the way he calls me Beck, even though we're virtually strangers. It's unbelievably sexy.

'Well,' I retort, breaking eye contact, 'you're one to talk. You sing like an angel. Like a . . . choirboy on acid.'

He laughs. 'You could work for *Rolling Stone* with soundbites like that.'

'Seriously, though. Did you ever think of giving music a go, professionally?'

He makes a face. 'Och, no. I never really wanted to be a pop star, if you can believe that.'

'Come on, everyone wants to be a pop star.' I flick at the icing on my cake with the prongs of my fork. 'Just seems to me that, with your talent, if you moved to, I don't know, Bristol, or London, or anywhere with a decent music scene—'

'Scenes aren't really my scene,' he says, with a wink.

'Smart-arse.'

He smiles at me. 'Who knows, maybe it's growing up on Shetland. My upbringing was . . . unstable, and since I've come down here, all I've wanted is to be normal. Find a nice girl, settle down.'

'And now you've found one.'

He gives me an odd look.

I press a hand on the table. 'Leanne, I mean.'

He picks up his coffee. 'Aye, Leanne. Exactly.'

I reach for my coffee, too, and we sip self-consciously at our drinks, surrounded by the clinking of cutlery and the babbling of toddlers. I stare out of the window, suddenly aware that the sun has faded and the sky has turned a mottled, battleship grey. The pier is still mostly deserted, save for the young girl from before, a handful of dawdling pigeons and someone loitering behind the fortune-telling machine. *Strange place to linger*, I think to myself.

'Beckett?'

'Huh?'

Kai's swilling a spoon around his drink, catching the foam. 'You were miles away.'

'Sorry,' I say, glancing at the window again. The figure behind Grandma has disappeared. 'What were we talking about?'

'My failure to become a pop star,' he says, slurping foam from his spoon.

'Ah, yes. Of course.' My cup chinks on the saucer. 'I don't know, maybe you've had the right idea all along. I spent my twenties manically chasing my career, like I was running away from something – from this town, to be honest – but now that I'm back, I'm starting to get it. Why people like it here, I mean.' I point at his coffee. 'Plus, now oat milk's arrived on the south coast, it's only a matter of time before Heaviport opens its first vegan brunchery. So who even needs London?'

Kai laughs at this, from his stomach, like he really means it.

'You wouldn't have been happy here,' he says, after a while. 'I barely know you, granted, but it's obvious. You're too creative. Too—'

'Selfish,' I say, thinking of my father, the word spitting from his tongue while I listened, terrified, from upstairs. *Too caught up in herself.*

'No, not at all.' Kai shakes his head. 'You know, you should really learn to see yourself the way other people do.'

My eyes dart around the room. 'You don't mean these people, surely?'

'No, not them. Your friends. Leanne.'

'She doesn't know me any better than you do, Kai.'

'Not now, perhaps, but when you were wee . . . ? You were best pals.'

I fill my cheeks with air, then let them deflate, gradually, like a wilting balloon. 'About that.'

'About what?'

'Me and Leanne. Our legendary friendship.'

Kai leans back in his seat, a faint frown on his face.

'OK, here's the thing.' I thread both hands through my hair. 'Until I came back the other week, I barely remembered anything from before I left for boarding school. It was just . . . blank.'

'Aye, Leanne mentioned that.'

'But being here, living in that house, things are coming back to me. All these different memories, fragments from my childhood.' I hold his gaze. 'And she's not in any of them.'

He works his jaw for a moment. 'And?'

'Don't you think that's strange? She tells me we were best friends, joined at the hip, but all I have is her word. I don't remember her at all.'

He shrugs, slicing into his carrot cake. 'That might not mean anything.'

'It might not. Or . . .'

He pauses, fork mid-air. 'Or what?'

'Or she's making the entire thing up.'

Setting the fork down, Kai runs a finger along his lightly stubbled jaw, then drops his voice again to that soothing, husky whisper. 'If that's the case – and I truly doubt it is – but if that is the case . . . does it really matter?'

'Of course it does.'

'Why?'

'What do you mean, why?'

'Couldn't you just . . . let her believe it?'

I make a short, sceptical throat noise. 'No, come on.'

'Why not?'

Now I'm the one lowering my voice. 'Because it's fucked up, Kai. That's why.'

'Look,' he says, leaning forward, elbows on the table, 'I know Leanne better than almost anyone, and there isn't a nasty bone in her body. If she *has* managed to, what, conjure up this friendship out of thin air, I'm telling you . . . she believes it. And if she truly believes it, then even if it is a fantasy, maybe that doesn't matter.'

I fold my arms, pressing them into my chest. 'It makes me uncomfortable.'

Kai glances out of the window, then back at me. 'You've probably figured this out already, but Leanne has a ton of issues. We have Sunday lunch with her folks now and again, and they're a real mess. Her mum's a kleptomaniac – she's mentally ill, if you ask me – but she's never been treated. And her dad? He's OK in the head, I suppose, but he's an old lech and a drunk. I'm surprised we didn't bump into him in the Wreckers on Friday; he near enough lives in there.'

I drop my head, picking at a thumbnail.

'All I'm saying,' continues Kai, softening his voice, 'is she's been through the ringer in life, and having you back here is, like . . . a glimmer of hope.' There's that word again: *hope*. 'So why take that away? She's not doing anyone any harm.'

I rub an eye with the heel of my palm. 'I guess you're right.'

'The Scots usually are.'

I take a long, slow gulp of coffee. 'I do think it's sweet, you know.'

'What is?'

'The way you look out for her.'

He stares at me, eyes glassy, and for a second or two, doesn't say anything. Then, almost to himself, he murmurs: 'Someone has to.'

A strange silence hovers between us.

The coffee machine squirts in the corner.

'You really *are* the perfect housewife,' I say, sticking a fork in my last dollop of carrot cake. A smile blooms on Kai's face. 'Call me Fanny Craddock.'

'And the music industry's loss is Leanne's gain.'

'I suppose it is.'

'Shame, though,' I add, my mouth full, ''cos your people are responsible for some of the greatest pop music of all time.'

Kai nods, sagely. 'That we are.'

'Biffy Clyro, Mogwai. Simple Minds.'

He points at me. 'Teenage Fanclub.'

'Jesus and Mary Chain.'

'AC/DC, they're technically Scottish.'

'Yep. And, oh . . . Primal Scream?'

'Primal Scream!' he says, clapping his hands. 'I grew up on that band.'

'*Screamadelica* is such a great record.'

'That album *was* my childhood, Beck. I can't tell you.' Kai's dark eyes are firing as he loses himself in the memory. 'My big brothers had this old cassette copy, and it's all I listened to. Hearing "Loaded" always takes me right back.'

'Totally, but for pure songwriting, you can't beat "Movin' On Up" . . .'

The rest of the afternoon slips away, effortlessly, in a haze of conversation, laughter and caffeine. I forget about everything – the cold, uncharted corners of Charnel House, the spectre of my father's death, my worries about Leanne. I forget it all.

Because the truth is, I haven't sat in one place and talked like this, with another person, long and deep and for hours on end, for many years.

And if it wasn't for the cafe eventually closing and Juliet near enough prodding us out the door with a broom, I'm not sure we'd ever have moved from that table.

LEANNE

'I'm sorry, Beckett . . . it's all a mess . . . you must hate me . . .'

'Hey, Miss. Wake up, Miss.'

Someone's talking to me. I open my eyes.

'You shouldn't sleep here,' says a voice from above.

I look up. 'What?'

There's a little girl standing over me. I touch the floor and feel wood.

'You shouldn't sleep here,' she says again. 'A man slept here when there were them mega floods and he got swept into the sea and now he lives in a cave.'

I sit up and my back scrapes against something large and metal. 'Wh . . . where am I?'

'You're with Grandma, Miss. Did you know you talk in your sleep?'

Holding on to whatever's behind me, I pull myself to my feet, shivering hard. When I turn around, I find the old fortune-teller staring at me from her glass cage.

Grandma. The cafe. I must've dozed off . . .

'Wait, no. Beckett—'

'She don't work, anyway,' interrupts the girl, and I notice that the Seafront doors have been locked. The building's empty. 'You won't hear her talk.'

I push my knuckles into my eyeballs. I'm so tired. I've barely slept since Beckett came back; I just lie awake at night, thinking of things I could say to her. Picturing her face.

'When did the cafe close?'

The girl shrugs. 'Dunno, just now.'

I take her by the shoulders. 'Did you see two people, a man and a woman, leaving together?'

'You're hurting me.'

'She's got short, dark hair, dark eyes, he's kind of stubbly—'

'Yeah, yeah. I . . . I saw them. Will you get off me?'

She tries to pull away, but I'm holding tight. 'When did they leave?'

'You're hurting me!'

'*Tell me.*'

'I don't know!' she cries, her eyes watery. 'I don't know, only just now.'

I let her go, scanning the high street. 'Which way did they walk?'

'That way.' She points past the ice-cream parlour, along the coastal path. Towards Kai's house.

I start down the boardwalk.

'You shouldn't grab people like that,' the girl shouts after me, but I'm running away fast, shoes slapping against the wood.

I might already be too late.

20.

BECKETT

'Fancy a drink?' says Kai, as we turn off the coastal path and into a sleepy residential road. He gestures up the street, towards the railway. 'My place is just the other side of the bridge.'

I swing my arms at my side. I'm not ready for the evening to end, but something is playing on my mind. 'Uh . . .'

I think of Leanne's freckled, girlish face. Her trusting eyes. On Friday, I made a casual comment about how good-looking her boyfriend was and I thought she was going to burst into tears. If she knew we were together now, she'd go to pieces.

Kai cocks his head, waiting for me to finish.

'. . . Y-yeah, sure. Drink sounds good.'

We push on in the dark, passing silent homes, the only sound the crisp slap of our shoes on the frosty pavement. As we walk, I text Zadie an update.

Beckett
The sexy Scot's asked me back to his. Is this a terrible idea??

Zadie
I've seen the pics, Bee. GET IN THERE. If I wasn't gayer than Christmas, that boy would be in trouble.

I chew at my cheek to keep from smirking. I feel like an awkward schoolgirl on a date with a dishy sixth former.

'Sorry,' I say, looking up, as I return my phone to my handbag. 'Best mate from home.'

Kai smiles. 'No bother.'

As we turn off the road and on to the railway bridge, I peer over the walled edge, tracing the line of the train tracks beneath us. Litter is strewn all around, crisp packets and laughing gas canisters. A single shoe lies between the sleepers, laces reeled out like spilled noodles.

'Don't suppose high-falutin' types like yourself ever deigned to set foot in the ghetto,' says Kai, once we've left the bridge behind and ventured into the housing estate beyond. 'Not unless you'd run out of crack, or illegal fireworks.'

'You've got me there,' I reply, glancing around. 'I don't recognise any of this.'

This small annex of Heaviport, quite literally on the wrong side of the tracks, seems even poorer than the rest of the town. Many of the houses look abandoned, their windows cracked and stained, front gardens cobwebbed with weeds. And Kai's right. Other than sneaking over the bridge to get to the lighthouse – a route that circumvented the estate anyway – I don't recall coming out this way as a child. Apparently, my father's 'man of the people' routine didn't stretch that far.

My phone dings again.

'One second,' I say, rummaging for it. 'I'll fob her off.'

Zadie
Soooo . . . any fresh intel on Leanne?

Beckett

Kai says her heart's in the right place. Reckons she's just got mummy/daddy issues.

Zadie

Maybe you should try and find her folks, then?? They still live down there? You need to talk to someone who knew her as a kid.

There's a sudden, stifled noise behind us. Almost a sneeze. I pause, swivelling on my heels.

'What was that?' I ask, peering down the street. It's a chilly evening in Heaviport, and I'd assumed we were alone.

Kai juts out his bottom lip. 'Fox, probably.'

I frown at him.

'Come on,' he says, picking up the pace. 'I'm just at the end of this road.'

In stark contrast to its neighbours, Kai's house is clean and well kept, an end-terrace Victorian with a painted green gate and an attractive front garden. There's a mat out front with the word 'Welcome' on it and a hanging basket by the door, overflowing with purple heather. I'm not quite sure what I expected from his place, but it wasn't this. It's very grown-up.

He lets me in and shows me to the living room.

'Make yourself comfortable,' he says, unbuttoning his coat, 'and I'll grab some drinks. What's your poison?'

'A wee whisky?' I reply, aping his accent.

He raises both palms in the air. 'That accent is woeful, but if you promise never to do it again, I have a bottle of Shetland malt in the back with your name on it.' He starts to leave, then leans back into the room. 'Provided your name is Saxa Vord Distillery, that is.'

I drop on to the sofa. 'That's actually my *Dungeons & Dragons* alias, so . . .'

He smiles and disappears into the hall.

Kicking off my shoes, I relax into the sofa and take in my surroundings. High ceiling, antique cornicing, stripped wooden floors. There's a whiff of paint and sawdust in the air, as if the building has been recently renovated, and the furniture feels new and sturdy beneath me. Kai may not live in the greatest neighbourhood, but his house is pretty and spacious. In London, it would be worth a fortune.

'I was saving this stuff for a special occasion,' Kai is saying when he reappears with two tumblers, quarter-filled with a dark, almost ruby-red whisky, 'but, hell, I suppose I could drink it with you instead.'

I give him the evil eye as he sits down next to me, passing me a glass. We clink.

'Cheers.'

'Cheers.' I gesture round the room with my drink. 'Excellent digs, may I say.'

'You may.' He swills his whisky. 'I just finished doing it up.'

He glances out into the hallway at a tidy pile of tools, gathered on a sheet by the stairs. Paint rollers, a sledgehammer. Stacks of sandpaper. A man of many talents.

'Big project, by the looks of it.'

'Well, these things take time. Worth it in the long run, though.' He collects my gaze. 'I know what you're thinking, by the way.'

'And what's that?'

'How can a guy who runs a seaside music shop and plays free pub gigs on the weekend afford to buy a three-bedroom house in this day and age?'

I pump a fist against my thigh. 'Wait, is that your day job? A music shop?' He nods, ruefully. 'Your place better have a snappy aquatic pun for a name, or I'll be very disappointed.'

He stares sheepishly into his drink. 'Soundwaves.'

'Oh, wow.' Laughter spills out of my mouth. 'That's even better than I'd dreamed.'

'Are you mocking me, Beckett Ryan?'

I drop my jaw in spoof indignation. 'Never.' I knock back a finger of whisky. 'Seriously, though, it's lovely here. Very homey.'

Kai casts an eye around the room. 'Probably seems a bit big for one person, but property's cheap round here.'

Don't I know it.

'Plus,' he adds, 'it's an investment. Big enough for a family.'

I scan the room, picturing it suddenly populated with the brightly coloured detritus of a busy young family. Duplo blocks scattered in front of the fireplace. Half-finished crayon drawings on the coffee table (*daddy werking in his shop*) and a food-encrusted baby bouncer in the corner. Leanne, lifting a rambunctious toddler to her hip, palm on her pregnant belly.

I tuck the tip of my fringe behind my ear. 'Can I ask you something?'

Kai lifts his drink to his lips. 'Sure.'

'Why doesn't Leanne live here?'

He drops his head back, massaging his eyes with thumb and forefinger.

'Sorry, should I not have asked that?'

'No, it's fine, it's just a . . . sore subject.'

I think back to the time I spent with the two of them at Leanne's place, last weekend. How I'd asked if they lived together, and he'd thrown her a look.

'How so?' I ask.

Kai gives a small, exasperated shrug. 'I've asked her to move in, more than once. She's in that wee rented flat all on her own, and I've got so much room here, but she's funny about it. Says she isn't ready.' He fingers the rim of his tumbler. 'I think she likes her own space.'

145

She's a real curiosity, that Leanne.

It's driving me crazy.

Rolling the remaining half inch of whisky around my glass, I think about Zadie's last message. *Maybe you should try and find her folks, then??* All I'm doing here is going round in circles, and Kai doesn't seem to know much more than I do. Then I remember something he said earlier – how he and Leanne sometimes have Sunday lunch with her parents – and an idea spreads roots in my mind.

I drain my drink. 'Any chance of a top-up?'

'You drink like an Islander,' he says, impressed. 'I'll bring the bottle.'

While Kai makes the short journey to the kitchen and back, I grab his phone – no passcode, luckily – and scroll through his contacts. Lance, Leah, Leanne . . . yes. Leanne's parents.

'You'd better not be about to drink me under the table,' says Kai, as he drifts into the room with the whisky bottle. I've already replaced his phone on the arm of the sofa.

'I make no guarantees,' I reply, watching him pour the reddish liquid. 'This stuff is fantastic.'

He shows me the label. 'Most northerly distillery in the United Kingdom.' He sets the bottle down on the coffee table and rejoins me on the sofa. 'A wee taste of home.'

I take another draw of the whisky and sink back into the sofa cushions. The buzz is beginning to kick in.

'Do you ever think about going back?' I ask.

'Hmm?'

I nod at the bottle. 'To Shetland.'

His face goes taut. 'I don't know, Beck. The coastline's beautiful, and it's part of who I am, but . . . too many bad memories.'

I drag my teeth across my bottom lip. He could be talking about my relationship with Heaviport.

He looks down into his lap. 'I don't want to get too serious, here, but my parents were . . . well. Let's just say they weren't cut out to be parents.'

I turn my body towards his. 'In what sense?'

'They were both drinkers, and daytime drinkers at that. They'd let us run all over town, making trouble, and they didn't care what people thought. My older brothers were rough as houses, and they learned that from my dad. He was a violent man.'

I think of Kai's face, outside the Wreckers, after he'd been slammed against the wall. Torn, bloodied skin, peppered with dirt.

'Did he ever . . . hurt you?'

'Often, aye. I was shy and wee, and kind of soft. Totie, we say in Scotland. And my dad, he was *big*. He had hands like spades, and he would—' He sucks in a quavery breath. 'Well, you know.'

I do know, of course, more than he realises. But I can't tell him that. Word travels fast in this town.

'Sorry,' says Kai, his cheeks colouring. 'I'm not used to talking about this kind of stuff.'

'It's fine, we don't have to.' I shift on the sofa, fingers twitching. I have this overwhelming urge to reach out and touch him. 'We could talk about my fucked-up family instead, if you like?'

Kai lets out a hollow laugh. 'One in, one out. Go on, then.'

'Where do I start?' I take a mouthful of whisky. 'Oh, OK. Here's one. They named me after my *grandfather*. They could've picked my grandma, Audrey, but my father chose Beckett, because he wanted a boy. And I am . . . not a boy.'

I gesture up and down my body, in demonstration of this fact, and as Kai's eyes settle on mine, I'm aware that my fingertips are resting, lightly, on my breasts. A visceral image fills my mind – he's tearing my shirt open and pressing his lips to my chest, breath hot on my skin. My hips arch against him.

'What was so wrong with having a girl?' he asks.

147

'He, uh . . .' I rub my eyes, chasing the image away. 'He had his heart set on a son, I have no doubt of that. But maybe if I'd been the right *kind* of daughter, it wouldn't have mattered. I could've taken up the mantle of headteacher at Heaviport Secondary anyway, as was my destiny, and become an acceptable face for the family.' I poke at a stain on the sofa arm. 'But I was not the right kind of daughter.'

'What kind were you?'

'Stubborn, head in the clouds. I was obsessed with writing little fantasy books. He called them "perverted".'

'Seems like those stories worked out all right for you.'

'Not the way my father saw it. See, our family has history with the town that goes back generations, and the Ryan men have always been headteachers here. All my father really cared about was raising a son to continue that tradition, and instead he got me. I torpedoed his legacy, and he despised me for it.'

Strangely, saying it out loud makes it real, and a bubble of emotion rushes up my throat. I take a gulp of whisky, drowning it.

'Beck, that's horrible.'

'Yeah. Yeah, it is.' My bottom lip quivers, and I clench my jaw to stop it. 'My parents weren't able to have any more children, and I guess it drove a wedge between them. I think he was pretty frosty to my mother as I grew older. From the few memories I have, anyway.'

'Were you close to your mum?'

'Barely.'

'Not ever?'

'Not that I recall. Things might've been different if she'd taken my side – if she'd fought my corner against him – but she didn't. She let my father walk all over us, and eventually, he grew tired of me and packed me off to boarding school. I wasn't even ten.'

'That must have been hard.'

'Actually, it wasn't. I was glad to be out of there. In my teens, I only came home when I absolutely had to.' I take another drink, perilously close to finishing my second glass. 'I'm pretty sure my father was as cruel to my mother as he was to me, but she never did anything about it. She never considered leaving him, or even confronting him, and I lost all respect for her. By the time I was old enough to move out for good, there was nothing left between the three of us. We'd gone cold.'

I pause, starting to feel drunk. Without asking, Kai tops me up.

'Don't get me wrong,' I continue, with a sip, 'I felt sorry for my mother, in my own way. And maybe she and I could've become close, as adults, if . . . if she hadn't . . .'

Kai inches towards me. 'Beck?'

I draw in a long, considered breath. Once I start this story, there's no going back.

'There's something I haven't told anyone.'

He blinks at me. 'You don't have to talk about this, you know.'

'I know. I know that.' His eyes, dark and comforting, do a little dance with mine, and I feel my chest spin. 'I should've shared it sooner, though. I'm carrying this cancerous thing around inside me, and I need to get it out.'

'Aye, sure. I get that.'

I lift my feet on to the sofa and fold them under my thighs. Kai sets his drink on the coffee table.

'Once I hit my late teens, their marriage was basically a charade. My father resented my mother for not being able to have more kids, but he kept the relationship going nonetheless, presumably for the benefit of his pristine reputation. Fast forward ten years and my mother was this broken shell of a woman who hadn't been loved – who probably hadn't been touched – in a decade.

'One day, I get a phone call from her. She rarely called me like that, not out of the blue, so I knew something was off. She said she

149

was thinking of coming to London to stay for a weekend, which was weird, but part of me thought, why not? Might be good for us.'

'Was it?'

I shake my head. 'We'd never "hung out" as adults, so we had no idea how to do it. We were like two embarrassed exchange students, circling Hyde Park, trying to make conversation.' I let out a puff of air. 'Anyway, on the Sunday, I take her to Paddington, and just as I'm saying goodbye, she loses it. Goes to pieces. She's beside herself, coughing and sobbing, and when I finally get her to calm down, she tells me the story.

'My father had retired by then – this was just before his dementia kicked in – and he was throwing himself into local politics, stuff like that. He was never around. So my mother discovered the internet.' An image pings into my mind of Diane Ryan staring, confused, at a screen full of kitten memes, and perversely, I almost laugh out loud. 'God knows how, but she ended up on a chat forum – lonely hearts, or something – and fell into conversation with a wealthy American naval officer, recently widowed . . . who was looking for love.'

Kai's mouth falls slowly open.

'Yep, that's right. Boomer gets online scammed: you've heard it all before. All in, she transferred tens of thousands of pounds in life savings to this person, thinking she was preparing them for a wonderful new life together, sailing yachts around the Adriatic.'

'God, no. That is awful.'

'Yeah. And it was stupid – so stupid – but I didn't blame her for it. I blamed my father. He'd starved her of love, over the years, and eventually she reached the point where she had to eat.

'Anyway, when she finally realised it was a scam, she was desperate. She was convinced my father would leave her if he found out, and she was terrified of being alone. She thought it might kill her.'

In the back of my mind, I can still see the indentation my mother left in the bed when she died: a curved, foetal hollow like a pebble might leave in the sand. I picture the empty bottle of sleeping pills beside her, the final remnants of powdery sediment coagulating at the bottom of her stained wine glass, and an uneasy feeling whispers over me.

It took less than a week for his death to overwhelm her.

'What a mess,' says Kai, running a hand across the top of his head. 'I'm guessing she asked you for money?'

'She actually took an interest in my career, unlike my father, and I was at the height of my earning power at the time. Tales of my riches were all over the publishing press.' I can feel the rage in me stirring, just a dull ache for now, but swelling by the second. 'Her whole trip to London, it was just a ruse. She was buttering me up.'

Kai's eyes pinch. 'You gave her the money, didn't you?'

'I was her only hope. And we both knew it.' I think back to sitting in my flat, making the transfer. Gazing at my almost empty bank account as my mother raced home on the fast train. 'At the time, my career was flying, but it didn't last long. When my sales dried up and the contracts stopped coming, I fell into debt, and quickly. Then, before she died, my mother donated their savings – the money I had secretly reimbursed – to a domestic abuse charity. Which, by the way, I fully support, but . . . now I live off noodles. And if it wasn't for the baroness buying Charnel House, the bailiffs would be taking my flat.'

I look down at my knee and notice that I'm pumping it, like a piston. I've never told this story before, but now that I've started, I have to keep going, right to the end.

'A few years pass, my father's mind goes and then he dies, suddenly, of a stroke. So my mother asks me to come home, to keep her company.' The dull ache has twisted, mutated and turned acidic, roiling in my stomach. 'This probably sounds cruel, but I was conflicted. I'm broke and screwed up, and it's her fault – his, too, but he's gone now, so I focused on her – and I was just so *angry*. I refused to come, at first, and I know now that must have crushed her. It must have snuffed out that last flame of hope she had, because she followed him five days later, and I will never forgive myself for that. I'd booked a train home, before I found out, but by then it was too late. The shock and the isolation and the . . . desperation had killed her too.'

Kai catches my eye, his gaze steady. 'You shouldn't blame yourself, Beck. It's not healthy.'

I look away, aware of my heartbeat in my throat. Maybe he's right, but I can't change the way I feel. I grind my teeth until I hear them squeak.

'So, let me get this straight.' Kai crosses his arms. 'You go into a career your dad disapproves of, and against all the odds, you do well. Like, *really* well. He never tells you he's proud, never even acknowledges your success. Then your mum falls for an internet scam and calls *you*, the daughter she's neglected for years, and asks you to replace the money so your dad never finds out and leaves her. You do that, but before you can inherit the money back, she donates it to charity, and now the only thing keeping you from financial ruin is the fact that the town is turning the family house, kind of ironically, into a children's home.'

I bob my head one way, then the other. 'That's about the size of it.'

'No wonder you couldn't stand the bastards.'

'Except, no,' I say, with a pained sigh. 'It was just money, at the end of the day, and we were broken long before all that. There was something deeply wrong with us, the Ryans. We were never a family.'

Kai charges my glass again. 'Well, either way, I think you need to give yourself a break.'

'From what?'

'From taking the blame.' He gives a sideways nod out the window. 'Leanne told me how the locals treated you at that meeting the other week. Like you're some cash-grabbing yuppie who never cared for her parents and only came back to clean up on a house sale.'

I roll my eyes. 'Yeah. That was a lark.'

'Weren't you tempted to tell them the truth?'

'It's too complicated. Too messy. And I guess I wanted to protect my mother . . . and my father, too. Their reputation was everything to them.'

Kai shakes his head, disbelieving. 'You're a good person, Beckett Ryan.'

'I'm really not.'

He finishes his whisky, smiling through the glass. 'Yeah, you keep telling yourself that.'

I glance at my phone, checking the time. I feel like I could talk to him forever, but at some point, I need to head home. I have a brisk start tomorrow.

'I'm scattering their ashes in the morning,' I say, emptying my glass again. 'Heading out to a . . . significant spot, I guess you'd call it, at the crack of dawn.'

Kai lifts his brow, nodding. 'That's good, right? Might give you some closure?'

'I'd rather not have to deal with it, to be honest, but I'm an only child, so . . . you know.' I look up at him. 'I always envied people with siblings.'

He rolls his tongue round his cheek. 'You might not've been crazy about mine.'

153

'Still, that's the benefit of having more than one, right? They can't all be rotters.'

He laughs, but his laughter has an edge to it. 'You're saying it's a numbers game?'

'Precisely.'

'Well, there were five of us, so—'

'Five? That must have been *fun*.'

'Depends on your idea of fun.'

I glance around the room, at the bookshelves and cabinets, then back at Kai. I tip my drink at him. 'Do you have any photographs?'

His eyes seem to grow in their sockets. 'Ah, no . . . no, you don't want to get into all that.'

'Come on, I've told you my life story. Now it's your turn.'

He gives me a slanted glare. 'Fine. I'll show you one thing.' He stands up from the sofa, pointing at me. 'But you have to promise not to laugh.'

'Oh, absolutely not. I cannot make that promise.'

'You are something else, Beck. You know that?'

'I do,' I say, as I follow him into the hallway.

LEANNE

I roll away from the wall and drop on to all fours, my hands pressed on the cold paving. My back is killing me. I've been leaning against the front of Kai's house for I don't know how long, under the window, and I'm aching all over. I wanted to move sooner but I couldn't. I had to hear everything.

Women stare at Kai all the time, of course. I'm used to it. They look at him, then they look at me, and I know they're wondering why he's with me. I know they *want* him. But this is more than that.

They were really *talking* in there.

My gut feels raw, like I've been sick. I know I shouldn't, but I can't help myself. I start crying, hot tears of anger and shame, dripping down my icy skin. Wetting my neck.

She's really into him: I can tell. She got tired of me because I'm dull and straight and boring and now she's moved on to Kai, with his guitar and his house, and his Shetland whisky. They're bonding, and it won't end here. They'll become a couple and she'll move in and we won't be able to stay friends because it'll be too awkward, and I'll never get to see her again.

And that's not fair. It's not fair because Beckett was my best friend in the world and I've only just got her back. I found her first, and he can't have her.

He can't have her.

21.

Beckett

'Do you hear that?' I say to Kai, as he stops by a small door, about waist height, underneath the staircase. He opens it to reveal a dark, cluttered alcove, and sticks his head inside.

'Hear what?'

'Sounds like . . . somebody crying?' I strain to catch it. 'Either that, or your neighbours have a very sickly cat.'

Kai pops his head back out again. 'Eh?'

'Do your neighbours own a cat?'

He looks at me oddly. 'Aye, tatty wee bastard named Leroy. Why?'

'I think he's ill.' I point into the alcove. 'So what are you hiding under there? Harry Potter?'

'In a way, yes.' He ducks back inside and his voice comes out, muffled, through the wall. 'Somewhere in here, there's a picture of me as a wee'un. Harry Potter specs, an' all. Here it is.' He re-emerges with a scrap of paper in his hand, about the size of a post-card. His expression has turned, his mouth a thin line. 'We weren't exactly a "happy snaps" kind of family, so this is all I have.'

He passes me the slip of paper without looking at it. It's a torn section of newsprint: a black-and-white photograph of Kai and his siblings, standing on a street corner in front of a building called

The Shetland Warehouse, two of them giving the finger to the camera. Beneath the image, a headline reads: 'UNRULY FAMILY BRANDED "TROUBLEMAKERS" BY POLICE'.

Feeling suddenly guilty for forcing him into this, I realise why he didn't want to show me. He's ashamed.

'Oh, yikes. That's not good.'

In the picture, there's Kai, bespectacled, aged maybe twelve or thirteen, with his three older brothers on one side and a kid sister on the other. His brothers are big and mean-looking, but Kai is fragile, skinny. I look at the way they tower over him, and a shiver ripples through me. Their father must have been even bigger.

'I shouldn't have pushed you on this,' I say, laying a hand on his arm. 'It's not actually that funny.'

'Come on, you weren't to know.'

He curves his fingers over mine, and my pulse quickens. I drop my hand.

'So, where is this?' I ask, studying the heavy brick warehouse in the photograph, and the quaint-looking shops behind. 'My geography of Shetland is non-existent.'

'Lerwick. Main town on the island.'

'That where you grew up?'

'Just outside, aye.'

I look again at his younger self, fascinated by his narrow shoulders, slender limbs. Fearful eyes trapped behind NHS frames. 'You got rid of the goofy glasses, then.'

'Aye, thank God. Contact lenses saved my life.' He expels a slow breath through his teeth. 'Shame the rest of my childhood isn't so easy to forget.'

We look up from the photograph at the same time, and I realise we are only inches apart. The heat from our bodies is mingling in the narrow space.

157

'Your past doesn't have to define you, you know,' I say, whisky burning in my chest. 'You're a different person now.'

'You think?'

'I know.'

I wet my lips.

His hand is in the small of my back. 'This is wrong.'

'Maybe,' I reply, against his mouth, 'but I say we do it anyway.'

He pulls me close, his grip suddenly firm, and I melt into him, shutting my eyes. Another flash comes, this one even more vivid. Kai's weight on top of me, my legs wrapped around him. Heels on his lower back.

I open my mouth to his, and the doorbell chimes loudly.

'Jesus,' he says, breaking away. His eyes are wide and blinking. 'Sorry, I . . .'

'No, no.' I make a fist, tapping it on my forehead. 'That was my fault. Fuck.'

The tuneless clang of the doorbell is still ringing in my ears, my lips tingling. Kai shakes his head. 'It's the whisky.'

'Right, yes! The goddamn whisky.' I force a laugh. 'What do they put in that stuff, rhino horn?'

His mouth curls into a regretful smile, and it makes me ache.

I point to the door. 'You need to get that. And I should . . . probably go.'

'Probably.'

I pluck my coat from the peg, heart racing. 'You see, *this* is why I'm still single,' I say, threading my arms through the sleeves. Kai is watching me with hunched shoulders. 'Think before you act, girl. For once in your life.'

'See you, Beck,' he says, opening the door.

'That Leanne, she is one lucky – fuck!'

My throat snaps shut. Leanne is standing on the doorstep.

'H-hi,' I say, but my voice is broken, husky, and barely makes it out of my mouth. Leanne doesn't reply. She just stares past me, into the house, wisps of her blonde hair twitching in the wind.

'You should come in from the cold,' says Kai, opening the door wider, and I realise that its window is made from frosted glass. Semi-transparent.

How long was she there?

What did she see?

'Well,' I announce, with phoney cheer, 'I really ought to be on my way. My merry way. Which direction is home, I wonder? It's all right, I'll just guess. I could do with a stroll.'

Squeezing past Kai, I drop down the front step and on to the path, until I'm level with Leanne. She looks at me, sort of blankly, but doesn't say anything.

I feel a chill on the soles of my feet. 'Would you look at that, people, I've forgotten my shoes. I'm not wearing any shoes. Would you credit that? Bloody . . . shoes.' Ducking inside, past Kai, I dash into the living room, slip my shoes on and rush back out, still muttering to myself. 'Got my shoes, got my phone . . . thanks, Kai, for . . . yep. Later, Leanne. Bye. Bye.'

Head down, hands clenched, I power along the garden path, through the gate and out on to the road, not caring which way I'm heading. The cool air on my skin is a welcome respite from the sting of whisky in my throat, and the hot rash of guilt on my face.

As I'm walking away, I can't help myself. I look back over my shoulder.

Kai isn't there.

But standing at the front window, watching me go, is Leanne.

22.

'Fuck, fuck, fuck.'

I close the front door at Charnel House, drop back against it and press my knuckles into my eyes.

She could see you through that frosted glass. She knows.

I spring away from the door and start pacing the hallway, hands splayed at my sides. What happens now? Will she confront me? Lay into me, even? She doesn't seem the type. She's more the sort to bottle it up, isn't she? To stew on it for weeks, having muttered conversations with herself in the mirror.

And what about Kai? Can I ever see him again? Because, despite everything – the mild terror banging around my skull, the beads of cold sweat on my forehead – I'm still turned on from that almost-kiss. I still want to feel his weight pressing down on me.

Sliding my phone from my pocket, I open my contacts and scroll to Leanne.

Texting her would be a bad idea. It would look too convenient, too slick. Like I have something to hide.

I close my eyes, the image of her standing on Kai's doorstep, staring at me, still flaring on my retinas. There was something menacing about the wooden look on her face as she waited for me to speak; something vacant and sinister, like a sleepwalker. I could have been imagining it, I suppose, but . . . should I be *afraid* of her?

I open my eyes to the harsh glow from my phone. Zadie was right: I have to talk to someone who truly knows her, and Kai can't help me. I need someone who knew her twenty-five years ago, when she claims we were inseparable. Someone who can tell me, once and for all, what sort of person she really is.

My thumb trembles over the screen, above the contact I stole from Kai. *Leanne's parents*. I glance at the clock on the wall: five past eight.

The phone rings for a good ten seconds before anyone picks up.

'Yuh.' A man's voice. Razor-edged, heavy with beer.

I pause, staring down the dimly lit hallway. Should I ask to speak to Leanne's mum, instead? It's a train-wreck of a choice: the incurable kleptomaniac, or the lecherous drunk. 'Um, hi. Is that . . . Mr Wilding?'

A very long pause. All I can hear is his breathing, low and phlegmy, against the mouthpiece. 'Who is this?'

'My name's Beckett. Beckett Ryan.'

Another pause. His breathing gets lower, and slower. 'I seen you in the paper.'

I rub a temple, silently cursing the perplexing popularity of the *Heaviport Gazette*. I thought local newspapers were supposed to line cats' litter trays. 'I was hoping I could ask you a few questions about your daughter, if that's OK?'

There's a fat, wet, slurping sound. He smacks his lips. 'G'on then.'

I suck in a breath, steadying my nerve. I can't do this over the phone. I need to see the whites of his eyes. I need to know if I can trust him.

'Could we meet in person? Tomorrow, maybe? I'll buy you a pint. And some pork scratchings.'

Leanne's father coughs up something, then sniffs it back. I can hear laughter from the television, thin and metallic in the background. 'I'll be in the Wreckers tomorrow, from four.'

I scrunch my face. Anywhere but there. 'I don't suppose we could meet somewhere else?'

'I drink in the Wreckers, gurl.'

'But—'

Bbrrrrrrrr.

The call dies.

I spend the evening writing, furiously. Something about being busted by Leanne – the nervous energy, the jolt of fear – has unlocked my brain, loosened my fingers, and I fill page after page, hands flying across the keyboard, eyes open wide in the glare from my computer screen. Leaving out only my father's violence, I write down everything I can remember: snatches of my parents, memories from the sleep clinic, fragments of my dreams, my nightmares. My mirror-image imaginary friend. I type frantically, the tap-tap-click unrelenting, as if it were the clacking of cogs inside my brain.

But then the whisky wears off, and I run out of steam.

Blinking in the dingy light, I wander into the kitchen, aware of a sullen grumble in the pit of my stomach. There's not much to speak of in the cupboard: a stack of noodles, an abandoned packet of Kettle Chips and half a bottle of wine. Retrieving the crisps and the wine, I set a glass on the table, pull the cork out with my teeth and give the bottle a sniff. My mouth snags at the corners. *Vinegary.*

Forcing down the first mouthful, I wince, toss a handful of crisps into my mouth and cross to the kitchen counter, where my phone is propped against the tiles, glowing with a message alert.

I stop chewing, the crisps turning claggy on my tongue. What if it's her?

Howard
Wotcha. Any news? Hx

My bones flood with relief. I need to settle down.
She isn't crouched outside the front door, waiting for you.
Unlocking my screen, I take a calming breath and wiggle a finger over Howard's name, tempted to break the habit of a lifetime.

'Beckett!' he announces, joyfully, when he answers the phone. 'You're calling me. You never call me.'

'You started it, texting me on a Sunday. On God's day.'

'You don't believe in God.'

'I believe in his day.'

Howard laughs his soft, rattly laugh. 'Still, can't a man check in with his favourite client, once in a blue moon?'

'Howard, we both know your favourite client is that guy off the telly with the showjumping Labradors.'

'They can balance crumpets on their noses, Beckett. Can you do that?'

I slump into one of the kitchen chairs. 'No,' I reply, wounded.

He clears his throat. 'So how's, uh . . . what's the place called? Heavitown?'

'Heaviport.'

'How's Heaviport?'

Gazing into my drink, I think of the look on Leanne's face as she watched me from Kai's living room window, hurrying away from the house. 'Have you seen *Fatal Attraction*?'

'Crikey, yes,' says Howard, alarmed. 'She boils the woman's bunny, you know.'

'Well, it's like that.'

'Yeeschk.'

I take an indulgent swig of wine. 'But the good news is: I'm writing again. Really *writing*.'

'Oh, splendid, I'm delighted.' Howard's chair creaks as he leans back in it, and I can hear the smile in his voice. 'When do I get to read some chapters?'

I scoff down the phone. 'There are no "chapters", How. This isn't a book, remember?'

'But—'

'*But* . . . I do want to send you something. Give me an hour and I'll ping it over.'

'Marvellous.'

'To be clear, this isn't a draft of anything. I just need to know if I've still . . . got it.'

Howard leaves a thoughtful pause. I hear him shift in his seat again. 'I haven't given up on you, you know.'

'That must be rather lonely,' I reply, draining my drink. 'Giving up on me is extremely fashionable of late.'

'Oh, don't be so dramatic. But a new book! How exciting.'

'Like I said, it's not a book.'

'What is it then, a sea bass?'

'Ideas. Childhood ramblings.' I thumb the outside of my glass. 'Therapy.'

'If you'd asked Joyce, he would've told you *Ulysses* was therapy.'

Reaching for the wine bottle, I chuck another generous splosh into my glass. 'Don't be cute with me, old man. I know what you're doing.'

'Is that so?'

'I'm not sending you this stuff so you can craft it into a natty elevator pitch and accost people with it in the Groucho Club.'

'I hate the Groucho.'

'That's not the point.'

'Well, look . . . forget all that. I'm just thrilled you're working on a new book.'

'It's not a book.'

'Right, sure. And how's everything else? Life in general?'

I fill my mouth with wine again, swilling it about. It's getting easier to drink with every drop.

'A bit weird, if I'm honest. They don't like me much down here.' I picture my sad tower of noodles in the kitchen cupboard. 'And I'm running out of money, too. If it wasn't for the local benefactor buying my family home for an inflated sum, I'd be on the streets by Christmas.'

'Oh. Oh, dear.' Howard gives a pensive sigh. 'Well, we can't have that.'

I lean my forehead on my palm, massaging my brow. My agent and I have always been close, but he doesn't need me laying my personal woes at his door.

'Sorry, that was too much information. Don't worry about me. I'm good.'

'Good. Good.'

Another pregnant pause.

'Well, keep me posted,' he says, eventually. 'Can't wait to read the book.'

'Not a book.'

'Whatever you say. Over and out.'

Arming myself with the rest of the wine, I plod back to the study and drop down in front of my laptop. Stretching out my fingers with a dry click, I lower my hands to the keyboard and begin to type.

> '. . . The truth is, my father never wanted me. He spoke about me as if I were worthless, a stain on his good name, and because I was too

young to process this, my overactive imagination dreamed up an evil double of myself – a manifestation of how he saw me – as a focus for my self-loathing. This doppelgänger was me, but a twisted alter-ego, the literal monster under the bed. She had my face, my hair, my eyes, my skin, but she lived in the shadows, and only came out in the loneliest hours of the night . . .'

2000

'Help!'

I shouted that word. Shouted it into the darkness.

I'm in my bed, and it's night-time. I know it's a dream, because I'm frozen, like the doctor said.

Your body is . . . para-lies.

All I have to do is close my eyes, and my arms and legs and heart and brain will go back to sleep, and it will be morning.

But when I shut my eyes, nothing changes. I still see everything. The walls of my room, the desk where I write my stories, the cupboard, the ceiling. And the ceiling is . . .

moving.

It's pink, like skin, and it's moving.

When I breathe faster, it breathes faster. When I stop, it stops. And now, bumps like worms are rising out of it, squeezing out of it, like when Teddy Mathers burned himself in cooking class. And the bumps make a shape.

A shape like an anchor.

'Mumma?'

It's rotting her brain. Feeding her sick imagination.

'Help m— h-help me . . .'

We should send her away.

'Please, don't.'

This is what you get, you little—

'Beck . . . ett.'

Whose voice was that? Who said that?

It came from underneath. A quiet, quiet whisper, from under my bed.

'Beck . . . ett.' Little fingertips, searching, up and down. 'It's dark down here.'

It's all in your imagination, Mumma says. *You're sleeping, you're dreaming. Close your eyes, it will go away.*

But my eyes *are* closed, Mumma. *My eyes are closed.*

'It's dark down here, Beckett.'

The voice is all mangled. It's my voice, but curly and strange, like it's from another world.

My eyes sting with tears. 'Mumma . . . please . . . she's here . . .'

My bedcovers rise up, and air rushes in. Then the covers sink again, all slow, and a body presses against me, warm and damp, like next door's dog.

It whispers in my ear. 'I can't sleep in the dark. Can you?'

2023

23.

It's a nasty, hacking morning and I'm carrying a heavy brass urn across an empty field, in semi-darkness, lungs burning in my chest.

Up ahead is the ocean, and the towering red cliffs of Heaviport. As the precipice nudges into view, I pause for breath, panting hard. The urn feels like an anvil in my arms.

WARNING

LANDSLIDES ON CLIFF EDGE

KEEP AWAY!

Passing the still-askew warning sign to my left, and the lighthouse on my right, I walk as close as I dare to the drop. Freezing rain dots my face, and wind flaps the lower panels of my winter coat.

I look down at the urn in my hands. They're in there, together: my mother and father. Their grey, powdery remains are united as one; forever joined in holy matrimony. Not even death did them part.

The official term is *commingled*. Reverend Worcester suggested it to me, the day after the funeral, when I paid her an abashed visit to apologise for my French exit from the cremato-rium. She wondered whether it might be appropriate, perhaps, if they were kept in a single urn? *Soulmates in life, so too in death*, she said to me, sweetly, and I nodded, sagely, as if that were in any way true.

Curling my fingers around the lid, I lift it off and peer inside. My father was grimly committed to their public image, the insepa-rable man and wife, right until the end, so perhaps *commingling* is exactly what he deserves.

He can't escape her now.

I stare out across the ocean, through the hanging mists, and watch the waves gnashing against each other. What was it that Leanne told me when we met here, after the cremation? *We thought if we shouted things loud enough, the wind would steal them away and throw them in the sea, and they'd be gone forever.*

Discarding the lid on the grass, I grasp the urn with both hands and give it a few strong heaves. It belches a large, billowing ash cloud into the air, and as I stand there, inches from the cliff face, the wind gyres my parents into a plume of smoke and whisks them out to sea.

LEANNE

I'm standing right behind Beckett. Close enough that I could reach out and push her over the edge.

Watch her drop into the water.

'Beckett.'

My voice is too small. She can't hear me over the wind.

'*Beckett.*'

She spins round. When she sees me, she drops the urn in surprise and a small pile of ash spills on to the grass. Rain soaks into it.

'Holy . . . Christ, Leanne!' Her eyes are huge. 'How long have you been there?'

'Not long.'

She shoves a wet hand through her hair. 'What on earth are you doing up here? It's seven in the morning.'

'I'm just . . . walking.'

Her face goes tight. 'How did you know I was coming here?'

My skin prickles. I have to lie. I can't tell her the truth, because the truth sounds crazy. *I sat outside Kai's house last night for over an hour, on a cold paving slab, listening to you two laugh and talk and swallowing my tears until they made me choke.*

But, then, they weren't just talking, were they?

'Earth to Leanne . . . ?' Beckett's head is tipped to the side. 'How did you know?'

I look down at the grey pile of deadness by her feet. Mummy and Daddy, being washed into the soil, ready for the gobbling worms.

I start to stammer. 'I-I . . . I didn't. Kai told me. He said you . . . told him you were . . . coming here?'

She glares at me, breathing hard. She doesn't believe me.

'A-anyway . . . Beckett, look, there's something . . . I . . .'

I reach into my handbag and search through the mess – tissues, earphones, some envelopes I stole from the corner shop on the way here – until my fingertips touch the leather binding of Beckett's diary. The one she's been searching for since she came back to Heaviport. The one I stole over twenty years ago, and lied to her about, and have been keeping on my bookshelf like a trophy.

It's time I returned it.

'Leanne, listen—'

'Just . . . wait. Wait a second.'

When I've confessed, she can forgive me for stealing it, and I can forgive her for falling in love with Kai, and we can all be friends again.

'There's something I need to talk to you about,' I say, as I begin to pull it from my bag.

'I can't, Leanne. Not now.'

'No, it has to be now.'

'I'm busy.'

'Please, just let m—'

'Enough, Leanne! Enough.' Beckett clamps her hands against her ears. 'I'm trying . . . fuck, I'm trying to *mourn my dead fucking parents here*, for Christ's sake. Would you just . . . would you leave me be?'

She drops to her knees, leans the urn upright and screws the lid back on. Then she picks it up and walks past me, rain running down her face like crocodile tears.

I watch her disappear into the mist and tears push from my eyes. Real tears, though, not crocodile ones. Hot and angry on my skin.

You're hurting me, Beckett. And the last thing I want is to hurt you back.

24.

BECKETT

The grubby St George's flag outside the Wreckers Arms thrashes at me in the wind, whipping back and forth with a belligerent snap as if trying to alert the town to my presence. I steal a look over my shoulder before slipping inside.

The pub is surprisingly busy for a Monday afternoon, though it's mostly old, single men sitting alone, staring into their pints. A few of them raise wrinkled heads as I walk in, like turtles on a beach, squinting at the sun. I keep my eyes low and make for the bar.

'You again.' The bartender gives me a sideways glance as she tears away the perforated opening from a box of cheese and onion crisps.

'Me again.'

She glares at me, cardboard disc in hand. 'You want something?'

'Just a bottled beer,' I say, pointing at the small fridge by her feet. 'Whatever you have. Peroni.'

'Stella.'

'Stella it is.'

As she bends down to collect my drink, I slip off my coat and cast an eye around the room. My date could be any one of these men.

'Hey,' I say, as the bartender plants a bottle opener against the lid of my beer. 'I'm here to meet some old guy – Wilding? Don't know his first name.'

She glances over my shoulder, yanking the top from the bottle. 'He's sitting beside the fruity, staring at your arse.'

I pivot, surreptitiously. At a small table by the fruit machine, a skinny, haggard-looking man in his mid-to-late sixties is nursing the dregs of a pint, beady eyes hovering lazily on my derrière. His gaze tilts to meet mine, and I see it. Something in his brow, the set of his mouth, that's Leanne. The woman who, in the early hours of this morning, crept up behind me on a cliff edge.

'Four-twenty, please.' The bartender slides my drink towards me, wipes her fingers on her top. Something approaching concern crosses her face. 'What you meeting Ronnie for?'

'Long story,' I reply, handing her a five-pound note. She takes it without looking, her gaze still trained on Leanne's father. 'Actually, what's he drinking?' I ask, remembering the promise I made him on the phone.

'Mild.'

'Pint of mild, then. And a packet of pork scratchings.'

She pulls a pint of watery-looking ale and sets it on the bar. I pass her another note and she rings it through the till.

'Watch him, OK?' she warns, her lips barely moving. 'Wandering hands.' She tosses a packet of pork scratchings next to the pint. 'And, look, while we're doing this . . .' She lowers her voice. 'Sam Hastings. The little lad with the temper – your sparring partner from Friday night – he's not here right now, but he comes in most days, so . . .'

I nod, gratefully. 'Thank you.'

She responds with an indifferent shrug, but her eyes are still narrowed with concern. Gathering up the drinks and the pork scratchings, coat hanging on my arm, I struggle over to Ronnie's table, shimmying my hips to get past the fruit machine. His eyes follow my midriff with dull, open-mouthed interest.

When I arrive, I table the drinks and force a smile. 'I'm Beckett.'

He looks me up and down, as if appraising a pig in a market. His greenish tongue sits between his lips. 'Sit, ma gurl.'

He reaches under the table and pats the seat beside his, and my brain flinches with recognition.

Where ya going, ma gurl?

I think this is the waster I saw rolling about outside the pub, the day I stepped off the train from London. He seems almost sober today, in comparison. Though the night is young.

'You're Ronnie Wilding, then,' I say, sitting across from him.

He bows his head, slowly, as if falling asleep. 'Very same.' He closes his dirty, slender fingers around his fresh pint. 'Famous round here, I am. People call me Casanova.'

If you so much as touch me, I will rip your dick off.

'That's nice,' I reply.

'Ay. Nice, it is.' His tongue is back between his lips. 'You look like a frisky one, gurl.'

'I'm really not.'

'Good, firm arse on you.'

I pull my beer towards me, biting hard on my tongue. I can't afford to let this old pervert get a rise out of me. 'That's . . . flattering, Ronnie, but I'm afraid I'm gay. And celibate.'

He takes a slow, wet sip of his pint. 'I like all sorts.'

'I'll cut to the chase, here,' I say, laying a splayed hand on the table. 'Since I've been back in Heaviport, I've spent a fair bit of time with your daughter, and she, uh . . . she says we were friends, when we were kids.'

He lolls his head back, considering my words.

I clear my throat. 'Best friends, actually. She says we were best friends, and we spent pretty much all our time together. At school,

179

and after school, and . . . well, problem is, I don't remember much from back then, and I can't seem to picture it. I just . . .' I rake a hand through my hair. 'I thought maybe you could . . .'

A sickly smile is spreading across Ronnie's wrinkled face. It hangs there, like a wound, and he doesn't say anything, for a long time. Then he begins to laugh: a rough, hacking laugh that sounds like someone trying to jumpstart an old chainsaw.

I shake my head, baffled. 'What's funny?'

'She says you were pals . . . ?'

'That's right.'

He laughs some more, his body starting to shake, and the laughter sours into a gluey cough.

I nudge my beer aside. For once, I'm not in the mood. 'What are you saying? Is she lying to me?'

Wiping his mouth with the back of his hand, he leans across the table and drops his voice to a low, crackling whisper. 'I'm saying that little whore has been lying since the day she slid out of her mother.'

I recoil in my chair. 'You don't . . . recognise me, then?'

Ronnie takes a long draw on his drink. ''Til they put your picture in the paper, I ain't never seen you 'fore in my life.'

'But . . . were there other kids, maybe, that Leanne brought home to play?'

He makes a dismissive sound into his pint. 'Leanne didn't have no friends. She's wrong in the head.'

'Well, maybe her mother might—'

'Aaah, don't you go bothering with that dried-up old witch,' he drawls, slamming his glass down hard enough to spill beer on the table. 'Shoulda never married her.' He points at my chest. 'I like girls with a bit of bust on 'em, like you.'

I fold my arms over my breasts, inadvertently hiking them up inside my jumper, and his nostrils flare in response.

I slide my chair back. 'Thanks for meeting me, Mr Wilding, but I think we're done.'

He picks up the packet of pork scratchings, indifferently, and drops it again. I'm already standing, putting my coat on.

'You looking for fun while you're here, gurl?' he says, leering up at me.

I pause with my arm halfway down my coat sleeve. 'I'm sorry?'

'Fun.' He leans forward, tongue pulsing against his bottom lip. '*Sucking and fucking.*'

My fists curl. 'I'm going now. Enjoy your pork scratchings.'

Heart thrumming, I sweep through the pub, ignoring the prying looks from other patrons. As I pass the bar, Ronnie fires a parting shot. 'Stuck-up bitch.'

I pause, fingers twitching.

Let it go, Beckett.

You've been here before. Literally, right here.

My jaw set, I carry on walking, heading for the door. But before I reach it, a second voice – a familiar voice – chimes in from the back of the room. 'He's right, an' all. You *are* a stuck-up bitch.'

I turn on my heel.

'I told you not to come here again,' says Sam Hastings, taking a step forward. 'Didn't you listen?'

25.

Emerging from the toilet, behind Sam, come three of his lackeys from the other night. They stand together, slackly eyeballing me.

I fold my arms. 'Only four of you?'

My voice sounds steady, but my heart is pounding. I shouldn't be goading him, I know that. I'm just not sure I can help myself.

'I don't want you in here,' says Sam, moving closer. He jerks a thumb over his shoulder. 'This is where I drink.'

I pull a face. 'What, the urinals?'

Someone behind me sniggers.

'You know what I meant,' Sam continues, walking towards me. 'The Wreckers is our pub, and we don't want your sort in here.'

'And what sort would that be? People who can read?'

He stops. We're less than a metre apart now.

'You think you're all that just 'cos you've written some shitty book.'

'Six shitty books, actually.'

'You mugging me off?'

'Wouldn't dream of it.'

He closes the gap between us. I can feel his hot breath on my face.

'You need to fuck off, Ryan, before I make you.'

I frown at him. 'I thought only cowards hit women.'

He hangs his head, shaking it. By his side, his fist pulsates like a beating heart. He looks up again. 'Maybe I changed my—'

'I think you should leave.'

All heads turn. The bartender has moved out into the main room, hands on hips, rolled-up dishcloth on her shoulder. She's looking in my direction. 'I mean you.'

My shoulders drop, and I search her face. She looks irked, but that ghost of concern is still there, drifting behind her eyes. I step away from Sam.

'Fine . . . fine. I'll leave.' I slip out my phone, check the time. 'When's the last train out of Heaviport?'

The bartender pulls the cloth from her shoulder. 'I didn't mean—'

'When's the last train out tonight?' I repeat, to no one in particular, as I'm buttoning my coat. There's an expectant pause, disturbed only by the clatter of fresh rainfall on the windows.

'Eight forty-five,' replies a greying, droopy-eyed man, sitting at the bar. 'Goes all the way to Lon'on.'

I consider his face. He looks like exactly the kind of person who would have memorised the local train timetable. I nod thanks.

'In that case, I'll be on the eight forty-five out of Heaviport.' I look around, feeling oddly like a disgraced prime minister vacating Downing Street. Every pair of eyes is on me. 'See you around.'

Reaching for the door and gripping the handle, I pause and aim a barbed look across the room. 'Oh, and Ronnie, just in case you didn't pick this up, let me make it crystal fucking clear: you're not a Casanova, you're a fetid little troll, and I would rather light myself on fire than go anywhere near what's in your trousers.'

He barks something indistinct at me, but I'm already stepping out of the Wreckers Arms, for the last time, and into the driving rain.

◆　◆　◆

The weather outside is wretched. The rain is diagonal, gathering in murky streams at the roadside, and the wind feels sharp and hard, like it has teeth. Clouds the colour of old meat are roiling in the sky.

Pushing up the hill, past the bank, the post office and the array of boarded-up buildings, I pull out my phone and scroll to my text conversation with Leanne. Raindrops pockmark the glass, and I text quickly before the screen is obscured.

I'm going back to London. Don't ever contact me again.

The sky lets out a deep grumble, as if in pain, and I drop my phone into my pocket.

I push on through the gathering storm.

My final hours at Charnel House are uneventful. I chuck my clothes and toiletries into my suitcase, straighten the sheets on my bed and wash up my solitary mug, bowl and fork in the kitchen. Avoiding my phone, which is on silent, racking up missed calls from Leanne, I use my laptop to book a train ticket on the eight forty-five and then just sit at the table, staring into space.

Counting up my reasons to leave.

Leanne is a liar and a fantasist. Sam Hastings has a price on my head, and my crush on Kai is like a lit match in a petrol station. As for my parents, and this house, if I'd ever dared hope that being here would bring me closure, that hope is gone. I made a whole show of traipsing to the cliffs this morning and flinging their ashes in the ocean, but it hasn't made a speck of difference. There's nothing and nobody here for me.

With one exception.

Gazing through the greyness of the kitchen window, I feel a twist of guilt.

Nadia's a good person, and she really seemed to think that staying in Heaviport would help me. But our passing friendship isn't enough to keep me in this town, not anymore. The truth is staring us both in the face: I don't belong here, and I never have.

Sitting up straight, I track an eye around the kitchen, following a long, spidery crack along the wall. Might she pedal backwards on the house sale when I break my promise? It was a deal, of sorts, after all. But she wouldn't cancel her plans for the children's home purely to teach me a lesson, would she?

The crack in the wall disappears behind the clock, and with a gasp, I realise what time it is.

Ten past eight.

Dashing into the hall, I reach for my suitcase and flick up the handle. *Too late to worry about that now.*

As I'm closing Charnel's hefty front door behind me, I take a careful glance over my shoulder, into the starved, empty darkness. A troubling scent eddies upwards, gamey and damp, and I'm reminded why I feel unsentimental about never seeing this place again.

I pass barely another soul on my journey through town. The storm has worsened considerably, and during my lonely walk down the hill, I get soaked to the bone, even through my winter coat.

I arrive at the train station to find it deserted and locked. A scribbled note has been taped to the inside of the rain-lashed front doors.

DUE TO EXTREME WEATHER CONDITIONS,
ALL TRAINS ARE CANCELLED UNTIL FURTHER
NOTICE

Standing there, dripping, I clasp my hands on top of my head, anger flowering inside me. It's as if some malevolent force is refusing to let me leave.

I close my eyes to the rain. *What now?*

'What am I supposed to do now?' I spit down the phone, pacing back and forth in front of the station doors. In the town square, a woman in a yellow mac hurries around puddles. 'I've had it up to here with this place.'

Zadie makes comforting noises on the end of the line. 'Hey, come on. It's only one more night.'

There's R & B playing behind her and I can hear the plasticky click of make-up palettes. She's getting ready to go out.

'I met him, by the way,' I say, hugging my chest, one-armed, for warmth. 'Leanne's dad.'

'Oh . . . and?'

'He's a sex goblin, Zade.'

She laughs at this – her infectious, mischievous chortle – and normally I'd play it up, but this isn't the time for banter.

'He didn't know me as a kid, as it turns out, and neither did Leanne. She made the entire thing up.'

Zadie pushes air through her teeth. I hear the pop of a lipstick cap. 'Sorry, Bee.'

'So now I've got nowhere to go and no one to see, and . . . and she's calling me every twenty minutes. I just . . .' I notice that I'm trembling slightly, though whether that's due to rage or the cold, I can't be sure. 'I feel *off*, you know? I need a distraction.'

Chair legs scrape, and the music cuts out. 'I'm running late, mate, but listen . . . you have to chill. Turn off your phone, go back to the house, open a bottle of wine. And stay out of trouble. Buzz me tomorrow when you're back. Mwah.'

She hangs up the call.

Honouring her advice, I power down my phone and gaze across the square into the empty arcade, listening to its haunting, jangly music. I think of the rows of glinting wine bottles that line the shelves at Poundpusher's.

Stay out of trouble, she says. Just for one night.

I think I can manage that.

26.

'So . . . we meet again.'

It's late, and I'm standing in the utility room at the back of the house, glass of wine in hand, shoulders hunched beneath a tortoise shell of blankets. The storm has been raging all night, and when I clomped upstairs to my bedroom a few minutes ago, it was icy cold, windows rattling in the wind. So now I'm back in front of the boiler, peering drunkenly at the controls.

There are two semi-circular dials on the outer casing of the unit, roughly at head height, and they're staring at me lifelessly, like big robot eyes.

I cock my head. 'Hey, don't look at me like that. I'll figure this out. I just need . . . instructions . . .'

Remembering the injury I sustained the last time I went fishing for the instruction manual, I lean over, cautiously, to peek into the narrow space between the unit and the wall. Grimacing, I slide my free hand into the gap, pushing through the prickly mess until I make contact with the corner of the booklet. I pull it out and flap it in the air.

'Yes!' I wave it in front of the boiler's unblinking eyes. 'We're in business.'

The boiler watches, indifferent, as I flick through the palm-sized manual, murmuring the chapter headings as I go. Pausing on a diagram of the control panel, I jab buttons and hit switches until the apparatus makes an abrupt sound – a sort of deep, mechanical chuckle – and a fragile blue flame springs up in the viewing window.

I take an exultant swig of wine.

Ffschklank, says the boiler, decisively, before emitting a throaty hiss, like a threatened cat. Water begins to travel down the crusty, skeletal pipes, heading for the rest of the house, and I'm about to stagger off when I catch another sound, barely there, beneath the trickling.

A whimper.

Like a lost child.

It's not real.

It's just the boiler.

FfssschKLANK.

Pulling the blankets tight around me, I turn and wheel away into the blackness of the hallway and an impossible sight stops me dead. A pale, scared-looking girl is standing outside the study door, watching me. Six-year-old Beckett.

FfssschKLANK.

Our eyes lock.

Then her little gleaming teeth appear, in the crescent of a grin.

'No . . . *no.*' I double over, gathering a fistful of my hair and squeezing it hard. 'Not now, come *on.* She isn't real. There's nothing . . . there . . .'

One more night in this house, I tell myself. *One more night, then never again.*

I force my head up, and she's gone.

Eyes open.

I'm not in my bed.

I went to sleep in her bed, in little Beckett's bed, but I'm not there anymore. I'm sitting on the landing, my back against the chest of drawers, hugging my knees. It's dark as hell outside, and the rain is coming down in sheets.

It feels like 4, 5 a.m.

Ffsschklank.

I lift an arm, slowly, into my line of sight, and regard it curiously. It's so . . . *small.* So clean and pale and small, as if I'm . . .

A child.

'Harold, talk to me.'

My head snaps up. That's Mumma's voice, coming from the kitchen. Muffled, like she's buried in a box.

'I'm busy, Diane. I missed a vital governors' meeting tonight.'

Daddy's down there too.

'They can survive without you for one evening, surely?'

I raise my other arm, drawing my hands together until my pinkies are touching, and stare at my palms in awe. They have no lines, no marks. The skin is tight and fresh.

'. . . We have to talk about Beckett,' Mumma is saying, in a secretive voice. 'About what the doctor said.'

The wind goes *tap-tap-rattle* at the windows. It looks bitterly cold out there, but inside, the house is hot. Burning hot.

Ffsssschklank.

Sitting up carefully, not making a sound, I pad across the landing on my hands and knees and peer down through the railings, into the hallway. A soft gasp falls from my mouth.

Something is wrong with the house.

'Fine, let's talk. Why is Beckett unhappy?'

I can see normal things down there – the green telephone, our shoes by the door, coats hanging on the rack, but the floor doesn't look right. The floor is different. And I can hear the sea.

'Well . . . you . . . you can be rather hard on her, sometimes.'

I've seen this floor before. Wide, rattly planks, with gaps so big you can spy the ocean underneath. I've walked those planks in my purple jelly shoes, on warm summer days.

FfsssschKLANK.

What is that sound? And why is it so hot in here?

'So this is my fault, is it?'

The sound is coming from downstairs. The heat, too. Maybe I should—

With a blink, I'm standing in the hallway, by the telephone table. I look up at the landing and see myself, nine-year-old Beckett, steal away into the dark, chased by a wicked little laugh.

The chandelier begins to sway.

'I didn't say that, but . . .'

I am walking along the pier. Looking down, I can see the water, and the wood is hot – almost scalding – on the soles of my feet. It must be summer.

'I do think Beckett feels, now and again, that you . . . you spend more time worrying about the children at your school than you do about her.'

Ffsssschklank.

That sound, it's coming from the end of the hallway. From something hidden in the shadows.

'My father was headteacher at Heaviport Secondary for twenty-five years,' comes Daddy's voice, still muffled, from the kitchen. 'My grandfather before him. My great-grandfather helped *build* the damn place with his bare hands, for heaven's sake . . .'

I slow down when I reach the kitchen. The door is shut.

'This is what our family *does*, Diane . . .'

Reaching for the door handle, I close my fingers around the familiar brass knob – oddly ribbed, like a beached jellyfish. But when I turn it, the brass warms and congeals into glutinous flesh, and I yank my hand away because the jellyfish is real now, it's slick and small and clinging to the handle, and as I pull backwards, long gobs of bluish mucus stretch between its tentacles and my fingers. The creature frees itself from the handle and drops to the floor with a thick splat.

FfssschKLANK.

I hear laughter. Sudden, happy laughter.

When I look up, the kitchen door is open. The room is clean and bright, beams of light pouring in through the window, and the table is humming with activity. With children. Some are drawing or writing, others chatting. The place is bustling and warm and full of sunshine.

Who are these children?

'Mumma . . . ?'

But my parents aren't in the room anymore. They're gone, and that's when I realise – this is the future. This is the future of Charnel House.

These are the children who will live here, one day, when it becomes a foster home, and they'll be playful and safe, and they'll stay up all night gossiping and have secret clubs and talk about their crushes and write in their diaries, and the house will be happy, *finally*, for the first time in years. My chest swells with hope.

And then their faces snap towards me. The sunshine is gone. The jellyfish twitches on the floor.

'Hello . . . ?' I say, in a weak voice.

The walls are dark again, rain on the window. The children just stare.

'Hello?'

They can't hear you. You're talking in your sleep.

The chandelier sways faster.

'This is what you get,' says one of the children, in a flat, sour tone. I drift backwards, but their faces only seem to grow larger.

192

'Wh— what?'

'This is what you get,' says another.

'This is what you get.'

A tall, slender girl stands up from her chair. 'This is what you g—reeeeuuhhhh,' she moans, her face elongating, jaw easing downwards, skin peeling from her skull.

'*This is what you get.*'

Tugging the door shut, I stumble away, my walk spinning into a run, but the hallway stretches as I go, never-ending, the sea wailing beneath me, the metallic clank growing louder, and louder, and—

Klank.

Ffssssch . . . KLANK.

Up ahead, a large rectangular box, metal and glass, is leaning at an angle against the wall. It wobbles precariously then slams back down on to the floor, rattling like a busted-up car.

Ffsssssschklank.

And there's a person inside it. Half a person.

ONLY 50p TO PLAY . . . IF YOU DARE!!!

Grandma. She's rocking the box, see-sawing it from one side to another.

Ffsssschklank.

Ffsschklank.

Ffsch—KLANK . . .

This time, the force of the impact sends the box careering all the way over and it crashes to the floor, glass walls shattering. Grandma snaps off her moorings and is left lying there, face down and legless, dotted with broken glass. A voice stutters out of her. 'Ah-ah-ah-ah . . . eh-eh-eh . . .'

I slow down, afraid to move any closer, and Grandma begins to shudder, violently. I look back and forth but the hallway simply tunnels away into darkness, in both directions.

Daddy's voice starts up again. 'She's obsessed with her stories, with this ludicrous imaginary friend . . .'

'Daddy? Will you help me?'

'Daydreaming will get her nowhere in life.'

'Ah-ah-*uh*,' says Grandma, bending her stiff old arms the wrong way over her head, until they're stretched out in front of her in a superhero-flying stance. 'Eh-eh-uh . . . eh-*uh* . . .'

'It's rotting her brain.'

Grandma bends her arms some more, forcing her half-a-body upwards, into a triangular tent shape, and as I watch, she begins to excrete long, bony limbs from the base of her torso. They extend from her body at sickening speed, like fast-growing stalks, three metres, four metres, five metres long, and then she heaves herself up on horrifying stilt-legs, bent hard at the knee like a spider's. She's higher than the house now, higher than everything, and as she looms over me, I realise a leathery flap is hanging from her mouth, just like on the pier that day. A lazy black tongue, lolling through her teeth like a piece of rotten meat.

'Ah-ah-uh,' stammers Grandma, voice stifled by the tongue, as she jerks towards me on her spider-stilts. 'Ah-ehk-it . . . Bah-*eckett*.'

'No wonder she doesn't sleep,' says Daddy, 'her head's full of nonsense.'

It's getting hotter. My skin is starting to crackle, like an oily pork joint.

'Baah-eckett,' chokes Grandma.

'We should send her away,' growls Daddy.

'I won't let you!' cries Mumma.

'I've made my decision.'

'You blame me, don't you?'

I want to run, but I can't. The chandelier is swaying madly.

'For not . . . giving you a boy.'

I can't run because, when I look down, I find that my right arm doesn't end in a hand anymore. Instead, my forearm fades into a thick chain, green with slime, and the chain is being pulled taut to the floor by a barnacle-encrusted anchor.

'Why shouldn't I blame you, Diane?'

Either side of me, the walls catch fire. I try to run, tugging at my chain-arm, but the anchor is too heavy and it won't budge. Grandma pegs towards me, still stammering around her black tongue, and underneath her, hundreds of glistening jellyfish writhe and flap.

'*It's your womb.*'

The floor is burning. Great, charred holes are opening in the wood like sores; furniture is falling through, tumbling into oblivion. Lamps, tables. Grandma's discarded machine.

I look down. I'm on fire. My flesh is bubbling.

'It's your wo-aaahmb. It's your wo-aaaahhhmb.'

And then I see her. In the dark of the hallway, behind Grandma. My imaginary friend. She's watching me burn, her eyes white pinpricks in the black.

'*It's dark down there, Beckett,*' she says, pointing to the floor. '*And I can't sleep in the dark. Can you?*'

With a splintering roar, the boardwalk collapses and I'm falling through the air, plummeting towards the ocean. I hit the water and it's fizzing with heat, the anchor dragging me through the murky depths and into the molten core of the earth until we finally come to rest in a hot, terrible cave, hundreds of miles beneath the surface.

This must be the place where I die. A quivering hellscape, its walls made of human flesh; a rotting womb where everything's burning, everything's alight, flesh peeling from my bones like pink slop.

I'm burning.

Let me die.

I'm burning—

◆ ◆ ◆

'Hhhhhhuuuuuhhh . . . !'

I take a sudden, rasping breath, sitting bolt upright in the darkness. My chest heaves up and down, like I've just run a hundred-metre sprint. My ears are pounding.

I pat the bedsheets around me, expecting flames, then drag a clammy hand up and down my arm, fingers trembling at the memory of my liquid flesh, oozing off like cream.

But there are no flames, and my body is intact.

I was dreaming.

Though it is hot in here . . . unbearably hot.

Tugging the duvet off my legs, I swing round and plant my feet on the floor. That rickety old boiler must be damned efficient.

Unless—

My heart begins to race. The soles of my feet are burning up on the wooden floor, as if I were stepping on to the boardwalk on a hot summer's day. The boiler may have been running full blast for several hours, but central heating can't be that powerful . . . can it?

Rising off the bed, I realise that, beneath me, in the study, I can hear things crackling and snapping. My nostrils twitch at the hint of smoke. Crossing to the window, I look down to find an eerie orange shimmer spilling on to the front lawn.

Oh, God.

The flames were real.

The house is on fire.

27.

Throwing on a T-shirt and jeans, I rush out of the bedroom and across the landing. I descend the stairs, slowing a little, aware of the heat becoming more intense, the skin shrinking on my bones.

At the bottom of the staircase, I pause, staring at the closed study door. Smoke is creeping out around the sides like ghostly grey fingers, and as I stand there, one foot on the stair and the other in the hallway, I'm captured by a single, fiendish thought.

What if I just let the house burn?

Dashing the thought away, I cross, unthinkingly, to the study door and open it, and a suffocating backdraught billows into me. I rear backwards, choking, and as I hit the opposite wall with a thud, I blink in disbelief at the sight in front of me.

The entire room is a hellish, pulsing orange; a screaming hive of flames. Furniture blackens, strips of ceiling wood drop to the floor like dead skin. And as I gaze, horrified, into the carnage, a grim realisation washes over me.

I did this.

I messed about with an old, demented boiler that I don't under-stand, and who knows how, but I must've drunkenly flicked the wrong combination of switches, because now, the future Heaviport Care Home For Children and Young People is about ten minutes away from ending its life as a raging inferno.

Then I notice that the study's bay window, which faces the street, is smashed. Straining in the darkness, I catch a petite, black-clad figure pelting off towards town, hair threshing in the wind. Shoulder-length, cappuccino-blonde hair.

My jaw falls open.

Leanne.

She's trying to burn me alive.

My phone. I need to call the fire brigade. Where is my phone?

I turned it off. I turned it off yesterday, and didn't switch it back on. *Because of her.*

I should never have trusted her.

I glance up the stairs, wondering if it's still in the bedroom, but there's no time. I have to call the fire brigade, I have to chase down Leanne. My phone takes, what, fifteen seconds to power up, and that's if I can even find it.

Whipping round, I cross to the telephone table by the front door and my heart sinks. Of course. My parents were the last humans on earth to own a rotary dial phone.

I jab my finger into the nine and spin the dial.

Clack-clack-clack-whrrrrrrrrr.

Nine.

Clack-clack-clack-whrrrrrrrrr.

Nine.

Clack-clack-clack-whrrrrrrrrr.

'Argh . . . Christ . . .'

A surge of acrid smoke burns my eyes, and I squeeze them shut, fumbling for the front door. As the line in my ear begins to ring, I turn the handle and kick the door wide open, sighing with relief at the cold, wet air rushing in.

'Emergency, which service do you require?'

'Fire . . . please.'

'I'm connecting you now.'

A pause, barely a second.

'Hello, fire service. Where are you calling from?'

I press the back of my neck. It's burning up. 'Er, Umber Lane, Heaviport. One Umber Lane.'

'And what's the nature of your emergency?'

Panicked, I glance over my shoulder at the encroaching smoke, the groping flames. I could swear the whole building is throbbing, like it's gasping for breath. 'My house . . . the house is on fire.'

'Is anyone injured?'

I think of Leanne, escaping down the street, leaving me to die. Anger simmers inside me. 'No, no . . . it's just me here.'

'OK. You need to leave the house and wait for the fire brigade. They're already on their way. What's your name?'

'Beckett Ryan,' I reply, feeling suddenly nine years old.

'Everything will be all right, Beckett,' she says, and my hand tightens around the phone cable as a dark vision rushes my mind. My imaginary friend, cowering in the corner of the study, being licked at by the flames. Her little body curling and shrinking like plastic in a microwave.

'Beckett?'

'Yeah, I'm here. Thank you. I'm leaving the house now. Thanks. Bye.'

Slamming the phone on to its cradle, I take one final look behind me, at the churning black smoke and the flames tonguing the walls, and tumble out into the night.

Before I know what I'm doing, I'm running, pounding the tarmac, puddles spraying left and right, raindrops pummelling my shoulders. In the distance, at the end of the long road that runs perpendicular to Umber Lane, I can just about make out Leanne from the pale flash of her hands in the dark, and the bob of her hair. She's beginning to slow, stopping now and again to rest her palms on her knees, but she doesn't turn her head. She doesn't want to see what she's done.

A stone jabs into my heel, making me stumble, and I suddenly realise that I'm barefoot. The road is filthy and wet from the storm, and I could run faster with shoes on, but when I look back at the house, it's obvious there's no point in returning. The study is a raging fireball, and the flames are scampering up the outside walls, craving a way in.

Besides, if I turn back now, I'll lose her.

'Hey!'

My sharp yell causes Leanne to flinch and almost turn round, but instead, she ups her pace and ducks down an alley. I've been gaining on her this whole time, and within seconds, I'm in the alley too, closing the gap.

We're three metres apart.

Two.

One.

'*Leanne.*'

This time she does turn her head, but before our eyes meet, I'm on her like a cheetah downing a gazelle. We pitch towards the wet ground, Leanne crying out, me clamping an arm around her neck, our bodies a clumsy bundle of limbs as we plunge to the concrete.

We land hard and awkwardly, both yelping, and skin is torn from my elbow. Leanne shields her face with her hand and starts to protest, wriggling underneath me, but I'm stronger than her, and feeling almost dizzy with rage.

I *need* to hit her.

To watch her bleed.

'You total . . . *psycho* . . .'

Straddling Leanne's back, I grasp her shoulder and wrench her over, bobbing upwards so her body can flip beneath me. She screams but she's too weak to stop me, and within moments, we're facing each other: me kneeling above, hand on her collarbone, her staring up at me, forlorn. Her chest is quaking with terror.

But as we lock eyes, I make a confusing discovery.

This is not Leanne.

'Wh—' I lift my hand off her neck. 'Who are you?'

She opens her mouth, quiveringly, as if afraid that I'm going to punch her just for answering.

In the distance, sirens.

'I'm . . . I-I'm Paige.'

My forehead slumps. 'Who?'

'Please don't hurt me.'

I lean down, and rain drips from my face on to hers. 'You just *set fire to my house.*'

'It wasn't my idea,' she blurts, desperately. 'I didn't . . . I wasn't . . .'

'You weren't what, exactly?'

She tries to raise her arms, but I'm kneeling on them.

'Please. It ain't what you think.'

I glance down at my curled fist, breath huffing out of me, the howl of fire engines reeling above our heads.

Am I *really* going to hit her? She looks so helpless.

'Grab her!'

Before I can finish my thoughts, I'm being hauled backwards and upwards, multiple hands clamped around my arms, my legs wheeling in the air. The hands set me down and my eyes dart about, brain scrambling to make sense of the action. Paige is dragging herself backwards in a frantic spider-walk, face stricken, while between us, four wild-eyed men form a wet, impenetrable wall.

Men I've met before.

'Sam?'

Sam Hastings, my old nemesis from the Wreckers, is standing on the far right of the group, breathing heavily through his nose. He's dressed in black, as are his henchmen.

'You're supposed to be in London,' he says, rattled.

'What are you talking about?'

He sticks his chin out. 'You wasn't supposed to be in the house.'

As I'm staring at him, I remember what Paige said to me, after I wrestled her to the ground. *It wasn't my idea.*

The longing to strike someone rears up in me again. 'You tried to kill me.'

Sam raises both hands, as if capitulating to a policeman. 'Hey, no. No. We thought you was on the train back to London. You *said* you was taking that train.'

I shake my head, bewildered. 'The train was cancelled. I could have died in there.'

I look past Sam, down the alleyway, and Paige's eyes catch mine. A wellspring of fresh anger rockets through me, and before I know it, I'm launching myself at her again, scrabbling against a wall of flailing arms.

'Sam, stop her!'

'That's my fucking house, you—'

'Get back!'

'We didn't know you was in there—'

'Let go of me—'

'Oi, calm down!'

'Stop touching me—'

'Your dad used to hit me.'

Silence. I stop struggling.

Paige is looking at me, childlike all of a sudden, her face chalk-white. Warily, Sam and the others back away, and I run a shaky hand over my wet hair. 'Sorry . . . *what?*'

She sniffs, fingers worrying against each other. 'Your dad used to hit me.'

I take a step forward. The men bristle.

'What the hell are you talking about?'

Paige starts to reply, but her lips tremble and her face folds, a string of spittle escaping her mouth. Her words are swallowed by sobs.

'Paige is my baby sister.' Sam's voice, now. 'She was at your dad's school. Your old man used to beat her up.'

Slowly, I turn my head to meet his. 'That's impossible.'

He works his jaw, gaze fixed on mine. 'It's true.'

'Wait, no. No.' My eyes drop to the ground. 'My father was many things, and trust me, I hated the old bastard, but he only hit . . . I mean, he wouldn't . . .'

As I'm saying the words, they begin to feel flimsy in my mouth.

'Honest,' pleads Paige, 'I ain't lying. I wouldn't lie about this.'

She's interrupted by the distant sound of a fire hose being turned on, spitting and gushing through the air. I think of my father's study, burning to nothing.

'But . . . if he hit kids at school, we'd know about it. The town would know about it.'

'Not kids,' says Sam, tightly. 'Just my sister.'

I look up, meeting his eyes, and something I told Kai, the night of the Shetland whisky, floats to the shoreline of my thoughts.

Harold Beckett Ryan wanted a son. He wanted a boy.

Girls must only be good for beating.

'He told me I was from a bad family,' says Paige, arms limp at her sides. 'He said he could do anything to me and my parents wouldn't care . . . and he was right.'

I look from Paige to her brother, feeling like my head is bobbing on a string. I'd always assumed it was just me, that I was his only dirty secret. But this town turned Harold Ryan into a demi-god, and it made him untouchable.

Playing judge and jury over other families, when his own was rotten to the core.

'He always hit me with the same thing,' continues Paige, her voice climbing in pitch. 'A belt, with a buckle on the end. Thick and heavy, it was, with a picture engraved. An anchor, like on the school badge.'

An anchor.

My head whips towards her. 'What did you say?'

'It h-had . . . an anchor on it,' she stammers, her eyes swelling with fear. 'That's what he hit me with.'

I feel a cracking sensation behind my ribs, like the snapping of sticks. Rotating away from the group, I press a fist to my chest, brain rushing with imagery.

An anchor, wreathed in thick ropes, green and sodden from the sea.

The school crest, carved in red stone.

A BETTER FUTURE FOR ALL.

'Oh . . . Jesus . . .'

A black leather belt, swinging gently above me, like the pendulum of a grandfather clock. Hanging on the end, my father's treasured belt buckle, the Heaviport anchor. A symbol of hope.

I'm eight years old, helpless on the floor of his study, purple arm splayed against the wood. Waiting for it all to be over. But the slaps, the skin twists, those weren't the worst parts. They were just the parts I remembered.

The belt was his grand finale.

Yesterday, on the boardwalk, Grandma wasn't trying to foresee my future – she was showing me my past. The black tongue easing from her mouth: a belt being pulled from its loops.

This is what you get, you little cunt.

'Beckett?'

I force my head up, one hand clutched to my stomach. Paige is standing in front of me, brow crimped. 'You all right?'

I clamp my jaw closed, swallowing hard. 'Uh . . . yeah. I'm fine.'

She drags a wrist across bloodshot eyes. 'We wasn't trying to hurt you, really. We thought you'd gone.'

I give her a cautious glance. 'It's OK. I believe you.'

'No one ever believed her back in the day, you know,' counters Sam, his eyes wild. 'She tried telling other teachers, but they just called her a shit-stirrer.'

Of course they did. She was a shy kid, from a difficult home. My father cherry-picked her because he knew she had no one looking out for her. That was his playbook.

Paige hunches her shoulders, shivering, and I'm struck by how small she is. How defenceless she must have been as a child.

'I stopped trying in the end,' she says, weakly, and her brother bares his teeth at me.

'Things he did to Paige, they fucked her up. She's never been right since.'

His fingers twitch, his body almost vibrating with nervous energy. His words ring in my ears.

Never been right since.

'And now—' Paige flails an arm in the direction of Umber Lane '—now they want to turn his house into a *children's* home, and that's just wrong, 'cos he hurt children. And I know I weren't the first, 'cos he told me. He said there was another girl, but she'd gone away, so . . . he chose me.'

I study Paige's face, the line of her jaw, the faint wrinkles by her eyes. She looks about my age, so she wouldn't have started at Heaviport Secondary until after I'd left for boarding school.

Without me around, he'd needed a proxy. A punching bag.

'I'm sorry, Paige. I really am.'

She jigs a shoulder. 'Ain't your fault.'

But that's the thing, Paige: it is my fault. Because you replaced me.

'Just 'cos he's your dad, don't mean we have to be angry at you, does it?' She levels a pointed look at her brother. 'Right, Sam?'

Sam crosses his arms and shifts his feet, avoiding my gaze. It appears our bar room spats may have been about more than a homophobic slur, after all.

'Yeah. Right.' He gives a reluctant sniff. 'Whatever.'

A chilly waft of drizzle passes over us, and I realise I'm riddled with goosebumps. Cradling my arms against the cold, I feel wetness on one elbow, and pull my fingers away. Blood, from where I crashed to the ground with Paige. The sight of it, fresh and gleaming, sticks in the back of my throat.

That need I felt, looming above her, to smash her, to cause her pain – I felt the same need last week, in the Wreckers. More than once. My father may be the abuser here, but he's lurking inside me, in my marrow. Like a cancer.

Maybe I shouldn't be concerned about forgetting him. I should be concerned about becoming him.

'I have to go,' I say, hurriedly, walking backwards from the group. Paige reaches out an arm.

'Sorry, again, for scaring you,' she says, her face pale with sympathy. Then it tightens with alarm. 'Wait, are you going to tell the fire briga—'

'No . . . no, I won't. Don't worry. I sort of feel like—' my eyes flick to Sam '—my family owes you one.'

Paige gives me the faintest, smallest smile. 'Thanks.'

Turning around, I begin the wet, lonely walk back to Charnel House, feet throbbing, teeth chattering with the cold, wondering what I'll find when I step back through that front door.

◆ ◆ ◆

As I draw closer to Umber Lane, the house looms out at me through the early dawn mist, its fires quenched, door still wide open from my escape into the night.

The front of the building is blighted by a charred hole where the study once was, smoking lazily like a gunshot wound in an animal. Where the flames fingered their way up the brickwork, a deep scorch runs at an angle towards the roof, giving the impression of a sly black grin, welcoming me home.

'Hey.' A stout, handsome firefighter is walking towards me, helmet wedged under his arm. Behind him, the lights from the fire engine bathe the street in a stuttering blue glow. 'You Beckett Ryan?'

I push my damp hair from my face. 'That's me.'

'We were wondering where you'd got to,' he says, with a slight frown. I glance over my shoulder, feeling caught out.

'Oh . . . uh, yeah. Sorry. I just . . .' I gesture at the house. 'This was my childhood home. I couldn't bear to watch.'

He nods, sympathetically. 'Sure, sure. Soph, can we get a blanket over here, please?' He receives a thumbs-up from his colleague, then turns back to me. 'Look, the fire's out now, and we've got the situation under control. The worst of the damage is limited to the ground floor, and while everything in the study was destroyed, the rest of your belongings should be roughly how you left them. Though they'll probably smell of smoke for . . . well, forever.'

I wriggle my hands into my pockets.

'End of the day,' he says, softening his tone, 'the building's still pretty much in one piece. I know this is a lot to take in, but trust me, it could have been worse.'

I stare at the house, into its watchful windows, and it grins back at me, darkly.

Part of me wishes it *had* been worse. Much worse.

'You're right. Thank you.'

He takes a breath, shifts his helmet from one arm to the other. 'Do you have somewhere you can go?'

I glance up and down the street. I'm not certain what time it is, but morning's definitely on its way. I could head over to the beach, catch the sunrise. 'I do, yeah.'

The firefighter nods again. Then his eyes flit, for the briefest moment, up and down my body, and it occurs to me that my bra may be showing through my wet T-shirt.

He clears his throat. 'Listen, if you hang around for a bit, we'll make sure everything's safe and then we can take you inside to fetch some dry clothes, a phone, whatever you need.'

'That'd be great, thank you.'

'Ed, here you go.' A second firefighter has appeared with one of those foil blankets they give to people who've just run marathons. She hands it to Ed, along with a blackened strip of material, then says something low into his ear.

'Cheers, Soph,' says Ed, wrapping the blanket around me. 'I'll be with you in a sec.'

As she pulls away, Sophie gives me a muted smile and slips out her phone.

'Is there, um—' Ed bobs the strip of material up and down in his gloved hand, as if weighing it '—is there anyone in this town who might want to hurt you, Miss Ryan?'

Only about eight thousand people.

'Not that I can think of,' I reply, casually, pulling the blanket tight round my shoulders. It crunches like a crisp packet.

Ed holds the material at arm's length, letting it dangle. 'This was found in your front room, a few feet from the broken window.'

I poke out my bottom lip. 'I don't follow.'

'Do you know what a Molotov cocktail is?'

I nod, hesitantly, my eyes drawn back to Sophie, who is standing by the front gate on a hushed phone call. I catch the word 'constable'.

'If this is what it looks like,' continues Ed, his voice lowered, 'someone may have been trying to harm you. Are you sure there's no one local who, say, holds a grudge?'

By now, Paige, Sam and their makeshift gang will be long gone, retreating through the Heaviport backstreets, heading for home. I think about the pain in Paige's face, the years of resentment baked into her. The anger she'll never shake.

When it comes to my father, she and I are not all that different.

'I doubt it,' I say, wondering whether Ed reads the *Heaviport Gazette*. 'I've only been back two weeks.'

He pumps air through his lips, then slides the scrap into a trouser pocket. 'Well, if you think of anything, you let us know, OK?'

'Of course,' I lie, enjoying the warmth from the crinkly blanket. 'I will.'

Half an hour later, when the house is declared safe, Ed escorts me down the garden path to the open front door. I hesitate on the threshold, one hand on the frame, reeling at the musk of burnt wood in the air.

The fire has turned the hallway into a black and dismal hollow, gnarled as a tree trunk. My parents' antique chandelier has been ravaged by the blaze, and for a moment, as I stare at it, I don't see a chandelier. I see a monstrous burnt spider, hanging upside down with its legs splayed.

'Miss Ryan . . . ?'

The fire rages across the ceiling, its flames unfurling like red-hot tentacles. In a distant corner, my imaginary friend, crouched in a black ball, pivots her head towards me, mouth open, eye sockets empty as caves.

'Are you OK, Miss Ryan?'

'Huh?'

Ed moves into my line of sight, brow pinched with concern. His eyes dart inside the house. 'I can go in for you, if you like.'

I suck in a breath. 'Oh . . . no, I'm fine. This is . . . this is fine . . .'

Stepping inside, I walk slowly towards the stairs, feeling the house creak and moan beneath my feet (more than before, I'm sure of it). I leave Ed at the bottom of the staircase and make my way to the landing, my hand hovering above the sooty, spoiled banister. At the top, I'm surprised to find the upper half of the house virtually unchanged, aside from the sharp smell of smoke and the odd ghost of a scorch mark on the floor. If I hadn't just walked through hell to get here, I might not know it had been in a fire at all.

In my room, I cross to my open suitcase and throw on some dry clothes, all the while glancing at my phone on the bedside table. I know I should switch it on, but I'm not ready to deal with the inevitable barrage of messages from Leanne yet.

One disaster at a time.

Sliding the phone into my handbag, along with my laptop, I leave the room and cross the landing again. As I'm passing my parents' bedroom, something inside catches my eye, and I stop in my tracks. Hanging on the chair, as it has been since the day I arrived, is my father's belt.

He always hit me with the same thing.

I peek over the railings at Ed, waiting for me below, faint bald patch on his crown. He seems content enough, so I pass quietly into the bedroom and approach the chair, my heart beginning a dull thud. As the details on the buckle – the regal curves of the anchor, the ribbed outline of the ropes – shift into focus, I feel suddenly short of breath, my lungs over-tight. I'm certain now, if I wasn't before, that I have been struck by this belt. More than once.

Biting down on my tongue, nearly hard enough to draw blood, I seize the belt by the neck, as if it were a venomous snake. Detaching the buckle, I slip it into my pocket and, impulsively, whip the belt across the room and on to the bed. It slithers off the mattress on to the floor, coiling sulkily.

I take a final glance around. This is the farthest inside that I've ventured since that first night, and it still feels eerie, interrupted, as if the death of my mother froze time within these four walls and I've stolen in here, uninvited, through the membrane of the past.

Her slippers, paired under the dresser, one turned on its side. The bedcovers still rucked up around her sad little imprint in the bed. Her ornaments and knick-knacks carefully arranged on the dresser: a wooden jewellery box with a floral-patterned lid, a drooping orchid, two or three tubes of hand and face cream.

And there, lying next to a glass perfume bottle, a photograph of my father.

My pulse lurches. I'm not used to seeing his face again, even after Nadia's home video, and a chill scuttles over me. How long has this been out here? Was this how my mother spent her final few days, sitting at the dresser, thumbing old photographs? Clinging to his ghost?

Part of me wants to turn and run. Get away from here, for good, and never come back. But another part, some deeper urge, needs to see that picture close up. To look him dead in the eyes.

Over the sound of a murmured conversation downstairs, I cross the room, handbag clutched at my side. Cagily, as if it might be electrified, I pick up the photograph and stare down at it, my breathing loud and thick inside my head. My father looks young, in his forties, handsome and clean-shaven, and from the hint of red brick and playing field behind him, I'd guess it was taken at Heaviport Secondary. He's gazing at some spectacle in the distance – a group of his beloved students, perhaps – and he looks happy, almost serene. His smile, much like the one I saw on the big screen in Nadia's cinema, is utterly sincere, and that's the worst thing about it. I'd convinced myself that the people of this town must have been tricked into their adoration for my father, but this picture tells a different story. So long as he was outside the walls of this house, Harry Ryan, Bobby Dazzler, was as real as the man who beat his daughter.

A jolt of sorrow rises in me. I choke on it, blindsided by the threat of tears, but then I feel the weight of the belt buckle in my pocket, think of Paige, and the feeling sours. I drop the picture and step backwards.

I'm about to turn away when I notice a second photograph on the dresser. A group picture, this time: a family portrait. My mother and father are posing in the garden at Charnel House, in front of the high, vine-webbed back wall, and I'm standing beside them, aged maybe seven, eight . . . next to Leanne.

A stone drops inside me.

She's been telling the truth all along. Her tales of our school days, her claims about our friendship, they weren't just some fantasy she cooked up. They were real, and this is the proof. The two of us, holding hands in a photo, squinting against the sun. A cute, dimpled grin on Leanne's face, a crooked one on mine.

I shudder at the memory of my last message.

I'm going back to London. Don't ever contact me again.

Oh, Leanne.

I shouldn't have gone behind your back. I shouldn't have met with your hideous father, or believed him when he said we were never friends. He wound me up and I lost my cool, but I took his word for it, and that was careless. He was probably drunk half the time when we were kids anyway, so even if I did go for play dates at the Wilding house, what are the chances he would remember me, nearly thirty years later?

Leanne is one of the few people who've been kind to me since I arrived here. I've been awful to her, and all she ever wanted was to be my friend.

'Miss Ryan? Everything OK?'

Ed's voice, from the foot of the stairs. I return the photo to the dresser, covering the one of my father, and call over my shoulder. 'I'm fine. Just coming down.'

I look again at the image of Leanne – at her sweet, happy face, dotted with freckles, and our little fingers, entwined – and my heart wrings in my chest.

Before I leave town, I have to make good on this. It's the very least that I owe her.

28.

A clean, tangerine light spills in through the windows of the Seafront Cafe, warming the tops of laminate tables, winking off chrome chair frames. In the distance, the ocean is unusually flat and serene, its blue-green surface undisturbed, save for the occasional splish from a dive-bombing seagull.

'You're up early,' says Juliet, raising impressed eyebrows, as she arranges various stainless steel implements on her coffee machine's drip tray. It's 7.45 a.m. and, staff aside, I'm the only soul in here.

'Too early,' I reply, lifting my purse from my handbag and suppressing a yawn.

'Flat white, isn't it?'

'Yes . . . yes. Double shot, please, with oat milk. To take away.'

Juliet busies herself making my drink. I offer her a five-pound note but she waggles a hand. 'Oh, no, no. We always give away our first coffee of the day. Company policy.'

'Is that so?'

She gives me a broad smile. 'It is.'

I doubt this is true, somehow, but I'm grateful for the gesture. 'In that case,' I reply, extending my arm over the tip jar, 'I shall accept your free gift, but I'm tipping you for the smile.'

I drop the note, and Juliet gives me a nod.

'Beckett?'

The voice behind me is warm and refined, with the trace of an accent. Turning, I find the baroness forming a one-person queue for the counter, her eyes pinched with worry.

'Oh . . . hello, Nadia.'

'Are you all right?' Her tone is far from casual.

She already knows.

'I heard about the fire,' she confirms, stepping closer to me. Behind, I sense Juliet pausing her work to listen. 'Just awful. Thank heavens you weren't hurt. How do you think it started?'

I shrug a shoulder. 'Probably just one of those things. Old houses.'

Her eyes draw into a slit. 'I'm told the fire service suspect arson.'

Reaching for my coffee, I take a foamy sip and study Nadia over the rim of the cup. She knows so many of Heaviport's secrets, and yet, when it comes to my father's abuse, she's as in the dark as anyone.

'I'll bet it was knackered wiring or something,' I suggest, blithely, keen to play it down. If this trail leads her back to Sam Hastings, and she discovers what my father did to Paige, she might pull out of the house sale altogether.

'I suppose it's possible,' she replies, distractedly, as if running scenarios in her head. She goes quiet, then catches my eye again. 'I gather you had another skirmish in the Wreckers yesterday. I'm beginning to worry for your safety.'

'Actually, now you mention it . . .' I pass a palm around the back of my neck. 'I know we had a deal, you and I, but I think it's time for me to go back to London. I'm ruffling too many feathers here, and the fire guy said it could be weeks before the house is habitable again.'

She makes a vague gesture out the window. 'You could stay at Anchora Park, if you like?'

'Oh, I . . . wouldn't want to impose.'

'Nonsense.' Her lips curve into a smile. 'I think I have the space.'

I glance at the floor, chewing my lip. The idea is almost appealing, but now is not the time. There's an anchor around every corner in that house.

'I might stick that invite on the back burner, if that's OK?' I say, wrapping both hands around my coffee cup. 'London's calling.'

She nods, lips pressed together. 'Fair enough.'

We lock eyes for a moment, and I feel a tickle in my chest: the unnerving sensation that the rug is about to be pulled out from under me.

'Listen, Nadia. About Charnel House.' My voice is lowered. 'With the fire and everything, and me leaving, are you still planning to b—'

'Oh, don't you worry about that,' she says, with a bullish flare. 'The fire is a minor hiccup. It may hold us back, but it won't hold us down.' She pulls in a long breath, then lets it out as a sigh. 'And I understand, Beckett. About you leaving. I know you've tried, and I appreciate not everyone in town has welcomed you with open arms.'

'I'm sorry if I've let you down.'

She laughs, gently. 'I'm not sure you have, exactly. That Leanne Wilding seems very sweet on you, for a start.'

Her mention of Leanne jabs at my chest, and I picture my phone in my handbag, still switched off. The messages piling up.

I will the thought away.

'Think I may have a friend in Juliet, too,' I say, scanning the room, remembering how she went against her husband to defend me. She's at a far window with a customer, admiring the sunrise. 'So that's two whole people.'

'Ah, yes. Heart of gold, that one. Husband's a bit of a handful, though.'

We watch Juliet for a while, as the sun climbs higher in the morning sky. The room swells with light.

'Hell of a storm last night,' says Nadia, her eyes on the sea. 'There's been landslides up and down the coast, and all kinds of trouble on the roads. But look at it now. So peaceful.'

Juliet gives us a wave as she makes her way back to the till. Nadia returns it.

'Well, I must push on with my day,' she says, gripping her handbag. '*Bon voyage*, my dear.'

She opens her arms and we embrace – not just a gesture, but a lingering hug – and it occurs to me that I haven't been properly held by another human being in a very long time. A lump forms in my throat. 'Thank you,' I say, blinking back emotion. 'For everything.'

'Do call me when you're settled back in London.' She takes out her purse and walks towards the counter. 'I'd love to tell you more about my plans for the home.'

'I will. Bye, Nadia.'

'And I meant my invitation,' she says, as I head for the exit, coffee in hand. '*Mi casa, et cetera . . .*'

The morning is about as beautiful as a November day can be, the air crisp and pure, the sky a raw, icy blue. After the storm, the town has the feel of a once-cluttered room that's been swept clean and emptied.

When I reach the end of the boardwalk, I look out across the sand dunes, tightening my scarf around my neck. Despite the cold, I'm determined to sit outside, at least for an hour or so, and write. My head is thick with fatigue, but I've got things to say – new things – and I need the wind to keep me alert.

I walk along the beach for ten minutes or so, eventually settling on a sandy knoll above a tumble of large, algae-scabbed rocks. I boot up my laptop and, while it loads, rest my phone on my fingers, thumb poised over the power button.

The screen flickers to life. I steel myself for a flood of messages, but none come, so I stand up, waving the phone in the air, and am rewarded with a single, lonely *blip*.

Leanne
I'm sorry, Beckett. I don't know what I did, but I'm sorry.

I rub my eyes, a low groan in my throat. At least if she'd flown off the handle about it – sent me hundreds of desperate, hysterical messages – it might have eased my guilt. But, no. Two sentences, contrite and humble.

I feel about four millimetres tall.

My MacBook fades into life and I look from its screen to my phone, face scrunched. I will make this right, as soon as I can. But not with a text message. I have to go and see her, and she'll have left for work by now.

I'll go early evening, when she's home. That's what people do in small towns, isn't it? Pop in for a cuppa. Face to face, so no one's misunderstood.

I'm about to lock my phone when I notice Zadie's text chat, sitting beneath Leanne's. I owe Zade a conversation, too. I need to tell her about the fire, of course, and Paige Hastings, but I feel like I haven't asked about her life in weeks. I've been absorbed in my own drama, blinkered by this place, these people.

Trains are back up and running – I'm on the late one home tonight. Free tomorrow for a catch-up? x

Zade'll be on her way to work now as well, earphones in on the Central line, engrossed in some impenetrable litigation case. I try to imagine her meeting Leanne one day, and the thought makes me smile. Those two could not be more different.

Turning from my phone to my laptop, I scroll to recent documents and open the file entitled 'Heaviport 2023'. The cursor blinks expectantly at me.

I begin to type.

> 'I discovered something, today, in the early hours
> of the morning. A secret that a little girl buried,
> deep under the foundations of her hometown,
> because she knew almost no one would believe
> her. It twisted my heart, this secret, because I
> harbour the same one, and it's about time I
> squared up to it. The truth about a man who,
> to most of the world, was a beacon of light, a
> symbol of hope – but to me, was the darkest,
> cruellest kind of monster, the kind that doesn't
> just know where you live, but lives there too . . .'

Fiercely, ceaselessly, I write. About my father's abuse, for the first time, about how my childish obsession with an imaginary friend became the catalyst for his violence. How that violence was the reason we never bonded – the reason why, all these years, I've been consumed by this black, mutating hatred for him, and why I couldn't bring myself to visit him, even on his death bed.

It doesn't take a doctorate in psychology to figure out why I have so few memories from the first nine years of my life. I was rejecting that part of me, papering over it the way you might hide damp in a crumbling house. But I was too young to be selective, so my brain scrubbed out almost everything, from my school and home life to my friendship with Leanne, and even now, I can't be certain those memories will ever return.

And then there's my mother.

Did she know he was beating me? She must have.

She *must* have known, and she never intervened. She never tried to stop him, and the only reason he eventually relented was that they banished me, ejected me from their lives. I was finally safe, but only on account of being hundreds of miles away in some huge, echoey boarding school.

I write about my father's split personality, about the unsettling difference between the man that Heaviport knew and loved and the one who laid his fists on me, behind closed doors. It was as if he *needed* to hit me, and Paige, so that he could be civil, even celebrated, to the rest of the world.

The harder he hit us, the softer he could be on everyone else.

Four hours pass in a blur.

Beckett
Howard, I've written a load more. Sticking it in an email for you. Morning, by the way.

Howard
Good Lord, woman. You're on fire.

I cringe at the accidental pun, and consider telling him. But he'd only worry.

Beckett
This is the proper juicy stuff, too. Brace yourself.

Howard
I am braced!

Beckett

To be real, there are things in here, explosive things, that I've barely told anyone. So this stays between us, OK? Not for public consumption.

Howard

Of course.

Sucking in a lungful of salty air, I hit send on the email.

Beckett

In other news, I'm coming back to London. Decided I couldn't live any longer without knife crime and artisanal cheese. Cocktails soon? B x

Howard

Splendid idea. Groucho? Chortle. H x

Slapping my laptop closed and sliding it into my handbag, I stand up and swivel on the sand, facing towards town. I imagine Leanne at work, beavering away at her desk, filing documents and sharpening pencils. Come five-thirty, I'll be paying her one final visit.

29.

LEANNE

I turn the shower dial up high, almost to the top, until the water is scalding. Until my skin goes pink.

I wish I could burn it all away. All the terrible things I've done, all the people I've let down. I want to start again. A different person.

I swipe a hand across the shower door, leaving wobbly finger marks on the plastic, and shut my eyes.

I just wanted to be friends.

Was that too much to ask? My phone tells me that Beckett's seen my reply, but she hasn't written back . . . and she never will, will she? I was too desperate, too needy, and now I've lost her forever. I've—

Wait.

Was that the doorbell?

I pause, hair in my fist. It can't be the doorbell. No one ever comes to see me, apart from Kai, and he's meeting a friend tonight. I must have imagined it.

I reach for the dial and turn the heat up, all the way.

BECKETT

I listen to the dying strains of the doorbell, chewing a fingernail. It's chilly out here, well past sunset, and the cold is trickling into my bones.

Still no answer.

I'm reaching for the intercom to try the bell again when the door jolts open, forcing me backwards. A young, fresh-faced man comes out, maybe mid-twenties, and gives me a surprised smile.

'Can I help you?' he says.

I ruffle my hair. 'I'm . . . not sure. I'm a friend of Leanne's, your upstairs neighbour? She doesn't seem to be in, though.'

The man laughs, softly. 'She's in the shower. I can hear it through the ceiling.' He gestures inside the hallway. 'Why don't you go on up? Her door's normally unlocked.'

So trusting, I think, as I brush past him, returning his smile. I could be anyone.

'Thank you,' I call after him, as he makes his way down the garden path, into the darkness.

He throws me a wave. 'Tell her hi from Pete, downstairs.'

At the top of the staircase, I knock, hesitantly, on Leanne's front door, but there's no response. I twist the handle and with a gentle snick the door yields, opening out into Leanne's snug little living space. I scan the room, feeling like an intruder. As a Londoner, I will never get used to this. *You've heard the cliché about towns where people don't lock their front doors?* repeats the baroness, in my head. *That's actually true here, or at least it used to be.*

The sound of the shower is spilling out from behind the half-open bathroom door. Steam drifts through the gaps.

223

'Leanne?'

There's a small commotion from inside the bathroom, and the gushing of the shower cuts off. 'Hello?'

'Leanne, it's . . . it's Beckett.'

A short pause, then her voice jumps an octave. 'Beckett, oh my God! Oh, wow. Wait, I'm all wet. I'll come out. Hang on—'

'It's fine,' I call back, smiling at her eagerness. 'Don't rush. You finish your shower, I'll amuse myself in here.'

The squeak of bare feet against acrylic. 'OK . . . OK . . . thank you . . . for coming round, I mean. I'll be quick. I'll be quick.'

I shift from one foot to the other, mentally rehearsing the little speech I've spent all afternoon preparing. Up until now, Leanne has been the awkward one, the stammerer, but now it's my turn to be uncomfortable. I can feel my back clamming up.

I walk over to Leanne's bookshelf and start fingering the spines. 'Pete from downstairs says hi,' I call, trying to sound relaxed.

Leanne's voice comes back to me through frantic splashing. 'Oh. Oh? Pete. Right . . . thank you.'

'Seems like a nice guy.'

'He is nice!' she squeaks, over-excited. 'He works at the petting zoo.'

I can hear her scrambling to finish, hurriedly rinsing, as I cast my eye along her modest assortment of novels. Aside from my complete collection, there's only a handful of titles on the shelf. *Robinson Crusoe. The Perks of Being a Wallflower. Eleanor Oliphant is Completely Fine.* All books about loneliness.

'I'm nearly done,' she calls, through the wall, as I pause on a thick, red spine: a spine that's oddly familiar. Something I've read before, I think, until I realise this is not a book, at least not a published one. It's a notebook.

Somebody's diary.

'Mumma!'

I can hear angry footsteps marching towards my bedroom. Leanne looks past me, along the landing, her eyes all big and worried.

'Don't shout like that, Beckett,' says Mumma, appearing in the doorway. She pushes hair behind her ear. Her fingers are shaky. 'What do you want?'

'I can't find my diary anywhere.'

She makes a clicky noise with her tongue. 'Well, you should've been more organised with your packing. You've known about the new school for weeks.'

I stare at her, squeezing my hands into fists. 'I am organised, but my diary isn't where I keep it, so someone must have stolen it.'

'Don't be ridiculous. Who on earth would steal your diary?'

I don't have an answer for that, which makes me even more annoyed. Mumma points at Leanne. 'Why don't you ask Leanne to help you?'

I twist around and scowl at Leanne. 'I *did* ask, but she's not trying very hard.'

'Hey,' says Leanne, in a sulk. 'I am trying, it's just not here. It's not anywhere.'

'Two minutes,' says Mumma, before clomping away, down the stairs. I look at Leanne, and all around us the house creaks in the wind.

She bites her lip. 'I'm sad that you're going.'

'I'm not,' I say, clamping my teeth together. 'This house is horrible, and this town is horrible, and it's good riddance, I say.'

Leanne swallows. 'Will you come back and see me?'

I shake my head. 'I'm never coming back here. When I'm grown up, I'm going to move to London and be a writer, and I don't care if I never see my family again.'

Leanne's mouth wobbles. 'What about me?'

'You can come to London, too,' I say, with a shrug. 'We can live together in a big house, with no parents. And no boys.'

A tear drops down Leanne's cheek, and she tries to smile. 'A-and . . . and we can keep secret diaries, and only share them with each other . . . and every night you can write in mine, and I can write in yours?'

I nod, reaching out my hand. She shakes it.

'You've got one minute.' Mumma is standing in the doorway again, stabbing at her watch. 'Your father's outside, and the car is running.' She looks at Leanne. 'Leanne, dear, you need to leave now. Beckett's going.'

I stand up. 'What about my diary?'

'Oh, I don't *care* about your diary, Beckett,' she snaps, grabbing me by the arm. 'Get outside, now.'

I tug myself away from her and stomp down the stairs, leaving Leanne behind.

'If you want a diary,' calls Mumma, after me, 'you'll just have to write another one. Now, let that be the end of it.'

I slide the chunky red notebook from Leanne's bookshelf and hold it in my hands, feeling its weight.

THE SECRET DIARY OF BECKETT DIANE RYAN,
AGED 8 9
TOP SECRET!! KEEP OUT!!!!

As the shower dial squeaks in the bathroom, and the patter of water slows to a stop, dots join in my head.

I never lost my diary.

Leanne *stole* it.

A flat laugh shoots out of me, and I stifle it. Should I be annoyed about this? It was a betrayal, I suppose, but an extremely small one. And kleptomania does run in her family.

I pass a thumb across the book's hard cover, exploring its grooves and dints. This explains so much. Leanne's strange, furtive behaviour over the last couple of weeks; that sense on the cliff edge, when I was scattering the ashes, that she had some big secret to reveal. If I know Leanne, and I think I'm beginning to, she'll have been feeling horribly guilty about this, ever since I arrived. She may even have been feeling that way since the day she took it.

In fact, weren't we sitting in this exact room, last Friday night, when I brought up how strange it was that I hadn't kept a child-hood diary? *And it was right here the whole time.* She'll have been having sleepless nights about this, I'll bet. Fretting about how to tell me, turning it all into a much bigger deal than it really is. No wonder she's been acting so screwy.

'Diary thief,' I joke, to myself, flicking through the pages. 'You funny old thi—'

My breathing stalls. I've stopped on a random date, a Thursday in October. Lines of my confident but wonky nine-year-old scrawl fill the top half of the page.

I hope I can sleep tonight. I feel very tired.

At night-time, bad things happen. I try not to get scared, but she is so so frightening. She won't leave me alone.

I hope I can sleep tonight.

The memory of those restless nights is still painful, but that isn't what's catching my breath. There's something here that shouldn't be. Underneath my entry is a second one, written – and drawn – in someone else's hand. A timid, babyish scribble, in arresting red ink.

My pulse is in my throat. Was this always there? Where did it come from?

There's a crude stick-picture of me in bed, asleep, three little zeds floating over my head, flat lines for eyes. A second stick-girl, this one with crosses for eyes, lies on the floor beneath me.

Six words are scrawled along the bottom of the page.

tonight i sleeped under her bed

Turning the page, fingers trembling, I stop on an almost identical entry from the following night. My bedtime musings, scrawled in black, and underneath, in my co-author's spindly hand, a red-ink picture – a stick-girl with crosses for eyes stands in the closet, while I slumber, unaware, beneath the covers. A message in red at the bottom.

tonight i sleeped in the cubbard

Page after page, it's the same.

tonight i weared her dresses

tonight i tutched her skin

tonight i standed up and looked at her all night

tonight i sleeped right next to her

My scalp crawls.

When I was sent away to boarding school, my nightmares halted, abruptly, for no obvious reason. Looking back, I probably chalked that up to being away from my father, to being free of Charnel House, with its looming shadows and moaning floorboards. I never saw her again, my menacing doppelgänger, and she soon slipped from my thoughts, silent and swift, like an eel disappearing beneath a rock.

But there's a reason my imaginary friend vanished the day I left Heaviport, and it's been staring me in the face for weeks. That eerie little girl wasn't a figment of my imagination. It was Leanne.

30.

LEANNE

My heart is thumping as I wrap the towel around me. I'm so excited, I want to sing.

Beckett didn't sound mad. She sounded . . . normal. Like maybe we can fix this. Like whatever I've done, we can fix it.

'I'm so pleased you came round,' I say, stepping out of the bathroom, 'because, look . . . whatever I did, I'm sorry. I can make it up to you. I know I ca—'

Beckett is looking straight at me. Her eyes are big. Her cheeks are pale.

'Beckett? Wh—'

I glance down. She's holding the stolen diary in her hand, open on a page I know well. The October 28th picture. The sleeping-right-next-to-her picture.

My skin goes tight.

She knows.

BECKETT

When I speak, my voice is strangled. Stretched thin. 'How . . . could you?'

Leanne swallows, one balled hand at her chest, gripping her towel. Her face is blotched pink from the shower.

'A-all . . . along,' I say, forcing out the words, 'it was . . . you?'

She extends an arm towards me. 'Yes . . . it was me. But—'

'Don't, Leanne. Don't touch me.'

I clutch at my stomach with my free hand, a cold terror stirring. I think of all the things she's done, the untold hours she's spent standing over me, in the dark, in that groaning old house. Just watching.

When I saw her red-pen entries in my diary, as a kid, I would have assumed my double was writing them. Bent over my notebook in the small hours, eagerly scribbling. I must have been terrified. 'I . . . came here tonight—' my voice thickens with emotion, but I fight it '—to apologise to you. For pushing you away, for not trusting you, but—'

'Please, Beckett. I know it looks bad.'

'Bad?' I shake the book at her, its pages rattling like dry leaves. 'Have you any idea how twisted this is?'

She presses both palms to her eyes, and a puppyish whimper escapes her mouth. 'I never meant to upset you,' she cries, letting her hands fall. 'I just . . . I wanted to feel close to you.'

'Close t—? Jesus *Christ*, Leanne.' I glower at her, open-mouthed, and with a clunk of gears, my fear turns to anger. I hurl the diary into an armchair. 'How the hell did this happen? How was it even *possible*?'

She stares at me, eyes like buttons. 'Your . . . your front door was often unlocked. I could just sneak in withou—'

'Fuck, no, stop it. *Stop it*. I don't want to hear any more. I don't want to know.'

A big, hacking sob bursts from her mouth, and she starts to cry. 'I-I'm so, so sorry, Beckett. I know it was wrong.' She drags an arm across her eyes, like a small child. 'But you were everything to me. I worshipped you, I . . .' She scrapes her teeth over her bottom lip. 'I wanted to be you.'

I pause, frowning, at her words. She's said that before.

I should've read the signs.

'We were never real friends at all, were we?' I say, dropping on to the arm of the sofa, fingers pinned to my forehead.

Leanne blinks at me, forlorn. 'What? No, it's not like that.'

'You were just some creep who hung around me, who stuck to me. And I had no other friends, so I just . . . put up with it.'

'We *were* friends,' she pleads, taking a careful step towards me. 'Real friends. A-a-and we still are. You mean everything to me. I don't . . .' She takes a quavering breath through the tears. 'I don't think I can live without you.'

I glare at her, astonished. 'Do you even hear yourself?' My voice is starting to crack. 'You're ill, Leanne. You need help.'

'That's right,' she says, her face lighting up. 'I need help, and you can help me. You can save me.'

She reaches for me with both hands and I leap up from the sofa arm, backing away. 'I can*not* save you,' I say, almost laughing. 'I'm not a psychotherapist, I'm a failed author.'

'You'll never be a failure to me.'

I clamp my hands to my ears, squeezing my eyes shut, and a muffled scream seeps out of me. 'Just shut up, OK? Shut up. This . . . this thing between you and me, whatever it was, it's over. It's finished.'

Brushing past her, I pull open the front door and clatter down the stairs. I can hear her following me, the slap of wet feet on wood.

'Where are you going?'

I look back up at her from the hallway. 'I don't know. I just need to be . . . away from here.'

She pauses a few steps from the bottom, clutching her towel. Her eyes fill with tears again. 'Don't you want to take your diary?'

I make a harsh, sarcastic sound in my throat. 'Funnily enough, Leanne, I don't. Because what you did *chills my fucking blood*, and I don't ever want to be reminded of it.' I toss a backhand wave up the stairs. 'You keep it. I'm sure you'll enjoy your little drawings far more than I ever would.'

She hurries down the last few steps, starting to protest, but I point a rigid finger at her.

'Don't you dare follow me, Wilding.' I wrench the door open, and before she can get a word in, I snap at her again. 'We are done, understand me? Done.' I slam the door in her face.

As I pound the deserted backstreets of Heaviport, turning this way and that, in random directions, I'm fizzing with rage. Who does that to a friend?

I wanted to feel close to you.

My night terrors destroyed me, as a child, and I'm not sure I ever recovered. They left me exhausted, confused and afraid; I didn't know what was real and what wasn't, and even as a kid, at the back of my mind, I wondered: *am I going insane?* I saw this ghostly little girl in my room, too many times to count, and she seemed so real to me, and I thought that meant I was disturbed. That there was something deeply wrong with me.

But there was nothing wrong with me at all.

There was only her, slinking into our house under the cover of darkness. Sneaking into my room and lurking beneath my bed, for hours on end, waiting for me to wake. Touching my things. Watching me sleep.

I feel my neck twitch and throw a panicked glance over my shoulder. What if she's out there, somewhere, following me? It wouldn't be the first time.

Ducking down a narrow side street, I drop back against a wall and gaze into the purplish sky, the breath escaping my mouth in chilly clouds. Where am I going, exactly? What's my move? My train leaves in a couple of hours, and my suitcase is still at the house. I should make my way back to Umber Lane.

I push on, drifting past bus stops, peering into kitchen windows at the glowing orange warmth inside. I think of my father, stalking the hallways at Charnel House, consumed with disgust for his aberrant daughter and her phantom twin, and a creeping despair sinks into me.

Without Leanne, he may never have started hitting me in the first place. He may never have hit *anyone*.

So many lives might have been different.

After a hazy period of time – ten minutes? Twenty? – I realise I've meandered past my parents' house without even noticing. I ought to turn back, grab my luggage from the bedroom and head for the station, but instead, I'm veering in the opposite direction, towards the railway. Crossing the bridge, eyes dragging the train tracks, where a lone white shoe still lies among the litter. Wandering into the backstreets on the other side.

Soon, I find myself outside a familiar home: an attractive, Victorian end-of-terrace with a tidy front garden and a doormat reading 'Welcome'. Hanging basket, teeming with heather.

I shouldn't be here.

I reach for the knocker.

31.

'Please be in,' I murmur to myself, knocking three times. 'Please be in.'

I squint through the frosted glass, searching for movement in the unlit hallway, and I'm reminded of Leanne. Standing out here last Sunday night, while on the other side of the door I pressed my chest against her boyfriend, his fingers in the furrow of my spine.

This is wrong, he told me, in his soft Islander brogue.

I knock twice more, somewhat slower. Still nothing. Stepping backwards off the welcome mat, I peer up at the first floor and a tightness crosses my ribs. There's not a single light on in the house. I try one more knock, limp and defeated, and my shoulders slump, forehead coming to rest against the cool glass. I think I'm going to cry.

'Beck?'

I start, hand leaping to my breast, and swivel round. Kai is standing on the garden path. He gives me a lopsided smile. 'You OK?'

I swallow the tears. 'Yeah. Yeah, sure.'

He looks me up and down. 'You seem . . . uh . . .' His brow dips. 'What happened?'

My eyes stray past him, scanning the road.

'Beck?'

His tone has changed, deepened. I tug my hair behind my ear and he follows my shaking fingers.

'I had a bust-up with Leanne. A big one. And I needed, I don't know, I needed . . . someone.'

He pleats his forehead, throwing a concerned look up and down the street. 'Look, come on in,' he says, pulling his keys from his pocket. 'Sorry I wasn't here just now. Went for a few pints after work. Wee bit tipsy, if I'm honest . . .'

Inside, he takes my coat and drops it on a hook, next to his. 'Can I get you anything?' He motions down the hallway. 'Something to eat, cup of coffee—'

'I need a drink.'

'Oh . . . aye. Sure.'

'Something strong.'

He forces air through his lips. 'I'm out of whisky, sadly, but . . . tequila?'

I nod, almost manically, and he backs out of the room. I drop on to the sofa, heart galloping, and listen to him clanking around with glasses and drawers in the kitchen.

'Now, this, believe it or not, is pretty decent tequila,' he says, as he reappears with a bottle and two short tumblers. 'Not the shit students drink, but—'

'Perfect,' I say, reaching out, hand snapping like a pincer. He passes me the bottle with a nervous smile and I whip the lid straight off, gulping the liquor down, relishing the sting.

Kai itches an eyebrow. 'You know, good tequila is really meant to be sipped, not . . .'

I glance at the label on the bottle. *100% blue agave*. I hand it back. 'Christ . . . sorry. I don't . . .' I shift over as he sits next to me. 'I just need to feel numb.'

'Hey, I can hardly judge,' he says, arranging the tumblers on the coffee table. 'I'm four pints and a chaser down. Cheap date.'

I smile, weakly, as he charges our drinks and slides one over.

'Beck.' He tries to catch my eye. 'Will you tell me what's going on?'

My mind turns back to Leanne, and her drawings in my diary. The thought of her watching me through the open cupboard door. Tugging on my bedsheets in the middle of the night.

'It's complicated.'

He lifts a shoulder. 'I've got time.'

I frown into my drink. 'She . . . look . . . Leanne *did* something, years back, when we were kids. I just found out about it, maybe half an hour ago. It's messed up.'

Kai blinks a few times, his dark eyes strangely pretty in the low light. 'That doesn't sound like Leanne. Are you sure?'

I bow my head, nodding.

'D'you wanna talk about it?'

'I don't know.' I knuckle an eye socket, and it feels raw. 'I think I just want to forget.' I'm sitting with my back to the window, and I can feel a bristling on my neck, as if she's standing right behind me. 'I do know that she needs help, though. Psychiatric help.'

'That bad?'

I press my lips together.

Somewhere in the house, a beam creaks.

'Look,' says Kai, edging towards me, 'I know what you mean about wanting to forget, and we can, if you want. We can drink tonight, and talk about it another time. But . . .' He softens his voice. 'Sooner or later, I'll need to know. She's part of my life too.'

I return my drink to the table.

He lets out a sigh. 'And, hey, I don't want to sound like some therapy nut, but the other day, after we talked about my family, I felt better. Shitty at first, then . . . better.'

He's looking at me so earnestly, so openly, that horribly, I laugh. I clamp a hand to my mouth. 'Sorry, sorry.' Kai frowns and

I raise a palm, chastened. 'I'm not laughing at you. I don't . . . I don't even know why I'm laughing, actually.'

The strangeness of my response is infectious, and he bites back a smile. 'Why *are* you laughing at that?'

'I wasn't really. I was just . . .' I pause, tongue pressed against my teeth. 'I don't know if this is weird, but I feel as if we're alike, somehow. You and me.'

His smile deepens. 'Aye. Aye, I know.'

I lean over to pick up my tumbler, draining it in one swig. My face puckers. 'OK . . . OK. Here's the thing.' Eyes on the tequila bottle, I refill our glasses, my hand unsteady, the liquid nearly spilling. 'Someone set fire to my house last night.'

Kai's mouth drops open. '*What?* Jesus, why didn't you say? Are you all right?'

'I'm . . . fine.'

His face is blanched. Sounds struggle from his lips. 'I don't . . . wh— is the house—'

'The house'll live, it's indestructible.' I table the bottle and snatch up my drink. 'But I found out, after the fire – and it's kind of a long story, how – but I found out that my father used to beat some random girl, over at the school.'

Kai touches fingertips to his brow. 'Beck, no.'

'And the thing is, the only reason he laid a hand on her in the first place was . . .' There's a quiver in my stomach. I wash it down with tequila. 'Well, it was my fault.'

Leanne's fault, if you trace it back far enough. But I'm not getting into that now.

Kai's face buckles. 'I don't understand.'

'I didn't tell you this before, because I've hardly told anyone, but until I left for boarding school, the person he was hitting . . . was me.' Weirdly, uncomfortably, I try to smile. 'So you and I, we actually *are* alike. We could start our own club.'

Kai pushes his hair back from his forehead and stares into the wall. 'I thought your dad was, like, the patron saint of Heaviport.'

'To most people, yeah.'

He shakes his head, disbelieving. 'Are you OK?'

I clench my jaw.

Kai sinks back into the sofa. 'I don't know where to start. I can't believe that bastard was hitting you . . .'

I look at him, studying his coal-dark eyes. Kai is the one person I know who'll actually understand what I'm going through with my father, and some day, soon, I'll talk to him about it. But not tonight.

'Lime and salt.'

Kai cocks his head. 'Huh?'

'We need lime and salt,' I announce, rising from the sofa. 'This is tequila, and we're not doing it properly.'

I sweep out into the hallway, bottle in hand. He follows. 'Thing is, Beck, it's actually sipping teq—'

'I know, I know, you said.'

We're both in the kitchen now, me opening and closing cupboards, Kai watching, bemused, from the doorway.

'You sure you don't want to talk about it?' he asks, scratching his head.

I pause with my hand on a half-open cupboard door. 'I do. Honestly.' I close the door and start rifling through the spice rack. 'But not now. Right now, I want to drink.'

'You are a bad influence,' he says, crossing the room towards me.

I look up from the spices. 'I try.'

Our eyes meet, locking in, and a twisted thrill shoots through me. The tequila is spiking my blood and I can feel my anger dissolving in its wake, like a bad dream in daylight.

Kai points. 'Lime in the fridge, salt by the hob.'

Minutes later, we are standing at the kitchen table, shot glasses scattered between us, lime wedges stacked in a small hillock next to Kai's novelty salt shaker: a chipped, smiling Santa Claus. The tequila bottle stands high and proud in the centre.

'To fucked-up childhoods,' I proclaim, raising my glass.

Salt, tequila, lime.

Slam.

'To . . .' Kai presses the back of his hand to his mouth, suppressing a hiccup. 'To a glorious waste of over-priced booze.'

Salt, tequila, lime.

Slam.

'To growing up in backwater seaside towns,' I say, pointing a crooked arm at the window.

Salt, tequila, lime.

Slam.

Kai squints, darkly, into his glass. 'To abusive fathers.'

Salt, tequila, lime.

Slam.

'Wait . . . wait.' I take Kai's wrist, pull it towards me and tap a small mound of salt into the dip between his thumb and forefinger. 'This one's different,' I say, the edges of my words beginning to soften and slur. 'This time, you lick my salt, I lick . . . yours.'

Kai screws his face up. 'Huh?'

I focus on Santa's smile, which has gone a little fuzzy, as I measure out a heap of salt on my own hand. Grains sheer off the pile and on to the table.

'We switch. I do you, I do me.' My lip twitches, like Elvis. 'Wait, no. You do me, I do . . . never mind. Here's the toast.' I raise my glass. 'To you.'

He sways, just a touch. 'Me?'

I don't know how, but suddenly, we're close. Pressed up against each other, his back to the table.

'To you. For being here for me, even though I'm . . . a stranger.'

Kai leans in and chinks his glass, softly, against mine. 'To strangers.'

I take his wrist to lick off the salt, but before I know what's happening, my mouth is travelling up his arm to his neck and his hands are behind me, fingertips squeezing my buttocks through my jeans. We've dropped our shot glasses somewhere and we're tugging, grabbing at each other, little yearning moans escaping my mouth as his strong hands pull my body into his.

We kiss, deep and eager, and within seconds we're grappling at each other's flies, laughing at the awkwardness, my hand desperately stroking at the growing hardness between his legs. Soon, we're hopping out of trousers and flinging them across the room, and then we're naked apart from his open shirt and my bra, our shoulders heaving with lust.

Switching places with me, and with unexpected flare, Kai jimmies me up, on to the table, and there's a clattering of glasses as his fingers slide around my bum and pull me to the edge, where he's waiting for me, unbelievably hard, his cock brushing my inner thigh. I grab the lapels of his shirt, tugging him towards me, and he buries his mouth in my cleavage, lips hot and wet against my skin. I feel him enter me, stopping my breath, and then we're rocking together, kissing hungrily, my legs wrapped around his.

As he thrusts, he unclasps my bra and tosses it aside, and we build to a furious rhythm. He dips a hand between my legs and presses a thumb in exactly the right place, with exactly the right pressure, and my brain splinters in seventeen places, like a window shattered by stones. I snake my arms around his neck, hands in his hair, cheek to his stubble, and he smells so good, *feels* so good, like he's home, like we already knew how to do this. And I know it's wrong, I know he's supposed to be hers, but as our mouths find one another and our sweat mingles, as we're both climbing to a shivering climax, I admit to myself that I don't care. The wrongness of it, the badness of it, *that's* the turn-on. She took something from me, she took my childhood, and now I'm taking something back. Something that will hurt her.

Something that will make her scream.

So, yes, it's spiteful of me, and sadistic, but I *like* it. It feels better, sexier, filthier, knowing that I'm getting my revenge.

Looking out over his shoulder, into the night, I think of her. Of her pale face, appearing at the kitchen window. Hair still wet from the shower, eyes blazing. Watching us fuck, watching Kai from behind as he drills into me, following my fingers as they rake down his back.

You asked for this, Leanne. It's what you deserve.

And I'm crying out, I'm shaking, I'm thudding a fist against Kai's chest as our rhythm slows, my eyes shut tight. Our bodies slump and we gasp together, hungry for air, slowly fading back into the real world. I open my eyes.

Behind him, at the window, there's nothing.

She isn't there, watching us.

And she never was.

Afterwards, we're upstairs, stretched out naked on Kai's bed, music playing quietly from his phone. Outside the window, the world is suede-velvet black.

'I just always found them a bit sappy,' I'm saying, lying on my side, head propped on one arm.

Kai's jaw drops. 'Sappy? Are you trying to tell me "Driftwood" is *sappy?*'

'I am. That is a sappy song.'

'Travis are an *extremely* important weave in the rich tapestry of Scottish pop,' he says, adjusting the pillow behind his shoulders.

I arch an eyebrow. 'I'm sorry, did you say "tapestry"?'

'Aye, I did. Wanna fight about it?'

He smiles, a playful, wicked smile, and the urge to feel him inside me again licks at me, like a whip. Rising up on my knees, I straddle him, planting my hands on either side of his head, and his gaze roves my body. I reach down to find him hard, strong and hot in my fingers, and as I bow to kiss him, he cups a hand around one of my breasts, giving it a sensual squeeze.

There's a sudden, savage knock on the front door.

'Who's that?' I say, straightening like a meerkat.

Kai tilts his head at me, amused. 'I may be many things, Beck, but I'm not telepath—'

'*Shh.*' I hold up a finger, head twisted to the side.

Somebody's shouting.

'Beckett!'

My throat constricts. It's her.

'Beckett!'

Kai's eyes swell and I roll off him, instinctively pulling the sheets up and over my body. Slipping off the bed, he yanks on jeans and a T-shirt.

'Fuck. Fuck, this is bad,' I mutter, heart going like a pneumatic drill. 'How did she know I was here?'

Even as I'm asking the question, I realise it's a moot point. She doesn't *know* I'm here, not for certain, but she'll have tried Charnel House and then, with all the pubs and cafes shut, she'll have been drawn to the only other place in Heaviport that she knows I'd consider safe.

'It's fine,' insists Kai, but his face says otherwise. 'I'll deal with it.'

He dashes from the room and Leanne bangs on the door, four times, then shouts through the glass. 'I know she's in there, Kai.'

His bare feet on the stairs, then a pause.

'Let me in.' Leanne again, but still muffled. He hasn't opened the door.

'I can't do that, I'm afraid.'

There's a different sound, this time, the sound of the door handle rattling. She's trying to force her way in. 'You *have* to,' she cries, her words cracking with emotion. 'I have to see her.'

She stops rattling the handle, and underneath, I can hear Kai's heavy breathing. 'I'm not letting you in, Leanne.'

A long, edgy silence.

'You fucked her, didn't you?'

The shape of her voice has changed, now. A steel edge.

'Look, Leanne—'

'I *knew* it.'

'I'm sorry it had to happen this way, OK? I truly am. I never meant to hurt you.'

'She's not yours, Kai,' says Leanne, and she sounds wild, almost bestial. 'She's *mine*.'

'Beckett says you need help, from a doctor. And we'll get you that help, we both will. You're not going to lose us. But, right now . . . you need to go.'

'Let me in. I want to talk to her.'

'Leanne, please.'

'I want to come in—'

'*Leanne*.' Kai's voice has dropped several tones. This time, he means it. 'Go home, or I'm calling the police.'

A minute later, Kai is back upstairs, perched on the edge of the bed, while I sit propped against the pillows, eyes wide and alert.

'You wouldn't really have called the police on her, would you?' I ask, gnawing on a fingernail.

'Och, no.' Kai rocks a little on the mattress. 'I just know what she's like. I had to be firm.'

'Are you certain she's gone?'

'Aye, she's . . . she's gone.' He twists to face me. 'And, look, I know Leanne can be full-on, but she'd never hurt anyone, least of all you.'

He reaches across to stroke my shoulder and his forearm brushes my nipple. We catch each other's eyes, remembering what Leanne's visit interrupted, but for now, the moment has passed.

'Do you think we should get some sleep?' says Kai, pressing a palm to his brow. 'My head's still fuzzy from the tequila.'

'Yeah. Yeah, I do.'

We dance awkwardly around each other in the bathroom, washing our faces, patting them dry. He lets me borrow his toothbrush. I stick my tongue out at him in the mirror.

Back in the bedroom, we're lying side by side in the low light, breathing together. The house is quiet.

'Night, Beck.'

'Night.' I run a finger, tantalisingly, along the ridge of his leg. 'I have some unfinished business with you in the morning, mister.'

He laughs, softly. 'Noted.'

I glance out on to the landing, where a lamp is still glowing. 'Should I get that light?'

'Oh . . . uh . . . do you mind if we keep it on?' he says, bashfully, and I shake my head.

'Course. Doesn't bother me.'

'Lame as hell, I know, but . . . I can't sleep in the dark. Can you?'

My body stops. Pauses. Like the blood has clotted in my veins.

Something about his voice, his accent, saying those words, was . . . what?

Familiar.

245

It was familiar.

As I'm staring at him, the most unsettling feeling gathers inside me, like my stomach is crawling with earthworms. Because my imaginary friend, sliding into bed beside me, all those years ago . . . that's exactly what she said.

I can't sleep in the dark.

Can you?

It was Leanne all along, of course. I know that now; it's written in my diary. It was Leanne.

But if that's true, then why are those words, those exact words, coming out of Kai's mouth? And why, in his curly, lilting accent, do they sound so much like they did in my nightmares?

I hear the rustling of sheets as he turns to me, eyes suddenly wary. He blinks. 'Why are you looking at me like that? Beck?'

32.

'. . . Beck?'

I cover my mouth.

It can't have been him. It doesn't make sense.

'What's wrong?' He looks worried. Intensely worried.

My hand falls from my face, and I force out words. 'I . . . er . . .' I cough, splutter. '. . . To go to . . . toilet.'

He watches me, forehead crinkled, as I slide off the bed. I'm naked, but it doesn't feel sexy anymore. I feel exposed.

Pulling a thin dressing gown from the hook on the bedroom door, I tug it over my body and pass silently on to the landing. From where he's lying, Kai can't see me now, which is good, because I'm not going to the toilet.

After click-closing the bathroom door, for show, I pad down the stairs, throwing looks behind me as I go. On the ground floor, I double-back on myself, take a few more steps and then stop, breath held, by the staircase alcove – at the small, waist-height door that Kai opened for me when I was last here.

It can't be.

Turning the handle, I open it and crouch down, peering inside. It's mostly full of random junk and piles of dog-eared magazines, but there's a bare bulb hanging from the underside of the staircase, a string light switch swaying gently next to it, and just about enough room for me to crouch inside.

It doesn't make sense.

Chest thrashing, I squeeze myself into the cramped space and close the door. I pull the string and the bulb winks into life with a tiny electrical sizzle. Its glow is weak, but it's enough to read by.

Please still be here, I pray, as I glance all around. The other night, when Kai reached in here himself, he didn't have to search long to find it.

And there it is, sitting on top of a pile of old music magazines. A black-and-white scrap, torn from a newspaper, featuring a photograph of the five Cunningham siblings, standing together in front of The Shetland Warehouse in Lerwick. 'UNRULY FAMILY BRANDED "TROUBLEMAKERS" BY POLICE'.

It just doesn't make sense.

Kai grew up hundreds of miles away from here, on the Shetland Islands. Yes, he moved down when he was older – when? I don't know, he didn't say – but as children, we were never in Heaviport at the same time, right?

Except . . . now that I'm looking more closely at the newspaper clipping, actually taking in the details, I notice something horribly important. Something I missed before. It's written in the header, above the picture, in minuscule type.

THE HEAVIPORT GAZETTE, 21st March 1997

No. No, no, no.

My gaze drops below the photograph, and I realise there's a caption.

Heaviport newcomers, the Cunningham siblings, pictured in their previous town of residence

– Lerwick, on Scotland's remote Shetland Islands.

They weren't branded troublemakers in Lerwick.

That happened *here*.

Jamming the heel of a hand into one eye, I brace my jaw. I can't stop now.

I look again at the picture. On the left-hand side of the image are Kai's three big, mean-looking older brothers, two of them flipping the bird. Next to them is skinny, fragile Kai, in his clunky Harry Potter specs, and on the end, a kid sister with long, dark hair and an identical pair of NHS spectacles perched, askew, on her face.

It's as I'm looking at her, Kai's little sister, that the realisation comes. A sick, creeping feeling, curling up my spine and over my shoulders like a poisonous gas.

Now that I think about it, Kai never told me he had a sister. I just *assumed* he did, because that slight, long-haired kid on the end, the one with the matching glasses, looks like a girl. A girl with long black hair and coal-dark eyes.

My fingers, hands, arms begin to shake. My gut tightens, and contracts.

Kai didn't have three older brothers: he had four. And that's not his sister standing on the end, there.

It's not a girl, at all.

It's Kai.

'Beck?'

My shoulders twitch at the sound of his voice, coming from the upstairs landing. I can hear the creak of floorboards under his feet as he knocks on the bathroom door.

'Everything OK?'

Leanne.

Oh, Leanne . . . what have I done?

Leanne doesn't have long, dark hair, like me, and she never did. When we were little, she had a blonde bob – she told me so herself. And she's always been smaller than me, anyway. We really don't look that much alike. So she couldn't have been my identical, imaginary friend.

'Hey, Beck, you OK in there?'

The house moans lazily above my head, and I begin to panic. He's about to realise I'm not in there. He's about to—

'I'm coming in.'

The bathroom door swings open, and the floorboards screech again. It sounds like he's muttering to himself. I wedge a thumbnail between my teeth.

'Beck?' he calls, out loud.

I don't have long, now. I have to think.

It can't be. It doesn't make any sense.

A loud, yawning squeak, inches from my face, sucks the air from my lungs, and I watch as a shower of dust floats down from the angled ceiling. Then another dust shower, and another, each accompanied by a squeak of the wood panelling above me.

He's coming down the stairs.

Suddenly, it's all rushing madly through my brain, every tiny thing I've got wrong, every clue I've missed.

The night we met, when I heard him sing. How delicate his voice was, how . . . feminine.

He sings like a girl, Sam Hastings said.

His accent – that unusual, old world, coastal burr.

His eyes, coal dark. Like mine. *Strangely pretty*, I thought of them, only this evening.

The way he shortened my name, straight away, to Beck. That instant familiarity, as if we'd met before.

And our attraction to each other: immediate, chemical. Animal. What is it they say about human sexual preference?

We are attracted to people who look like us.

My gut rolls and I retch, loudly. I cover my mouth.

Footsteps above my head.

'Where are you?'

Then, finally, the way I felt when he was inside me, barely an hour ago. Thrusting and slamming, my cries mingling with his, our bodies slick against each other.

He smells so good, feels so good.

Like he's home.

'Seriously, Beck. Where the fuck have you gone?'

The footsteps stop, a metre or two away, at the base of the stairs. He flicks the hallway light on and I hold my breath, chin trembling as I strain to stay quiet.

'This is really starting to freak me out, you know.'

He's walking in this direction, about to pass the alcove. I ball my fists. I should've turned off the bulb in here, but it's too late to do it now. If he hasn't spotted it already, he might hear the click or notice the light disappearing.

'Is this some kind of . . . sexy . . . game?'

The footsteps draw closer, passing right by me, and I sit stock still, gulps of hot breath trapped inside me. Several agonising seconds go by, and then I hear him in the kitchen, pouring a glass of water.

I take the risk. I turn off the light.

'D'you want some water, Beck?'

He's still in the kitchen, clanging around with glasses. I don't have long before he realises something is very wrong.

Could I ease open this little door and run from the house, out on to the street? No . . . no. The staircase is visible from the kitchen, so he would see me, or hear me, the moment I made a move.

I'll have to stay here, ride it out.

'I'm bringing you some water, wherever you are.'

And when he's back upstairs, I'll bolt.

'This is . . . very . . . odd . . .'

My thoughts careen to Leanne, and our argument. When I was yelling at her, I barely stopped to let her answer, and I didn't listen, not properly, to what she was saying. But if I had, I might have realised that the crime I was accusing her of – sneaking into my room at night – and the crime she was apologising for – stealing my diary – were two different things. And then maybe I wouldn't be here, cowering in this dusty cupboard, hiding from a monster.

The monster under the bed.

'I'm going upstairs,' calls Kai, with pantomime absurdity, 'so, you know . . . you can come out, now, wherever you are.'

Hiding from the nightmare that I thought was a figment of my screwed-up brain. My sickening mirror image with her other-worldly voice.

In a pinch of light slicing through the door frame, I stare at the quivering newsprint, gaze fixated on Kai. The way his girlish hair falls in front of his face, all black and scraggly. His skinny arms, pale skin. The tortured intensity in his eyes.

He crept into my room, night after night, and lay beneath me, waiting for me to wake.

He stood at my bedside, watching me sleep.

He climbed into bed with me, warm and damp, and touched my paralysed, hallucinating body.

He was the pair of eyes, shining in the dark.

No, no, no, no, no, no, no, no.

'You're in there, aren't you?'

My heart stops. He's outside the door.

'That light was definitely on a second ago . . .' He laughs, low and rough. 'Is this grown-up hide and seek? 'Cos if it is, I'm about to win.'

Desperately whipping my head left, then right, I notice half a broom handle propped against a pile of old towels, the broken end splintered and cracked.

Lightning quick, I jam it under the door handle.

Silence.

Then, the faint crack of Kai's knees, as he crouches down.

'I'll huff, and I'll puff, and I'll . . .'

The handle begins to shake.

And shake, and shake. Violently, like someone trying to escape the doors of hell.

Then, suddenly, it stops.

'Beck? What's going on?' He pushes out a breath. 'What are you doing in there?'

I shift around until I'm on my knees, palms on the ground, like an animal about to pounce. So I'm ready.

'*It was you.*'

My voice is hoarse, the words snagging on the fine layer of dust that's coating my throat. I sound feral.

'Wh— huh? What was me?'

Tears fatten in my eyes. 'Under the bed.' The tears bulge, then cascade down my cheeks. 'Under my bed, when we were kids. I thought I was losing my mind, going insane, because I saw this horrible little girl in my room at night, but all the time . . . all that time . . . it was you.'

He lets out a flat, mocking laugh. 'I have absolutely no idea wh—'

'*Don't* lie to me, Kai. Don't even bother. I found my old diary, with all your . . . your drawings, and I'm looking at you in this photo from the *Gazette*, and it was you. It was you. *It was you it was you it was y—*'

'Fine!' I hear him standing up, clamping his hand on the banister. 'Fucking . . . *fine*. It was me. You happy, now?'

Hearing him actually say it, actually *admit* it, hits me hard in the chest and I scurry backwards, as far as I can go – which is no more than half a metre or so – into the back wall. I'm scrabbling at whatever's behind me, eyes smarting with tears, gut lurching.

'But I only did it . . .' He pauses, then softens his voice to that hypnotic, Highlands sigh. 'I only did it because I was in love with you.'

I let out a desolate sound, almost a bark, then double over, vomit exploding from my mouth and splattering on the floor. As I watch it mingle with the dust and detritus, I start to weep, great sobs hitching up my dry, stinging throat. 'No . . . no . . . please . . .'

'Don't go judging me, there, Beck.' His voice turns away from me and I hear a heavy shuffling sound, as if he's sliding down the alcove door and sinking into a sitting position. 'You don't understand what my childhood was like.'

I wipe my mouth with the back of my hand, spreading the sticky mess everywhere. My skin glistens with saliva.

It smells awful in here.

'I was a sad wee boy, y'understand me?'

It sounds like his cheek's pressed to the wood. I can hear the points of his stubble prickling against it.

'We moved down here, to this town where I knew nobody, and thanks to my brothers, everyone hated us. Shoplifting, starting fights, an' that. And that wasn't me, you know? I was sensitive. I *felt* things.'

I curl back into a ball, starting to feel the cold again. My head throbs from the alcohol.

'My brothers were cruel, they were *bastards*, teasing me for my glasses and long hair. "Pretty little thing", they used to call me. Hissin' it through their teeth. *Kai's a pretty little thing*. And my dad, he beat me so hard that my ears rang, so one night, I just left, I ran away and I wandered all about the town, in the dark, cryin' my wee heart out, because I knew I was alone, and I'd always be alone.

'I ended up at your house, and I thought . . . that looks like a place where a real family lives. A family where there's love and laughter, not . . . hatred and fear.' He pauses, as if acknowledging how far from the truth this actually was. I hug my knees to my

254

chest. 'The door was unlocked, so I went in and walked around, looking in all the rooms, touching stuff. I went up the stairs and found your bedroom, and you were in there, sleeping, and you were the most exquisite thing I'd ever seen. I wanted to be your friend.'

He coughs, bitterly.

'But you wouldn't want to be my friend, if we ever met in the daylight. I knew that. 'Cos I was a weirdo. So, instead, I kept coming back, in the night, and lying on the floor underneath you, or watching from the cupboard, or standing at the end of your bed. I'd take off my specs, 'cos they didn't do much in the dark, and that made me feel free. Normal, like.'

(*tonight i sleeped in the cubbard*)

'And sometimes you'd wake up . . . sort of, but not really. You were in these trances. It was kind of beautiful, the way you were all twisted and frozen in the bed, like Snow White.'

An involuntary whimper rises in my throat. I swallow it down.

(*tonight i weared her dresses*)

'And I wanted to touch you.'

I cover my eyes, the air sucked from my lungs as graphic flashbacks hurtle through my brain. His teeth around my nipples, nails on my skin. The feeling of him sliding into me.

'I didn't touch you, though.'

The flashbacks subside, and I draw in a deep, uneven breath. I close my eyes, wishing this was a dream, or one of my hallucinations. Wishing I was about to wake up.

'Not at first.'

My eyes snap open.

Something clicks inside me.

Some infernal engine fires up in my belly, all the fear and disgust and sadness hardening inside me, clotting into anger, and I rise up on my knees, planting my fists against the door. 'You're pure evil, you know that?'

He laughs that flat, mocking laugh again. 'There was nothing evil about it, Beck. In fact, when you think about it, isn't it sort of . . . romantic?'

My fists splay, fingers stretching out along the wood like two giant spiders waking from a deep sleep. I'm almost pushing against the door, almost daring it to open so I can fly out there and rip his throat out. '*Romantic?* Are you out of your mind?'

A pause. He shifts too, on the other side, and I sense that he's turning around. 'We're two sides of a coin, you and I.'

I scoff at him. 'I'm nothing like you.'

We're face to face, now. I can feel it. Only a plank of old, dried-up wood between us.

'That's not what you said earlier, though, is it?' he says, and I squint into the door.

'What?'

'"We're alike, somehow." That's what you said to me, less than an hour ago. Right before I stuck my dick in you.'

I thump the wall, hard, and a puff of dust settles in my hair. 'I'll go to the police. I'll tell them what you did.'

He laughs again, and it turns into a snort. 'I was, what, nine? There's nothing they could do, even if you had proof, which you don't. And anyway, what was my crime, exactly?'

'I don't know . . . breaking and entering.'

'Your door was unlocked.'

'It's still trespassing. Stalking.'

'You can't prosecute a kid for . . . stalking,' he says, though he sounds unsure. 'And you can't *blame* me, either.' His voice sounds muffled, suddenly, but it's also jumped in volume. He must be pressing his mouth against the alcove door. 'You can't blame me for what I did, because I had no fucking choice, did I? My dad was a vicious motherfucker, and I was terrified of him. *Ter–ri–fied.* Some nights, I thought he was gonna kill me.'

'Hey, you know what, Kai? My daddy beat me too, in case you'd forgotten.' Now I'm pressing *my* mouth against the wood, spittle shooting out as I talk. 'But I didn't go around sleeping under other people's beds like a *FUCKING PSYCHOPATH.*'

Silence. A long, strange silence.

I listen, intently, my ear pressed to the wood, but I can't hear a single thing. Not his body shifting, nor his breathing, nor his footsteps.

I need to make a plan. I need to know what I'm going to do when I get out of this alcove, because I can't stay here forever.

Kai's creepy, and he's screwed up, but he's not violent. I may not know him as well I thought I did, but I know that. The night we met, in the Wreckers, who was the one who confronted Sam Hastings? Who started that fight? Kai took a punch to the gut and a bruise to the face, and never even threatened to hit back. Not me, though. I would have fought that homophobic little prick all on my own, if I had to.

If it comes to it, I think, my ear still pressed to the alcove door, *I'll stand up to Kai. I'll give him everything I've got.*

If it comes to it.

Thhwack!

I topple sideways, snapping a hand to my ear, as the most almighty sound reverberates inside my head. Dazed, I press myself against the pile of towels at the back of the alcove, pulse machine-gunning.

'You know, Beck, I think I've had my fill of home improvements,' comes Kai's voice, strained, 'but I knew there was a reason I kept this sledgehammer lying around.'

Thhhwack, it comes again.

The door begins to crack.

33.

'Wh— Kai, what are you doing?'

He makes a strangled heaving sound, as if lifting the sledge-hammer above his head. 'Be quiet. I'm working.'

Thhwack.

The door yields further, the crack almost doubling in length. Inside the alcove, I'm frozen in place, eyes unblinking.

'And . . . *and* . . . while I work, I've a story to tell you.'

There's a small, metallic *dnk*, the sound of him resting the head of the hammer on the wooden floor.

He gathers his breath. 'Once upon a time, a wee Scottish boy from the magical island of Shetland was torn from his home and sent far, far away to a strange town where he had no friends, and nobody to talk to. His daddy was evil – ooh, children, he was one evil *cunt*, you take that from me – and he'd spawned a whole brood of evil wee fuckin' bastards in his image, so even though the boy lived with his family, he was lonely, so very lonely, and scared. Scared that, one day, his daddy would hit him so hard that his fuckin' wee head would fly clean off, and roll away into the sea.'

That strangled sound again.

A pause, then . . .

Thhhwack.

'Now, you might think this is gonna be a sad story, children, but you'd be wrong. Because one night, when he was walking the streets, alone, the wee boy came across a house, a big, fancy house on a fancy street, and he went inside, and he crept upstairs, and in the bedroom he found the . . . most . . . *beautiful* girl he'd ever seen in his short, miserable life. She was sleeping, so peaceful, and he didn't want to wake her, so he just watched her sleep, and she looked so perfect, and smelled so sweet—'

'Stop. Please . . . just stop.'

A silence, and then that metallic *dnk* again, but this time, three, four times in a row. Like he's thinking. Then his voice, up against the door. 'It . . . is . . . *rude* to interrupt a story, *Miss Ryan*.'

I hold my breath, my addled brain gripped by the desperate, irrational notion – a child's notion – that if he can't hear me, he can't hurt me.

Backwards footsteps, his throat straining, and then—

Thhhwack.

Dnk.

'And the wee boy, he fell in love with the girl, but he couldn't tell her 'cos she was always sleeping when they were together, and if she saw him in the daylight, she'd think him queer, a freak. So he bided his time. He waited until he was a man, and had grown handsome and clever and strong, and he saved all his pennies – because *many a mickle macks a muckle*, as my people say – and he bought a house, a beautiful house to rival the one the girl was born in, so that maybe, just maybe, he could tempt her there, to marry him, and to live happily . . . ever . . . after.'

Thhhwack.

Dnk.

I try not to think about him buying an entire house, just for me. All that effort, all that money, for someone he barely knew and might never see again. I can't let that distract me, not while I'm still in danger.

Beyond the door, his breathing has become husky. He's getting tired.

'Trouble is, the girl had left town, disappeared, and he didn't know where to find her. Because, you see, she didn't *want* to be found. She had run away.'

Thhhwack.

I stare at the crack, mesmerised, noticing a sliver of movement through it.

The wood is breaching.

'And so he moved into the house, the house he had bought for her, and he worked day and night to make it fit for a princess. He sanded, he painted, he sweated . . . and he waited. For fuckin' *years*. But a man has needs, children, so one day, he found himself a sweetheart, and she wasn't so bad, right enough, but she wasn't his true love. She was his true love's shadow.'

Thhhwack.

The door's going. Two, three strikes at most.

'By this time, his true love was a celebrated author, known throughout the land, and while she may have been famous, she was also famously elusive. No literary festivals, no book signings. She did not wish for her past to catch up with her, and so it didn't. At least, not yet.'

Thhwack.

'You see, the man, he knew, in his heart, that one day she would come home.'

Thhhwack.

His voice against the wood again, a dreadful giddiness in his throat. 'Because, eventually, Beck . . . everybody . . . comes . . . *home*.'

Thhhhwack – the door splinters and squeals and the grey head of the hammer bursts through, marooning itself in the open crack. Behind it, through the fissure, I can see Kai's face, his cheeks ruddy and streaked with sweat, eyes huge beneath raised eyebrows.

'Hello,' he says, in a horribly jolly tone, giving me a wink.

Then, gripping the handle of the sledgehammer with both hands, he tugs at it, puffing through tight lips, until the heft of the hammer and the weight of his body pull the entire door off its hinges and send it shooting across the floor. He drops the tool and staggers back against the wall, wiping an arm across his forehead.

Ten seconds pass, maybe fifteen, as he waits, bent over, for his breathing to slow, hands planted on his thighs. I'm still huddled in the back corner of the alcove, feeling like one of those long-missing people that the FBI find cowering in a maniac's basement.

I don't know what to do.

Should I run, fight, cry?

'Hey.' Kai has dropped to his haunches in the hallway. Giving me a dashing smile, he unfurls an open hand, like some nightmare vision of Prince Charming. 'Out you come, then.'

Soon I am standing opposite him in the narrow hallway, dressing gown tied messily across my waist, nakedness barely concealed. My arms are wrapped around my chest.

'So, here we are.'

He says this conversationally, as if this were merely the slightly awkward conclusion of a first date. I keep my eyes fixed on his, like a cat taking the measure of an unfamiliar human, and something I told him last weekend, after we talked about his father's violent rages, throbs in my mind like a neon sign.

Your past doesn't have to define you.

'Beck—'

'Don't touch me,' I blurt out, my hands leaping in front of my face. My fingers are trembling. 'I swear, if you . . . if you hurt me—'

'I'm not going to hurt you.' He angles his face away from mine, just barely, and half smiles. 'Why would I do that? I'm in love with you.'

His eyes flit up and down my body, tracing my curves, and I press my back into the banister. I can feel the wooden angles against my spine. 'Y-you're . . . you're keeping me here, in this house, like some kind of prisoner—'

'Am I?' He looks around, as if addressing an invisible audience. 'I don't believe I ever said that, did I?'

'No, Kai. You can't gaslight me like tha—'

'Of course, if you do leave,' he says, stepping away, 'then I may have to tell the Right Honourable Baroness Nadia Jhaveri about Harold Ryan and his . . . extra-curricular activities.' He shakes his head, imitating regret. 'Which would be an awful shame, because who, in their right and sane mind, would open a children's refuge in the home of a child *abuser*?'

I stare at him, breathing shakily.

He pushes his hands through his hair. 'The deal will fall through, you'll lose your flat, and you'll have nothing left but Charnel House . . . a home that will never sell.'

I tug at the dressing gown, pulling it tighter. He has me cornered.

But then I remember Paige, and how she tried to ring alarm bells about my father, back in the day. How her teachers refused to listen because, like everyone else in Heaviport, they didn't want to hear the truth.

I lift my chin in defiance. 'No one will believe you, you know. This town has been in denial about my father for years. And you have no proof.'

He tuts at me. 'Now that, I'm afraid, is where you're wrong.' Leaning against the wall, he slips his thumbs into the waistband of his jeans, like a cowboy. 'I've read your new book.'

My eyes leap around, searching his face. *How could he possibly know about that?*

'Harrowing tale, of course. But very illuminating.'

Did he find it on my laptop, somehow? He can't have done. When would he have gotten access, without me knowing? Unless—

I lift a hand, slowly, to my mouth. I sent those documents to my agent. 'Did you . . . hack my emails?'

Kai bows his head, lips pressed together. 'Aye, I did.' He points at me. 'But I'm only telling you that 'cos I care about you, Beck. Because honesty is the bedrock of any relationship.'

Honesty? Really? You mean, like not telling someone you're fucking that you used to creep into their house at night and watch them sleep?

'Point is, I could email your wee memoir to Nadia in a flash, and this whole house of cards would come tumbling down. No sale, no money, no life, no good.' He brings his palms together in front of his face, eyes suddenly alight. 'But, see, I have a *much* better idea.'

He inches closer and I try to retreat, but there's nowhere to go. I'm pressed against the stair rails.

'We've something special, you and I. You have to admit that.' He waves a hand backwards, into the kitchen. 'What happened on that table earlier, that was *real*. And you feel it too, in your gut.' He sinks into me, easing a leg between mine. 'We are fuckin' explosive together.'

My head starts to shake, shudder, like I'm a small child in a doctor's office, terrified of a looming needle. 'No. No, n—'

Kai silences me with a finger to my lips. 'We sell Charnel House and your London flat and you move in here, with me. Then we get hitched and make beautiful babies together and live a normal life, a perfect life, and we forget our fathers, the mother*fuckers*, we forget them – and we win, because we didn't let them screw us up, y'understand? We win.'

For the oddest, eeriest second, I feel a flash of attraction, an ephemeral trace of what I saw in him, that first time we met, in the Wreckers. But it pushes bile up my throat, and I swallow it down. 'No. I won't . . . you have to let me go—'

'You've got no one now, Beck.' His lips stretch back from his teeth, his patience beginning to thin. He talks into my cheek. 'Your parents are gone, and you can't be friends with Leanne anymore, not after what's happened. You *need* me.'

My face is turned from his, but I can't escape him. His musky scent, his groin pressed against mine, beginning, repulsively, to harden. His voice is a whisper now.

'I was there, all those years ago, through the dark nights, when you were afraid and seeing things. I was right there, underneath you, beside you. Holding you.' His fingertips climb my thigh like a hairless tarantula. 'I'm the closest thing you have to family.'

I can hear my heartbeat in my ears, and a feeble, strangled sound in my throat.

I can't stay here with him. Of course I can't. Even if he's serious about sending my work to Nadia; even if it bankrupts me, and I lose everything. But what do I do? Call his bluff, try and make a run for it? Or do I wait until he's asleep, then sneak out of the house?

Because, the thing is, I don't believe him. When he says he's not going to hurt me, I don't believe him anymore . . . because it's in him. It's in his DNA. I know that because I felt it too, last night, when I knelt above Paige, fists curled and lusting for blood. The urge to make her suffer.

The sins of our fathers.

'It's bedtime, Beck,' says Kai, his fingers closing around mine. 'What do you say we lock all the doors and windows . . . just to be safe?'

♦ ♦ ♦

I'm standing on the threshold of Kai's bedroom, aware of his presence behind me, herding me forward. My eyes are drawn to the bedside table. 'Wh— where's my phone?'

His breath is on the back of my neck. 'You don't need a phone.' I feel five firm points, his fingertips, around my spine. 'Go on.'

As I shuffle towards the bed, he hurries me with his fingers and I almost stumble on to the mattress, clutching at the sheets. I cross to the far side and half sit, half lie there, stiff and afraid, like a child bride.

'You not taking the gown off?' he asks, unbuttoning his jeans.

I clutch at the cord, knotted tightly around my waist. 'I might get . . . cold.'

'Suit yourself.' Pitching his clothes into a corner, Kai squirrels his big bunch of keys under his pillow and slides beneath the covers. The bed frame moans under his weight. 'Course, if you need warming up, there's one very effective method for that.'

I swallow, two, three times, forcing back panic. I fake a shrug. 'Maybe in the morning? I'm tired.'

His eyes narrow, glinting in the semi-darkness. 'Aye. In the morning.'

I press my head against the pillow, reluctant to move under the sheets. I don't want any part of him touching me.

'Sleep tight,' he says, closing his eyes.

'Yeah. Night.'

After a minute or two, his breathing turns steady and slow, and I stare wide-eyed at the ceiling, watching the restless shadows of trees as they spasm back and forth in their uneasy, nocturnal dance.

I'll wait.

I'll just wait, for however long I need to, and when he falls asleep, I'll run. I'll find a way out. He may be stronger than me, but I'll have a head start and I'll run, and I won't stop until I lose him.

If that wrecks my life, so be it.

'I'm an insomniac, by the way,' says Kai, and my skin tightens, arms rigid at my side. 'I mean, back when we shared a bedroom, I barely slept at all. I just used to lie there, listening to you.'

Everybody sleeps, I think, desperately. *He has to go eventually, and when he does—*

'And even when I do sleep,' he continues, shifting under the duvet, 'boy, is it light. I wake at the smallest sound. The smallest . . . wee . . . sound.'

I keep my eyes fixed on the ceiling, on the dancing tree shadows, and it feels like they're speeding up, becoming frenzied. Madly they swing, matching my heartbeat. Wind keens through the branches.

'You sleep well, now, Beck,' says Kai, patting the sheets beside him.

Quite how long I lie awake for, I can't be sure.

I'm aware of time passing, but I don't have my phone and there's no visible clock in the room. All I know is that the house is dark, and the streets are silent.

Kai's breathing is calm and smooth – tranquil, even – and as I turn towards him I feel a faint but focused anger warming inside me.

Not much of an insomniac, are you?

This could be my chance.

Soundlessly, I reach out an arm to steady myself and rise from the mattress like a slowly lifting drawbridge. But before I'm even upright, Kai's hand shoots out and grabs a fistful of dressing gown, stopping me dead.

'We'll have ourselves a wonderful time,' he says, dozily, pleasantly, and I rotate my head to stare wide-eyed at him, my flesh crawling, his grip tightening on my skin.

His eyes are closed, and the corners of his mouth are curled into a placid smile. 'She's dancing in the sun,' he says, flatly, and lets out a fey little laugh. 'Showing herself to the men.'

Is he talking in his sleep?

'We'll have ourselves a wonderful time,' he says again, and I lie back down, next to him, shackled in his iron grip, eyes filling with cold, emotionless tears.

I can't escape him.

I can't escape this house.

34.

Eyes open.

My muscles seize with terror as I find his face, looming and pale, hovering above mine.

Don't hurt me. Please don't hurt me.

But as my brain wakes up, I realise I am lying on my side, facing him, and my shoulders relax. His eyes are closed, his breathing low and throaty. It seems we both drifted off.

Beneath the duvet, my bladder is achingly full. I look past Kai, towards the open bedroom door. The toilet's only on the other side of the wall.

Millimetres at a time, I slide my legs along the mattress, shooting glances at his face and trying not to tug on the bedcovers. But he doesn't move. His face is as lifeless as a waxwork.

Touching my soles to the cool floorboards, I rise off the bed and pad around it, scanning for my phone as I go. I'm not sure what time it is, but maybe someone in this town will be awake? Leanne, Nadia. The police. I recce the bedside table, the shelving units, squinting in the bluish dark. Kai must have hidden both our phones last night when I was downstairs in the alcove – he clearly suspected I was on to him, even then – but where?

It's dark down here, Beckett.

My gaze falls to the bed. Or rather, the floor beneath it.

I was there, all those years ago . . . I was right there, underneath you . . .

Keeping my eyes on Kai until the very last second, I lower myself on bent knees, hands splayed on the floor, then crouch on all fours and lift a chilly flap of duvet. It's dim and musty under the bed, but I can just about make out a pair of slippers, some balled-up socks and a dusty tennis racket. And stowed a little further back in the murky black, a lidless shoebox.

Chest thumping, I stretch an arm under the bed, breath held. When my fingertips nudge cardboard, I feel for the lip of the box, raise it off the ground and pull it out, careful not to rattle the weighty objects inside.

A thrill charges through me.

My phone is lying, switched off, next to Kai's Samsung, among a random collection of keepsakes. As I lift it out, my gaze is drawn to a ball of lacy blue cotton, nestled in the corner of the box. Is that my . . . underwear?

My scrabbling fingers, tearing my knickers off, casting them to the kitchen floor.

His hands, pulling my body across the table.

He must have pocketed them last night, before we came upstairs, and stashed them in here.

And there's more.

A torn, empty sugar sachet from the Seafront Cafe. The whisky glass I was drinking from on Sunday night, unwashed. A dry, browning lime wedge, teeth marks in the flesh.

Suddenly, the very touch of the underwear turns my stomach, and I drop it like a dead thing, back into the box. He's been *collecting* me, ever since I came home. Gathering souvenirs.

'Urngh,' burbles Kai, shifting on the bed, and a needle of ice shoots through me. Warily, I loom up in the darkness to peek over the nobbled ridges of his toes.

He's still sleeping.

Remembering the throbbing pain in my bladder, feeling almost woozy with it, I stow the shoebox under the bed and pluck my clothes from the back of Kai's chair. Clutching my phone, I creep from the room.

Don't think about the shoebox.

Don't think about him.

Will you tuck me in tight, Mumma?

As I lift my palm to push open the bathroom door, I pause. This is a Victorian house and the wood is old, so I have to take this slowly, deliberately. The slightest noise could wake him.

The door barely creaks when I open it, but as I elbow it closed behind me, it lets out a curving squawk like a coffin lid in a horror film, and I freeze on the spot, eyes wide with dread.

No sound from the bedroom.

I give it ten seconds.

Crossing to the toilet, I drop a thick layer of tissue on the surface of the water and let the pee out strategically, gingerly, my whole body sighing with relief. I power up my phone and rest it on the toilet tank, and while a shred of signal kicks in, I discard Kai's gown and throw on my clothes, pulling at zips and threading buttons. The time is 6.15 a.m.

Leanne, 2.28 a.m.

I know you don't want me contacting you, but I'm so confused. What did you mean by drawings??? I didn't do those drawings.

Leanne, 3.08 a.m.

I should never have stolen your diary. I feel awful. I just want to be your friend, Beckett. Please forgive me.

Leanne, 3.47 a.m.

Please.

My heart pulses with guilt. She must be going out of her mind.

I jerk my head upwards, deer-like, at a shuffling sound behind me. Was that in the walls – the rustling of a pipe? Or could it have been him, waking up?

I don't have a second to waste, now. I may have a phone, but the adjoining wall is too thin to risk making a call, especially on threadbare reception. If I try to leave the room, that door may creak loud enough to wake the living dead – and this time, I might not be so lucky.

I think about the fat bunch of keys wedged underneath Kai's pillow. Yesterday, when he led me around the house, ceremonially locking the front and back doors and any window big enough for a person to squeeze through, he only covered the ground floor. I guess he didn't think I was crazy enough to climb out of a first-floor window. Crossing the bathroom, I peer through the grubby glass, throat shrinking at the view. How far down is that? Six, seven metres?

But then I notice the greenhouse, jutting out from the rear of the building. Its roof, slightly pitched, almost halves the distance from the bathroom window to the ground. If I could hang out of the window and lower my feet on to the metal trusses between the panes, I could crouch there, catch my balance, and spider my way down.

I glance over my shoulder at the closed bathroom door. It's now or never.

Lifting the window, I drop one leg out, straddling the frame, and frost seeps into my jeans. I duck low, manoeuvring my upper body through the hole, until only my right leg remains inside.

Don't look down, now.

I look down. *FUCK.*

Sunrise is over an hour away, and it's dark out here, but I can see enough to imagine the mess if I get this part wrong.

Lifting my right leg through the window, I manage to half kneel on the ledge while stretching down, at an angle, towards the greenhouse roof. A vertical plastic gutter and some jutting pipes provide makeshift foot and handholds, and after ten or fifteen nervy seconds, I manage to toe the very edge of the greenhouse, one hand still clinging to the ledge above.

I test the metalwork, nudging it with my foot. It feels sturdy, but that doesn't mean it'll take my weight. The large glass panes are green and filthy, diseased with mould, and hairline cracks fork across them like varicose veins.

There's no going back, though.

I'm too deep into this.

One, two, three.

I let go of the window ledge, and his cold fingers seize my wrist.

35.

I look up, heart hurling itself against my ribcage, to find Kai's silhouette in the window. As his grip tightens around my arm, twisting and beginning to burn, I make a decision.

This is the last time you will ever touch me.

I tug, with all the strength I have left, and the force of it takes him by surprise, rocking his body forward and propelling his forehead into the window frame with a loud crack. He lets go, collapses, and I free fall into the greenhouse roof.

The next sound I hear is like splintering ice.

Blackout.

◆ ◆ ◆

The world is a deep, speckled grey. I am groaning, softly.

Where am I?

My eyes are closed as I grope left and right, fingertips brushing against cold slabs – sandstone, perhaps? – that suggest I'm outside. But my back is bent, uncomfortably, over something curved and soft, something other than stone, that seems to have cushioned my landing.

My *landing*. Did I fall?

At the prick of broken glass, I snap both hands to my sides and my eyes pop open, everything swimming back to me.

I fell through the glass. Through the greenhouse, on to the floor.

Kai was upstairs. I knocked him out, against the window . . . maybe? Or did he spring up again, seconds later? He could be thumping down the stairs to find me, at this very moment, blood boiling with anger.

I have to move. I have to get out of here.

Gritting my teeth, I lift the upper half of my body, swallowing a guttural cry of pain. I look down and my eyes bulge. There's a shaft of glass quivering in my torso.

'*Fuck*,' I exclaim, in a lacerated whisper, fingers trembling around the long, glistening shard protruding from my stomach. I stare at it in stupefied disbelief. It must have dropped down after I fell through the roof, the tip sticking in me like a javelin. But, curiously, now that I'm actually looking at it, I feel no pain, as if my nervous system is shielding me from it. As if the actual pain would be too much for me to bear.

I suck in a tight breath, steadying myself on the floor. I don't think it's gone too deep. I can pull it out.

Eyes darting around, I spot a large, cabbage-green leaf lying nearby and scoop it up, wrapping it around the shard to protect my hand. Then, still listening for footsteps inside the house, I close my grip around the glass, squeeze my eyes shut, and pull.

A primal, inhuman noise erupts from my throat, flooding the air, tears wetting my cheeks. I cast aside the scarlet-tipped shard and it clatters against the stone.

The wound is bleeding, but not profusely. I don't think it's going to kill me.

But *he might*.

With a squashed yelp, I roll off the pillow-like object that broke my fall – a grow bag, as it turns out – and, resting on all fours, race to catch my breath. Blood speckles the paving slab beneath me and I press a hand to the gash, wondering whether any vital organs have been punctured.

I whip my head up. Was that a creaking on the staircase?

I have to run *now*.

◆ ◆ ◆

The sleeping backstreets are purple-blue in the pre-dawn gloom, barely a window alight as I fly along the pavement, exposed feet picking up wet dirt and grit, palm turning sticky against my stomach. The terraced houses of Heaviport's far east end are a castle of darkness around me, half the buildings derelict, front doors spattered with graffiti. I pick up my pace.

I need to get to town, across the railway bridge, to safety. Someone will be awake on the other side, surely. People leaving their houses for work, de-icing their cars on the driveway. It can't just be me out here, in the frost.

I lift my phone – that sliver of signal has vanished – and my head spins, fast and then suddenly slow, like someone turning a tombola. I picture broken glass, sharp and glinting, the weeping wound in my belly. I'm feeling faint. My arms and legs are weightless.

Which direction am I heading in?

Is this even the way to the bridge?

◆ ◆ ◆

The road is steep now, steeper than it should be. I've lost my grasp on time, but I must have been going for a while because Kai's housing estate is long gone and my run has wilted into a lurch, knees threatening to buckle at any moment. My gut is a barbed knot of pain.

I search about in the low light, straining to make out my surroundings. How am I not at the bridge yet? And why is the air getting colder?

Slowing down, I lean on my knees, wheezing hard, and familiar shapes form around me. A fence post, a stile. Tattered hedgerows and a black expanse of fields, stretching into the distance.

I press a hand to my mouth. I've come the wrong way.

The railway bridge is back down the hill, a good ten minutes from here. *Of course it is.* I must have hurried along a random back lane, somehow, up a bridlepath, dragged off course by my muddled, dehydrated brain. I try to swallow but my throat is parched, and I feel weakness creeping over me. I know I'm losing blood.

I could turn back towards the bridge, but what if I make another wrong turn? What if I collapse from exhaustion, or pass out entirely? I can't let him find me like that. I can't let him find me at all.

Gazing across the empty fields, I think of the abandoned lighthouse, standing alone on its wind-lashed precipice, and Leanne's words float into my mind.

This was our secret den, when we were kids.

I can hear her voice, dreamy and close, inside my head.

If you climb to the top of the lighthouse, to the old control room, there's a hatch you can lock from the top, so no one can get to you. That was our hideaway.

There's a faint sound on the road behind me, and my spine locks. Footsteps.

Without looking back, I reach for the stile, clamber over the splintered steps and drop on to the grass on the other side. The storm has churned up the soil like a toddler playing with mashed potato, and as I struggle across the field, frigid clods of earth jab at my tender soles. I allow myself a backward glance. The light's too poor to make out anything beyond the hedgerows, but if those footsteps were his, he'll be gaining ground.

I push on up the hill.

As the field begins to level out, I pull my gummy hand away from the patch on my shirt and draw in a hissing breath. Fresh blood on my fingers. Without stopping, I slide my phone from my pocket and check the signal: a single, winking bar. I try the emergency services, then Leanne, but the calls drop before they can latch on. With one shivering hand, I tap out a series of typo-ridden texts.

leanne,,. its becktt, im in tourble. kais going tohurt me
im at ther old ligthouse..' pleqse come
i have tgo run. call police. come to thelightoiuse

Seeing her name on the screen brings the threat of tears to my eyes, but I urge them away. There's no guarantee she'll see these messages any time soon. She may not even be awake.

I have to find better reception.

Glancing up, I spot the domed tip of the lighthouse, peeking out over the horizon, and a surge of energy powers through me. What I need is altitude.

When I reach the flat, open plain beyond the hill, the wind rushes towards me like an old friend. Ahead of me is the English Channel, brooding and sleek, and to my right is the lighthouse, a cracked, looming tower against the sky.

Willing myself to move faster, despite the pain, I begin to jog and then run towards the building, glancing left and right as I go. Something feels different about this place – subtly wrong, like when you walk past a house you used to live in and someone else's car is on the drive – but there's no time to dwell on it so I shelve the thought, pressing on towards the lighthouse. At the open doorway, I lean my good hand on the rotted jamb, snatching a moment of rest, then pass over the threshold into the gloom.

I crane my neck upwards. A beautiful, decaying spiral staircase winds its way through the building from top to bottom, twisting into infinity like the swirls of a giant seashell. As I make for the bottom step, a buried memory bobs to the surface: dashing in here with Leanne, laughing breathlessly, school bags bouncing on our backs.

Race you to the top . . .

Slow down, Beckett! Wait for me . . .

I climb, steadily but urgently, sometimes taking two steps at a time, always with a protective hand pressed to my wound. The soft, rhythmic padding of my feet bounces off the tapering lighthouse walls as I ascend, and the higher I rise, the louder and more ill-tempered the wind becomes, hissing in tight loops around the building.

Eventually, feeling bobble-headed with fatigue, I reach the perforated metal platform at the top of the staircase and a hacking cough barks out of me. I lean against the railing, gulping down breaths, and against my better judgement, peer over the edge. My head swims at the dizzying drop beneath my feet.

That would be a very long way to fall.

Backing away from the railing, I turn to find a short ladder set against the wall, leading to an open hatch. I'm only moments from our hideaway, now. I have to get up there before I black out.

'Beck!' comes a resounding voice from the ground floor, and I feel my insides pucker.

Those footsteps on the road – they were his.

36.

'Beck, what the . . . what the fuck . . .'

Kai's voice vaults upwards from below, his distinctive Islander lilt pinging off the walls. For a beat, I tense up, stricken by the recollection of his fingers around my wrist, the flash of his wide, staring eyes through the hole in the alcove door. But then I remember why I came here, why I climbed all those stairs, and my muscles spring back into action.

Careful not to send any clanging footsteps back down the building, I stumble to the ladder and scale up it, emerging through the open hatch into a small, circular room full of dials and switches, vertical cables bundled on the walls like columns of spaghetti. An open door leads to the outer balcony, and beside it, another ladder leads up to, presumably, the lantern room, but I'm already as high as I need to go.

'Don't run away now,' calls Kai, from below, his breathing strained, a threatening jollity in his voice. It sounds like he's already a third of the way up. 'Fuck, these . . . fuckin' . . . *stairs.*'

As I stand, legs apart, above the hatch, I can hear him speeding up, cursing to himself, and it sends a skitter of insect legs up my spine.

No one can get to you, whispers Leanne, in my head.

I kneel on the sheet metal floor, wincing at the grinding sensation in my stomach, and cautiously lower the heavy steel hatch, holding its protruding handle with both hands until it clicks into place. Once it's closed, I slide the thick barrel bolt into its casing and give the hatch a quick, quiet tug, just to be sure.

Resting for a few seconds on hands and knees, I glare down at the locked hatch, a crooked smile tickling my mouth.

Try sledgehammering through that, asshole.

It sounds like Kai's calling to me again, but his words are muffled now, cocooned in their own echoes. Heaving myself to my feet, I cross to the open door and emerge into the freezing air, grasping for the balcony railing as the immense altitude hits me like a shot of cold vodka. From this height, the sheer volume of sea and sky is giddying, impossible to take in, and with the dawn drawing ever closer, the famous red cliffs are gilded in a brittle, steely light. It's a sight so arresting that I temporarily forget why I'm here, goggling at the view as if I've just arrived at the climax of the Heaviport lighthouse tour.

Checking myself, I reach into my pocket for my phone. Full bars appear, and in a rush of buzzes and pings, the phone delivers six missed calls from Leanne. She must be sick with worry, but I have to raise the alarm first.

Nine-nine-nine. I can't believe I'm dialling it again.

'Emergency, which service do you require?'

'Police, please.'

'I'm connecting you now.'

I glance over my shoulder, chewing my bottom lip. How long before he makes it to the hatch? Minutes, even seconds.

I did lock it properly, didn't I?

'This is the police. What's your emergency?'

Which one do you want to hear first?

'I, uh . . . I'm being chased. By a . . . stalker . . .'

Some typing. In the background, I can hear faint conversations, other emergencies. Other lives.

'What's your location?'

I let out a clipped, inappropriate laugh. 'This is going to sound odd, but—'

Clank.

The words stall in my mouth. That noise was metallic. He's at the hatch.

'Hello? Madam?'

The operator's voice turns tinny and distant as I lower the phone from my ear and gaze in horror at the hatch jumping, jiggering, as if being electrocuted from underneath.

'Beck. Beck, it's me.'

'Madam, can you hear me?'

I'm frozen on the spot, eyes bulging at the spasmodic jolting of the small metal trapdoor. I should reply, but I can't risk Kai hearing my voice. The voice in my phone grows more urgent.

'Hello? What's your location?'

'Open up, Beck. I know you're there.'

I steal back into the control room. Blood pounds in my ears as I approach the hatch, staring intently at the locked bolt, sitting in its neat, sturdy casing.

Kai laughs, but it sounds forced. 'That's more exercise than I've had all year, you know . . . Jeez. I thought I was gonna have a heart attack. Come on down, now, Beck. Come on now.'

I'm standing a few centimetres from the hatch, one hand clutching my phone, the other bunched into a trembling fist. Kai slams again, with both palms, and the bolt rattles in its keep.

What I hear next can only be described as a growl.

'Fuckin' . . . *hell*, Beck. *Come on.*' Another two-handed slam. 'Leanne told me about this place, you know. Said you came here all the time when you were wee, to hide away.' A spluttered cough, a catching of breath. 'So I know you're there, and I'll get in eventually. You may as well open up.'

If he saw me on the way up the hill, then he knows where I'm hiding. But if heading for the cliffs and climbing the lighthouse was just a lucky guess, then despite what he says, he can't be certain that I'm here.

Not certain.

Which would mean it's simply a matter of who breaks first.

'You know what you are, Beck? Eh?' His voice is a tremulous, ragged whisper, pressed up against the metal. 'You're a dumb . . . fuckin' . . . whore. Y'hear that? A rancid whore.'

I close my eyes and take a steady, silent breath.

He can't break through solid steel.

'I promise I won't hurt you,' says Kai, his tone suddenly as gentle as warm milk. 'I'll never hurt you, Beck. I love you. I love you so fuckin' much. Please . . . pl—'

His words turn woolly and broken, and he begins to make a high-pitched mewling sound, like a distressed dog.

Is he . . . crying?

'Please. *Please*, talk to me . . .' The hatch starts to tremble, slowly, like he's giving it weak little nudges. 'Open up, Beck. Come on. If you don't, I'll—' the hatch rattles harder '—if you don't, I'll go back out there, and I'll . . . I'll throw myself off the cliff. Don't think I won't. Please . . . open up . . .'

The movements intensify, the hatch clattering violently, and soon he's thumping it again, shrieking in mangled, primeval rage.

'GET THE FUCK DOWN HERE YOU DUMB CUNT OR I WILL TEAR OUT YOUR FUCKIN' THROAT, YOU HEARTLESS BITCH, I WILL KILL YOU AND THROW YOU IN THE SEA, YOU PIECE OF SHIT.'

The clanging stops, and Kai's breathing sounds tattered as he struggles to fill his lungs. I realise I am huddled against the wall of the control room, tears brimming in my eyes.

That's not the man I met in the pub on a quiet Friday night. The singer-songwriter with the heartrending voice; the man who drank whisky with me and listened as I spilled my secrets, and laid myself bare. The man I fell for. That's his father talking.

I hear footsteps. Kai is retreating, descending the ladder and dropping to the metal platform, making his way down the building.

He's really leaving.

Drifting out on to the balcony, I crouch down beside the iron railings and check my phone. The screen is blank – I must have lost the call when I walked inside – so I redial, passing through the emergency preamble with a robotic calm, like an actor rehearsing a too-familiar scene.

'A *stalker*, did you say?'

I'm staring through a gap in the railings. A crescent of ice-yellow sun is peeking its head over the horizon. 'Yeah . . . sort of. He's . . . he's dangerous. I think he's losing his mind.'

'What's your location? Are you somewhere safe?'

'I'm at the disused lighthouse . . . the one at the end of Shotts Lane, across the field. I'm on the balcony, but I've . . . I've bolted the hatch. I'm safe.'

Some typing. 'Do you know the man stalking you?'

I thought I did.

'We're . . . friends, I guess. H-he wanted to hurt me, but he can't get to me, so . . . I don't know . . .'

I brave a downwards glance and my head reels with a sickening vertigo, vision contracting then expanding like the aperture of a camera. But I force myself not to look away, because any second now, Kai is going to emerge from the lighthouse door, his small form scampering over the grass.

'Stay where you are, Miss Ryan. We're sending officers now.'

'Just hurry, OK? I think he's going to do something crazy. I think—'

A prickling wave of realisation washes over me.

The operator clears her throat. 'Miss Ryan?'

My nerve endings are alive, exposed wires under my skin. 'Yes?'

'Is everything OK?'

'Everything's . . . fine,' I say, blankly. 'I'm safe. Just come quick.'

'They'll be with you very soon, Miss Ryan. I'm going to hang up now, is that all right?'

'All right. Goodbye.'

Letting my phone fall to the wet floor, I lean forward, heartbeat juddering, and survey the miniature scene laid out far below me. When I arrived here, I felt that something was wrong. Something intangible. But up here on the balcony, I have perspective, and I can see what's changed.

The inclining metal sign that once warned of landslides has fallen flat, probably in Monday night's gales, and is lying face down in the wet grass. If you were coming here for the first time, as Kai might be, you would have no idea of the danger.

But that's not the real change.

When I bumped into the baroness at the Seafront Cafe yesterday morning, she mentioned that the storm had caused multiple landslides, all up and down the coast. And as I trace an eye along the precipice, I'm struck by the outline of the cliff edge. Where it used to be convex – as it was when Leanne and I first met here, and when I scattered my parents' ashes – it is now concave, a vast, serrated chunk of grass and dirt gone missing, as if a lumbering giant has risen, dripping, from the sea, and taken a bite from the rock face.

This almost certainly happened within the last thirty-six hours.

The ground could still be loose, just like Nadia warned. *One of these days, a young kid, or a local drunk, or just someone who isn't in their right mind will walk past that sign and the ground will give way, and they'll be tossed into the sea . . .*

My heart is gripped, abruptly, as if by an actual fist, and I rise above the railing, my face immediately battered by the buffeting wind. It's at that moment that Kai finally materialises at the base of the lighthouse, tearing across the grass like a mouse scurrying from its hole, heading for the cliffside.

'Kai!' My voice is so weak, so thin and reedy against the wind, that I can barely hear it myself. 'Kai! Stop!'

A gust whips along the balcony and wheels around me, almost knocking me off my feet, and I seize the railings with both hands, blinking wildly. *'Kaiii!'*

It's no good. I'm too high, too far away from him, and the elements are drowning me out. My voice is exhausted from stress and lack of sleep, and my feeble calls evaporate on the air.

Kai draws closer to the precipice, stumbling a little, almost tripping. When he reaches the edge, he stops, gazing out to sea, the wind batting his hair left, right, back and forth.

I shake my head, retreating to the wall. I can't watch this.

But then he swivels, spotting me on the balcony. He animates, shouting uselessly like a lost child in a fairground, and I wave him away from the edge, but he doesn't budge. He just yells up at me, fists balled, arms rod straight at his side. I can't make out his words, so my imagination does the work for me, his voice suddenly inside my head – as if I'm standing right there on the cliff edge and he's whispering in my ear.

I'm going to jump, Beck. I'm going to die, horribly, and it's your fault.

My body will smash against the rocks and be pulled apart by the sea, and it's all because of you.

Goodbye, Beck. Good luck sleeping in the dark.

And that's when the ground gives way beneath him.

It's a short, sharp, downward shunt, like one of those drop-tower rides at a theme park where they tease you once or twice, before the big plummet. The patch of earth that Kai is standing on falls by half a metre or so and then stops, almost as if settling, and he spins, panic-stricken, on the spot. Back bent, hands clasped on his head.

Even from up here, I can read that body language.

He was never going to jump.

He was so desperate, so frantic, that he thought threatening to commit suicide was the only way to force me to open that hatch, but it didn't work. And now it's too late.

A low rumble sounds in the earth, fissures forming along the ground beneath him. As his fragile platform begins to disintegrate, I rotate away, unable to bear it, fixing my eyes on the lighthouse wall. There's a deep, horrifying crack, and I drop to my knees.

I hear him calling my name.

And then . . . nothing.

I shake my head, over and over, hands pressed to the rough, peeling paintwork. I'm too frightened to look over the balcony, to face the yawning hole on the cliff edge. *This can't be happening. This can't be real.*

At my feet, my phone rings.

'Beckett?' says Leanne, when I finally pick up. 'Oh, gosh, Beckett. Is that you? Are you OK?'

I inspect myself, my blood-stained fingers and mud-caked clothes, as if seeing it all for the first time. The wound in my stomach has dried up. 'I . . . I'm OK.'

'Thank God, I was so scared. Where's Kai? Did he hurt you?'

I will tear out your fuckin' throat, you heartless bitch.

'He's gone, he . . . fell. From the cliff. He's gone.'

She doesn't say anything, for several seconds. I hear her swallow against the mouthpiece. 'Are you safe? Where are you?'

'In the lighthouse.'

'I'm coming to get you. I'm on the road, by the stile, I'll be there any minute. Just don't move.'

But I have to move. I have to go down there, and see that he's gone with my own eyes.

I hang up the call.

Back through the control room, with its levers and buttons, and on to my knees at the hatch. Unlock the bolt, scramble down the ladder. Round and round the spiral staircase, flinching with every step at the pain in my belly, then on to solid ground and out into the cool, fresh air. The pinkish glow of the rising sun. Across the grass and towards the cliff edge, but not too hasty, not too close. It could still come apart at any moment. One wrong move and I would join him down there, gasping for air as the riptide pulls me under.

At what feels like a safe distance, I peer over the precipice. I can't see the coastline from here, but there are clumps of dirt and sod bobbing about on the waves, like shipwreck survivors, and the water is cloudy and brown from crumbling mud. The sea lurches every which way, as if angry with itself, belching gasps of dirty foam into the air. No person could survive down there, no matter how strong a swimmer.

He must be drowned by now.

Backing away, trying not to think about how cold the water must be, I realise my own hands are turning numb and bury them in my pockets. My fingers connect with something metallic and chunky, and when I pull it out I find my father's belt buckle, the Heaviport anchor, lying in my palm.

'Beckett!'

Spinning around, I see Leanne struggling over the brow of the hill, waving at me. She's short of breath, her face warped with anguish, and as she draws closer, the sight churns me up inside. I never allowed myself to trust her, not properly. I don't let myself trust anybody.

I don't think I know how to.

Before I can swallow it down, emotion erupts through me and I begin to sob, inconsolably. My chest heaves with grief and sadness as I picture a different life, one I didn't get to live – where Kai never stole into my room, never became my imaginary friend, never drove my father to violence. Would I be a better person, if none of this had happened? Would Leanne and I have built a lasting friendship, something actually meaningful, rooting me to my home town? Would my family have stayed together?

Leanne's eyes widen at my obvious distress, and as she breaks into a run, I turn back to the water, retract my arm as far as it will go and, with a wounded cry, catapult the buckle into the sky, watching as it clears the cliff edge and disappears from view.

. . . We thought if we shouted things loud enough, the wind would steal them away and throw them in the sea, and they'd be gone forever . . .

I feel arms curling around me from behind, Leanne's arms, and her comforting voice in my ear. 'It's OK, Beckett. I've got you. I promise, I've got you. Everything's going to be all right.'

As the sound of sirens rises in the distance, I collapse in her embrace and we concertina into a tangled ball on the ground. Tears scything down my face, I hold her tight, as tight as I can, while somewhere out in the ocean, my father's anchor sinks to the sea bed.

DECEMBER

37.

On the walk back to Waldorf Rise, I take the Portobello Road, even though it's not really on the way, so I can be lost in a sea of people.

Christmas is in full swing on Portobello. Feet jostle for space among the market stalls, a busker belts out Mariah Carey, merchants mull giant vats of wine. The coffee houses are steamed up and packed with fashionable twenty-somethings, swiping idly at their phones.

I catch myself in a shop window, and my reflection glares back at me.

After all that time in Heaviport, a town I had barely lived in for over twenty years, I had to return to my real home, the place I know best, to feel anything close to anonymous.

I dump my suitcase on the sofa and flop down next to it, glancing around the living room at the paraphernalia of my former life. A framed poster of Terry Pratchett's *Reaper Man*, signed by the author. An abstract painting that I bought in New York, on a whim, for a ludicrous amount of money. My dusty awards on the bookshelf, facing each other in a semi-circle, like embarrassed teenagers.

In my gloved hand, I'm clutching a fat pile of unopened post. The letter on top, stamped 'Past Due', will be another angry warning about my mortgage arrears, a final demand for payment. For the first time in months, I know how I'm going to settle it.

In the kitchen, I sip an espresso and reach across the table towards the heap of envelopes. A twinge of pain flares in my abdomen and I finger my T-shirt, probing the rough landscape of the bandage underneath.

I wonder if I'll have a scar there.

After the police rescued me from the cliff edge, I spent a couple of days in hospital, in Exeter. It wasn't an especially serious injury, but it had festered, unattended, for nearly two hours, collecting sweat and dirt and grit, and the doctors wanted to be sure I was in no danger of infection. Back in Heaviport, they searched for a body, sending out dinghies and specialist divers, but he wasn't found. I shouldn't think he ever will be, unless, by some unlikely twist of fate, he washes up on a shore somewhere to be sniffed out by a curious spaniel.

It's unnerving, having no physical proof of his death, but the police told me that nobody could survive a fall from that height. Not with water so wild, or rocks so lethal. By now, he's probably in pieces on the sea bed, having been gnawed to shreds by hungry mouths.

With a shudder, I take a gulp of coffee and gaze down at the mess of post on the table. It's bills, mostly. Bills that, only a few weeks ago, I would have ignored, shoved in a drawer. But with the proceeds from the sale of Charnel House finally cleared in my bank account, I can actually start paying my debts. Credit cards, mortgage, the lot.

Picking one up, I'm about to pop the seal when my eye is caught by something odd, semi-obscured in the pile.

A postcard.

I frown at the peculiar photograph on the front: a taxidermied fox, standing upright and wearing a top hat and monocle. Flipping the card over, I find a single sentence written on the back.

Give me a ring, you ninny. Howard x

I laugh to myself. I suppose this is one way of cajoling me into returning his calls, and I can hardly blame him. He tried me several times while I was in hospital, and I didn't even text him back.

I've been in a strange place.

Standing up, I dial his number and wander across the room, stopping at the window to peer down on the street below. A supermarket delivery van is struggling to reverse into a tight space.

'Beckett Ryan! I'll be damned.'

'Hello, Howard.'

'Where have you been? Are you roasting me?'

I smile down the phone. 'It's "ghosting", How.'

'I've been calling all week, you know. A man might worry he's not wanted.'

'Simmer down, it's nothing like that.' I pull in a breath. 'I was in hospital.'

He goes quiet. A motorbike passes outside. 'Oh . . . oh, my dear. You should've said. Nothing serious?'

I press my fingertips to the glass, debating whether to start this now. The window is cool to the touch. 'No . . . nothing serious. But, hey, I received your monocled fox in the post. Ten points for creepiness. What can I do for you?'

He clears his throat, scratchily, then leaves an uncharacteristically long pause.

'Howard?'

'Don't hate me.'

'What?'

'Just . . . don't hate me.'

My brow pinches. 'You'll have to tell me what you've done first.'

A muffled, nervous laugh. The creak of his office chair. 'I, uh . . . I had lunch with one of my favourite editors last week. Maggie . . . Whitstable, at Shepherd.' He's stumbling on his words, which is unlike him. I drift back to the kitchen table. 'Just a catch-up really. We gassed about the merger, the new office *et cetera*, and then she asked about you.'

I lower myself, slowly, into a chair. 'OK . . .'

'She's always loved your writing, Maggie. Frankly mystified that you fell off the publishing map, as we all are, and . . . well, long to short . . . I know I wasn't supposed to, but I mentioned your new project.'

I stiffen. 'Howa—'

'It wasn't a pitch, honest to God. But her ears pricked up and I told her more, and she requested a sample, and one thing led to another . . .'

I tilt my head. I told him to keep this between us.

Not for public consumption.

'What are you saying?'

'She was bowled over by it. Said it was raw and immediate, unlike any memoir she's ever read. And she loves the angle, too.'

'The *what*?'

'Oh, you know: "former best-selling author, struggling with inner demons, sets aside the, uh, the fantasy worlds that made her a superstar to confront the very real abuse in her own past". Or words to that effect.'

A short, throttled sound escapes my throat.

'Sounds crude, I know,' continues Howard, 'but then these things always do.' He coughs a few times. 'Headline is, they'd like to make you an offer. To publish next year. I wrestled with it for days, because I know it's not what you'd planned, and if I've overstepp—'

'You had no right to do this.'

The line goes quiet. My fingers tighten around the phone.

He mumbles a reply. 'I, um . . . no . . . of course.'

'This isn't a *book*, Howard. I made that clear from the start.' I push the chair back with a loud scrape and pace the kitchen. 'It's not supposed to be out there, in Sainsbury's, like some lurid exposé. It's not *for* anyone else.'

Even as I'm saying it, I can't be certain that it's true. I feel as if the person I'm trying to convince isn't Howard, it's me.

'The thing is, my dear, I'm worried about you. The money troubles you mentioned on the phone, and you've been sounding so . . . so down. They'll be offering a hefty advance—'

'This isn't *about* money, can't you see that? I trusted you to keep it private.' He mutters something to himself, a whispered reproach, and I feel bad for snapping at him. But I can't stop myself. 'For Christ's sake, they're building a children's home down there. Did you know that? They're building it in our old house – in his house – because, as it turns out, my father was a hero to those people, and I don't think they'd appreciate the scoop. Unless, what, you're suggesting we call the council and ask them to hammer up a blue plaque by the front door that says "come one, come all, Harold Ryan adored young people, shame he used to beat the crap out of them"?'

'I had no idea. I'm sorry.'

'I just . . . I can't have this conversation right now. I have to go.'

'Beckett, pl—'

I hang up, blood singing, cheeks hot. Heart thrashing in my chest.

Minutes go by. I try Zadie twice, but she doesn't pick up. I lock my phone and chuck it on the sofa.

Glaring out of the flat, across the road, I find myself watching the small crowd of drinkers in my local pub, sipping pints and chatting. The windows are pleasantly steamed, orange lamps aglow. They know me in there. They don't know who I *actually* am, of course, but they serve me cheap house red and keep the fire burning and don't ask any questions.

I throw on my coat.

◆ ◆ ◆

When I lumber back through my front door several hours later, I'm not drunk, exactly, but I'm far from sober. I've had three conversations about government corruption, played a game of poker with a woman claiming to be Sinatra's ex-lover and lost forty-five minutes petting a Border collie while trying not to think about the publication, or otherwise, of my so-called 'memoir'. About how it would detonate like a grenade inside the lives of several thousand strangers.

Former best-selling author, struggling with inner demons, sets aside the fantasy worlds that made her a superstar to confront the very real abuse in her own past.

Crude, said Howard. And it *would* be crude, wouldn't it? To advertise my grief like that. To spill my family's secrets, upset an entire town, and for what? Some misguided quest for closure?

Huffing, I nudge the door shut with an elbow and set about unfastening my coat, swaying slightly against the wall. As I free the final button, my eye is caught by a flash of white on the floor: a lone envelope, lying on the mat. I must have dropped it on my way down the hallway this afternoon.

I sink to my haunches and pick it up. The address is handwritten, the penmanship neat and elegant. Breaking the seal, I pull out a sheet of plush cream notepaper and the letterhead stops my heart.

A trio of anchors.

ANCHORA PARK
Heaviport

Beckett,

My builders spotted the enclosed while clearing out the master bedroom at Charnel House. Thought it only right to pass it on.

Have a lovely Christmas,

Nadia

I picture my parents' dark, miserable room with its empty bed and coiling shadows. The faces that once peered out from inside it. I agreed with Nadia that she should keep everything in the building that could be useful for the children's home – furniture, toys, white goods – and then dispose of the rest. But I don't envy those builders, rifling through it all. Disturbing the swamp of my family's past.

Tabling Nadia's note, I return to her envelope and find a second one inside, also stamped and addressed to me. My spine turns to ice. The handwriting is my mother's.

I don't think she ever sent me letters, even when they packed me off to boarding school. In fact, if it wasn't for the occasional birthday card, I'd barely know her writing at all.

I open it, neck hairs bristling. As the paper unfolds, I catch the faintest trace of her perfume.

10th November 2023

Dearest Beckett,

This might seem strange, me writing to you. I know it's not something I've done before, but I have meant to, for some years.

I've been looking through old photo albums this week. Harold stored that sort of thing in the loft and I haven't seen them, many of them, since you left. There's one here of us all in the garden with that lovely friend of yours, Leanne. Shame, her parents were dreadful, and she didn't get much of a start in life, but I know your friendship meant the world to her.

The photograph. The one I found on her dresser, the morning after the fire. My intuition was right. She must have spent her final few days reminiscing, combing picture albums, trying to make sense of where things had gone wrong for us.

Anyhow, the picture reminded me that we <u>were</u> a family once, in our own way. And I suppose a part of me hopes that, with your father gone, you might find it in your heart to come home, one day. I would so love to see you.

Dementia takes the person you knew away, and while that was horrible, I have to admit that on some level it was a relief. The man who resented me was gone, replaced by a confused child, and I became a parent again. I know I was a poor mother to you, Beckett, but I tried. I think I was kinder this time round. I cared for him as best I could.

This afternoon, I donated what's left of our savings to a local domestic abuse charity. I know a great deal of that money was really yours, but I'm sure you won't mind. You're doing so well with your books, and the solicitor tells me that Harold made provision for you in his will, with the sale of the house. The charity were overcome with gratitude, of course, but the truth is, I had to do something with all this guilt, this shame for not speaking up over the years. For letting him do that to you.

Of all my mistakes, that was the worst. I knew that Harold was hurting you and I should have done something about it, but I couldn't, because he hit me too, sometimes, and I was petrified. But I will never forgive myself for staying silent. I couldn't protect you from him, and that weighs on me every day.

A small, involuntary sound falls from my mouth.

Of course she knew.

She knew but was powerless to stop it, just like Sam Hastings and his little sister. And she'd lived in Heaviport long enough to understand that, if it was Harry Ryan's word against hers, she would lose.

I picture my mother, years back, standing at the sink as I eat my dinner. The smell of toast, rumble of the washing machine. Her silhouette against the window.

Silence was her only option. She didn't have an agent, a publisher, the promise of a lucrative book deal. She only had me – this sad, angry little stranger with a head full of nightmares – and a husband who hated us both. All drifting about in that desolate house.

These days, I just feel tired. I don't expect I will see you again, and that's not your fault. I need to accept that you probably won't be coming back to Heaviport unless it's to bury me, and maybe not even then.

I'm lonely, but I'll get through. Folks from town come to visit, now and then, and there's a nice young Scottish man who's been extra helpful this year. His name is Kai—

Something rises inside me: a shock of heat, a jagged stitch in my belly. My grip tightens.

His name is Kai. He's a friend, I suppose – I met him at a town meeting. Such a sweet boy. Anyway, he pops over to help with chores and the like, and often we'll have a glass of wine together before he goes home. Sometimes he stays over, in your bedroom. I've told him your old bed must be rather small for a grown man, but he doesn't seem to mind.

I'm blinking, stunned, at the letter. The person who made my childhood bed, who left it looking so pretty and dainty for my arrival on that cold day in November . . . it was him.

Acid curdles in my gut.

*I really must go to bed now. Kai just left, and the wine has
me feeling very sleepy. I love you, my sweet girl. I'm sorry I
never told you that enough.*

I check the date at the top of the letter: 10th November. The
night she died.

A sick horror rushes my blood.

The wine has me feeling very sleepy.

Even now, when Kai's body is rotting somewhere in the English
Channel, nearly two hundred miles away, he has found a way to
hurt me. A way to tell me *Listen, Beck – I'm still in your head, here,
I'm still inside you, I've slept in your bed and poisoned your mother and
there's absolutely nothing you can do about it.*

The room tilts on its axis.

'Oh, God. Oh . . . Christ . . .'

Suddenly, something Kai said last week, in the hallway of his
house, crystallises in my head. He told me that he knew I would
come home, one day, because eventually, *everybody does.* I'd assumed
he was just rambling, mouthing off, but he wasn't. He knew I'd
come home because he had murdered my mother, and soon there
would be business to attend to, affairs to settle, and I was the next
of kin. He set the trap, and I walked right into it.

I think about being backed up against that wall, half naked,
as his fingers climbed my inner thigh and he purred, seductively,
in my ear.

You've got no one now, Beck.

I feel light-headed. Could I have stopped this, somehow? If I'd
booked that train one week earlier, would she still be alive?

I'm the closest thing you have to family.

There was always a part of me that thought it unlike my
mother, jarringly out of character, to take her own life. She was too

refined for that, too stiff-upper-lip. But I ignored the instinct and now it's too late, because you can't charge a corpse with a crime; you can't punish the dead. I can only punish myself.

Casting the letter aside, I rise from the table and make for the cupboard, for the cheap, nasty gin that I know is in there, hidden behind the spaghetti jar.

But then I think about the razor-sharp edge of Sam Hastings' cider bottle in the Wreckers Arms. About the sweet tang of the rum I drank, the night I started a fight with the boiler, convinced I could hear laughing, somewhere in that empty house. Hallucinating my younger self after too much Malbec, throwing tequila down my throat at Kai's place. The glass of wine that killed my mother.

This has to be the end of it. I can't keep drinking myself to sleep.

Leaning on the table with both hands, I stare down at the letter, picturing my mother's despairing face.

I love you, my sweet girl. I'm sorry I never told you that enough.

Salt tears sting my eyes. I'm sorry too, Mumma.

JANUARY

38.

Unless I have a heavy suitcase, I always walk to Paddington station. It's only about twenty minutes on foot from Notting Hill, and if you take the back roads, the streets are clean, peaceful and tree-lined.

I have excess energy to burn, too. Sober since December, I'm sleeping through the night now, waking up clear-headed and craving exercise, and the walking gives me purpose. It helps me to think.

Five weeks have passed since I read my mother's letter. In the hours immediately afterwards, I sat completely still in the dark, wine buzzing in my veins, the memory of her words looming above me like shadows on the ceiling.

I will never forgive myself for staying silent.

I should have done something about it.

As time went on, it became harder and harder to ignore the truth – that telling my story isn't really about me. It's about my mother, about Paige and Sam Hastings, and a small, forgotten town that chose a comforting lie over an ugly truth. I don't love the idea of my deepest secrets being shared with the world, but if that's what it takes to bring this to an end, so be it. I might be the only person left who can hold my father to account for what he did.

Eventually, I called Howard back and apologised for flying off the handle. He grovelled some more, promised to stop hawking my work around without telling me and then took me for crispy duck in Chinatown, where we talked about the old days and sang Noël Coward songs in a rickshaw. Afterwards, I holed myself up in my flat for a week, sifting over my work, drafting new passages, coming to terms with the idea of one day allowing strangers to read it. Then I made some calls, held my breath, and by that weekend, Shepherd Publishing had bought *Sleeping In The Dark*, my tell-all childhood memoir (I've grown accustomed to calling it that, now).

The news broke and I found myself back in the publishing press for the first time in years, hearing from people I had almost forgotten existed. I got invites to parties, launches, bookshop openings; I even went to some of them, made small talk and drank endless lime and sodas. These days, I'm spending my time ploughing through the manuscript, sculpting it from a muddled stream of consciousness into an actual, readable book, and Maggie has turned out to be my dream editor. She's tough and vivacious, whip-smart, and always speaks her mind. It's not an easy book to write, of course, but neither should it be. I'm going to dedicate it to my mother.

Before I inked my name on the contract, I called Nadia. I told her everything – about Kai, Leanne, my father – and I promised I wouldn't publish the book, I wouldn't go public with the truth, unless she signed off on it. And I meant it.

'Today is a good day,' she said to me, one icy morning last month, on the first of my return trips to Heaviport. We were standing on the driveway at Charnel House, wearing hard hats and hi-vis jackets, watching a crew of brawny workmen dismantling the charred remains of my father's study. 'I always love the beginning of a new project. The sense of anticipation.'

'We'll make an MBE of you yet,' I replied, and she laughed, knowingly, as a pair of builders lobbed a filing cabinet into a skip. 'I can't believe how fast it's all moving.'

'Well, I don't hang around, as you know. But I went back and forth over the idea, for a while. The news about your father was . . . unexpected, and I wasn't sure how people would respond.' She glanced at the house. 'We had it all out at the town meeting, though. We needed that, as a community.'

I thought of the meeting I had attended the month before. The way people had stared at me from behind their tea cups, the brittle tension in the air. How quickly it had descended into a pile-on.

'I was half expecting to find a burning effigy of me in the station car park this morning.'

Nadia raised a finger, that singular habit of hers that reminded you she was a lawyer, and smiled. 'Actually, you'd be surprised.' Her smile flattened. 'There was dissent, at first, of course. People don't like having their core beliefs challenged, and this idea of Harold as . . . well . . . some kind of monster, it upset people. One woman even suggested you were making it up, to cover your back. But Juliet, from the cafe, she stood up and fought your corner. She's taken a shine to you, clearly, and she's even brought her husband round, which is no mean feat. She and Joseph know a thing or two about small-town hostility, but they're very influential in Heaviport now, and their endorsement made a real diff—'

'Watch your backs!' The bark of a nearby workman was followed by the shrill reversing signal of a flatbed truck, stacked high with scaffolding poles, as it made its juddering way along the drive. Nadia and I back-pedalled to the front lawn.

'What was I saying?' she asked, as we watched the driver manoeuvring over the gravel, his colleague plodding alongside him.

'About Juliet.'

'Ah, yes. I was heartened by the response, actually. By how many people spoke up, after her, to support you. Perhaps they'd backed you all along, but been too intimidated by the mob to say so.'

The truck driver shut off his engine and jumped down from the cab. As his rigger boots crunched on the stones, he looked in our direction and gave Nadia a nod.

'Is there anyone in this town you don't know?' I asked, amused.

'I don't believe there is.' She laughed at herself. 'Anyhow, by the end of that meeting, I'd decided that the home *should* go ahead, as planned. If a town like Heaviport can turn itself around like that, after the way they'd treated you only a month earlier, it goes to show how powerful community change can be. And if Harold Ryan is no longer fit to be a symbol of hope for this place, then perhaps his house can be one instead.'

We both turned to look at the building, at its gaping, charcoal war wound, scorched innards and the network of burns twisting up the brickwork like black vines. Charnel House had always been a miserable place for me, a locus of terror and sadness, but on this clear, frosty morning, as it stood proud and indestructible against the icy-clean sky, I could imagine, for the first time, seeing it differently.

'I have a suggestion,' I said, gazing into my old bedroom window.

Nadia cleared her throat. 'Go on.'

'Have you found anyone to run the home yet? On a day-to-day basis, I mean.'

She raised her eyebrows, then shook her head.

'I was wondering if you might consider Leanne.'

Her mouth opened slightly.

'She doesn't really have any experience,' I continued, with a frown, 'and she has no idea I'm asking you this, but . . . I think she deserves a break.'

There was the clink of metal behind us, and the sound of two men sharing a joke. Nadia crossed her arms. 'Where's she working at the moment?'

'Not sure, some office in town. She may not even want the job, for all I know, but I have a feeling she'd be good at it.'

Nadia nodded, pensively. 'I can't make any promises—'

'No, no. Of course.'

'But I'll give it some thought.' She adjusted her hard hat. 'You're a good friend to her, you know.'

'I'm trying to be.'

A group of men stomped by us, carrying scaffolding poles towards the house. As they passed the front door, I noticed two gulls perched side by side on the portico, fussing with their wings. One nuzzled the other with its beak.

'I think I owe you an apology,' I said, folding my arms.

Nadia creased her brow. 'What on earth for?'

'I know how important the home is to you, and my book . . . it put you in a tricky position. I honestly didn't plan—'

'Beckett.' She shook her head, eyes fixed on mine. 'If anyone should be apologising here, it's me. Your return to Heaviport was supposed to be a long weekend, nothing more, and since I strong-armed you into staying, you've been physically threatened, fled a possible arson attack – still unsolved, to our shame – and, well . . . all the horrors with Kai Cunningham. I can't help but feel partly responsible.'

I raised a peaked hand to my forehead, shielding my eyes against the sun. 'Call it even?'

She smiled, extending an open palm. 'Even.'

We shook hands. She gestured around the side of the house. 'Shall we head round the back? I want to show you where we're building the tennis court . . .'

◆ ◆ ◆

'*The train now arriving at platform ten is the 12.34 Great Western Service from Exeter St David's . . .*'

Crossing the Paddington concourse, I dodge through the crowds, breath steaming in front of me, as the train hisses in. I stop at the ticket barriers, a tremor of anticipation in my belly.

The doors open and Leanne emerges from one of the middle coaches, struggling with the handle of her suitcase. The momentum of the herd sweeps her along, her innocent, doe-eyed expression oddly striking in the sea of blank faces.

'Leanne!' I call, raising an arm, as she slows for the ticket queue. Her gaze meets mine and she gives me a nervous smile, fishing for her ticket.

On the other side, we hug, awkwardly.

'Hey.'

'Hi.'

Two men in suits whip between us. I drop my hands into my pockets. 'So how was—'

'Thanks f— sorry. You go.'

'No, you go.'

She looks around, blinking at the size of the station. 'It was nice of you to meet me. I've never taken the Tube before.'

'Oh, you're in for a treat,' I say, scratching an eyebrow. 'London on your doorstep.'

She glances past me. 'Is . . . are we near the Hard Rock Cafe?'

'Sorry?'

'The Hard Rock Cafe. I've always wanted to go.'

I bite back a smile. 'I think that can be arranged.' Commandeering her suitcase, I tip my head at the escalators. 'Let's get your stuff back to the flat, then make a plan. But for tonight, I have something a bit . . . different in mind.'

Shepherd Publishing is housed on the top floor of a shiny modern office building, all glass and chrome, on the banks of the Thames. The reception area is spacious and pristine, dotted with exotic-looking plants.

'You must be Beckett,' says the receptionist, with a bright smile, as we approach the front desk.

'Apparently so.' I unbutton my coat while he taps away at his keyboard. 'I have a plus one: Leanne Wilding?'

'Course. She's on the list.'

I turn on my heel. Leanne is craning her neck to gaze up into the open-plan tower, at the huge windows and multiple lift shafts, the colourful bookshelves lining each floor.

'Here you go. Enjoy.'

The receptionist passes me the lanyards and I hand one to Leanne. She stares at it as if it were a backstage pass to a Beyoncé concert.

'Gosh . . . will there be celebrities?'

I give her a wry smile. 'You've never been to a book party, have you?'

She shakes her head.

'No celebs, I'm afraid. But if you're into awkward conversation and warm white wine, you'll have the time of your life.'

As the lift climbs, soundless, through the building, Leanne fingers the corner of her laminate, a faint frown on her brow. 'So this whole party is just for you?'

'Sort of. Maggie says she wants to "welcome me back into publishing", but really it's just an excuse to eat vol-au-vents and gossip about writers.'

She glances at her reflection in the mirrored walls. 'Will people expect me to know about books? What if I sound stupid?'

'You're not stupid, Leanne. We've been over this.'

Her frown deepens. 'I've been thinking about Kai again.'

'Leanne—'

'I was with him for a whole year, and I had no idea. I should've known. I should've broken it off—'

'I missed it too, remember?' I say, a hand on her shoulder. 'We all did. But he's gone now. Just try and enjoy yourself tonight, OK?'

She nods, pawing at her hair.

The lift slows to a stop.

As we walk through the double doors into the Shepherd offices, there's a hubbub of smiles and greetings and a subtle movement of people in our direction. The room is laid out like every publishing social I've ever attended: the improvised drinks table in one corner, mini buffet in another; the clutches of smart-casual employees, standing in broken circles, nodding politely at each other. Down one side of the room, floor-to-ceiling windows showcase a panoramic view of the river, the water choppy in the blustery gloom.

'Beckett, hi!'

Maggie is leading the charge towards us, small and green-eyed with her crop of bouncing blonde ringlets. She is flanked by four keen-looking juniors.

'Thank you so much for coming,' she says, giving me a quick squeeze. She smiles at Leanne. 'I'm Maggie, Beckett's editor.'

Leanne offers a timid hand, and they shake.

'Leanne's from Heaviport,' I explain, to nods from the juniors. 'We were close when we were kids, so she's been helping me . . . reconnect.'

Maggie leans back, her face opening. 'Leanne, of course. Can I get you both a drink?'

'Done and done,' comes a grandfatherly voice from behind Maggie, and Howard weaves into the circle, grinning, holding a

314

triangle of champagne flutes. Zadie strolls in beside him, dressed in a purple trouser suit.

'Aha, fizz,' exclaims Maggie, her eyes sparkling. 'Well played, How.' She touches my arm. 'Beckett, love, we'll catch up in a mo. Come and see us when you've had a chance to grab some food.'

She drifts away in the direction of the buffet, juniors trailing her like ducklings. Howard gives Zadie a sideways nod. 'This one's a troublemaker. I've only been here fifteen minutes and she's already got me squiffy.'

'Publishing parties are just so genteel,' replies Zadie, conspiratorially. 'At a law bash, we'd be on the vodka luge by now.'

She pulls me in for a hug and I inhale her familiar scent, grapefruit and orange blossom. As we disentangle, she looks me in the eye, speaks under her breath. 'You good, kid?'

Zadie knows that tonight is a big deal for me. A book event, in my name; the kind of evening I once took entirely for granted. I had no idea how lucky I was, back then.

'I'm good,' I reply, and we share a smile.

She turns to Leanne. 'Hi, I'm Zadie. Friend of Beckett's.'

'I'm . . . Leanne, friend of Beckett's,' parrots Leanne, cautiously, and Zadie throws me a secret look. I eyeball her to behave.

A prim silence settles.

'So how's about a toast?' suggests Howard, passing Leanne a glass. He floats one in my direction but I hold up a hand.

'I'm dry tonight.'

'Good Lord. Still?'

I pump out a laugh. 'You don't think I can stick to this, do you?'

He gives Leanne a jovial shrug. 'Stranger things have happened, I suppose. They found a whale in the Thames once.' Tabling the unwanted flute, Howard swipes an orange juice from a nearby waiter and gifts it to me. 'To *Sleeping In The Dark*, the memoir of the moment.'

We all touch glasses.

'So,' says Howard, sipping his drink, 'you're the famous Leanne.'

Leanne knits her brow. 'Famous?'

'Well, in a manner of speaking. From the memoir.'

Her eyes pop, like a startled animal's. 'I'm in the book?'

I glare at Howard, then turn to Leanne. 'I was going to run it by you, I promise.'

'The, uh, buffet looks good, don't you think?' stammers Howard, pulling an *oops* face. I shake my head at him. 'Shall we get some food, Zadie? They have these tiny little pork dumplings . . .'

When they're gone, I discard my orange juice and press my hands together, as if in prayer. Leanne watches me, patiently.

'Listen . . . Leanne. The book. I wa—'

'You don't have to apologise.'

'No, I'm . . . ah, Christ.' I massage my temples. 'I was going to run it by you this weekend, honest. And there's nothing bad in there, but I can take it ou—'

'It's fine,' insists Leanne, almost laughing. 'Really.'

I tug a hand through my hair. 'You're not upset?'

She lowers her glass. 'I'm not sure if you know this, but having you as a friend again, it's kind of . . . changed my life. So if I'm in your book, I'm happy to be there.'

I let out a breath. 'You're sure?'

'Of course.' She glances at her drink, cheeks pinked. 'Besides, I think I owe you one.'

I cock my head. 'What on earth for?'

'My new job. At the children's home.'

I think of the baroness, in her hi-vis jacket and hard hat, that chilly morning back in December. I had no idea whether she'd even consider the suggestion, let alone see it through.

A smile lifts my cheeks. 'The management job? That's amazing news.'

'I know it was you who got me the interview.'

I puff air through my lips. 'Well . . . in a way. But, still – congratulations.' I pick up my orange juice. 'I'd say that deserves a second toast.'

She points at my glass. 'You're really not drinking?'

'I know, it's a drag. But I've been so well behaved.'

A familiar peal of laughter breaks out across the room – Zade, of course – and my eyes flit to the abandoned champagne flute, standing on a nearby table. My throat tingles. 'Although . . . I suppose *one* wouldn't hurt . . .'

Reaching over, I pick it up and peer into the golden-yellow liquid.

Leanne lifts her glass. 'To new beginnings.'

We clink.

'New beginnings.' I take a draw on the bubbles and feel instantly soothed. I nod at the buffet. 'What do you say we go eat our body weight in dumplings?'

◆　◆　◆

I'm laughing – a gleeful, childish laugh – as I struggle to skewer the keyhole outside my flat. After a few attempts, Leanne leans into me from behind. 'Let me try . . .'

I twist my neck to look over my shoulder. 'Hey! Hey. Thanks, Leanne.' She curls her hand around mine and we slide the key into the slot. 'Nailed it.'

Inside, we clump up the communal stairs, Leanne behind me, pressing an occasional palm to my back. Whether that's to steady herself or me, I can't be sure.

'S'nice having you to stay,' I'm saying to her, the words treacly in my mouth, as we reach the small landing at the top of the staircase. We're pressed together in the cramped space, hot breath mingling. 'I mean, you're good at keys, and you love the Hard Rock Cafe, and . . .' I squish my eyes half closed, trying to focus. 'I might be a bit tipsy here, but I want you to know something.' I point at her chest, accidentally poking her boob. 'You . . . you . . . are a true friend.'

She smiles back, but I can barely make it out. She's blotting like a watercolour painting.

'I'm quite tiddly too,' she says, with a giggle. 'Your book people drink *so much*.'

'S'cos we're creatives,' I say, lifting my tinkling bunch of keys. I fiddle for the right one. 'Bloody keys again.'

Once we're inside the hallway, I drop sideways against the wall, a dizziness washing over me. I can feel moisture on my brow.

'We should get some water,' suggests Leanne, a fuzzy shape in my periphery. I nod, but it's an effort to even lift my head. Apparently, going sober for a month seriously lowers your tolerance.

'I've . . . have some in the bedrooms,' I announce, flapping a hand in the direction of the spare room, as if she might have forgotten where it was in the last five hours. I think about moving, but nausea ripples in my gut, like a lazy tentacle. I close my eyes. 'Think it's . . . bedtime.'

Behind my lids, the darkness throbs.

'Whoa . . .' I stumble, almost falling, as the floor seems to tilt beneath me. Reaching out, I grab the nearest object, a table lamp, knocking the shade askew.

'You OK?' asks Leanne, her voice distant and echo-ringed, like she's at the bottom of a well.

'Oh, yeah. Jus' out of practice.' I jab a finger in the air. 'Off to bed with you.'

She touches my shoulder. 'You call if you need me, though. All right?'

I give her a wonky thumbs-up. 'Night, night.'

Her hand slips off me and she drifts from view, her shape shrinking away down the hall. I push words from my mouth.

'Sleep . . . well . . .'

Using the wall to keep myself upright, I stagger to my bedroom and lurch through the doorway, dropping like a startled toddler on to the bed. I sit there for several minutes, barely moving, and then, with a suddenness that shocks me, my stomach hitches and I retch, clamping a hand to my mouth.

What is happening to me?

I don't get sick from drinking. I never have, not even as a teenager.

Perched straight-backed on the edge of the mattress, I squint through the open door, trying to focus on the soft orange light from the hallway lamp. The shade is still pitched at an angle from where I snatched at it, giving the impression of a stranger in a jaunty hat. I'm motionless on the bed, but in my mind, it feels like I'm floating closer to the lamp with every second, as if I'm a camera zooming in, and in, until I'm pressed right up against the light bulb.

Kai's voice is in my head.

We sell Charnel House and your London flat and you move in here, with me. Then we get hitched and make beautiful babies together and live a normal life, a perfect life . . .

These past few weeks, I'd pushed my memories of that night to the back of my mind. The blur of lust and tequila, the rush to feel his body on mine. It never happened, I told myself.

But it *did* happen. We slept together, and afterwards, I never once thought about protection, or the morning-after pill, because why would I? He was threatening to kill me. Safe sex was the last thing on my mind.

I look down, fingers cradling my aching belly, and panic slices through me. *My period's late.* I've been so focused on the book that I lost track of time; I hadn't even noticed I'd missed it.

I've been late before, of course. It shouldn't be a big deal.

Except this time, it feels different.

Desperately, I clatter through my bedside drawer, scrabbling for the spare test from last summer's pregnancy scare. Plucking it from the mess of balled receipts and tangled earphones, I stagger to the loo, sweat sheening my forehead.

Three minutes later, I'm back on the bed, eyes glued to the tiny screen.

A knotted lump rises in my throat.

'Leanne . . .' My voice is cracked, and barely travels. I try to raise a shout. 'Leanne!'

After a pause, I hear the pattering of socked feet down the hallway. She pokes her head through the door. 'Everything OK?'

I gaze up at her, feeling like a scared child who just called for her mother in the night. She reads the look on my face and her eyes seem to double in size. 'What's the matter?' she asks, ducking into the room and sitting next to me. I point to the test and her mouth blooms open. 'Oh my goodness, Beckett!' She takes a gulp of air. 'Is it Kai's?'

'It . . . has to be, yeah. S'been no one else.'

My eyes dance along the walls, head a jumbled mess. My speech is still slurred and my brain is running slowly, stutteringly. None of this seems real.

Leanne lays her hands on mine. 'This was meant to be.'

'Huh?'

She wraps my fingers in hers and I notice, for the first time, how dainty they are. Like a child's fingers.

'All of this, you going back to Heaviport, meeting Kai, sharing a bed with him, and making a baby . . . it was all *meant to be.*'

Eerily, she begins to smile, a big, toothy grin stretching wide across her face, like bunting being hung between her ears.

She tightens her grip on me. 'And I made it happen.'

39.

LEANNE

Beckett looks at me, her face frozen. She seems scared. 'Leanne, please. I'm feeling . . . weird, and sick, and . . . you're not making any sense.'

I squeeze my eyes shut. I have to remember – she doesn't know what went on before she came back to Heaviport. She doesn't know any of it.

I wasn't going to tell her on this trip. I was going to wait a while, until we were as close as close can be, so I could be certain of her trust. But now there's a baby on the way, and that changes everything. She's all alone up here, she needs a friend by her side, and Zadie's no good for that. *Zadie* is too busy partying and wearing purple suits and being a hot-shot lawyer, but I can give Beckett everything she needs. I can move here and live in her flat and help look after the baby, and she needs to know that.

She needs to know what I did for her.

'It's OK, Beckett,' I say, opening my eyes again. 'I'll explain. There's so much you don't know, but I'll explain. I promise.'

She's hugging her belly with one arm, and I picture the tiny foetus in there, floating around in its gloop. Swollen head, like an alien.

'It all started last summer, when your dad took a bad turn.'

Beckett sits up straight, very suddenly, her face all tight. My chest swells with pride. I'm the storyteller again. I love being the storyteller.

'One night, your mum came to speak at a town meeting. She told us all that Harold's dementia was getting worse, and he might not be himself if we saw him around town. We might not see him around at all, for much longer.' I think of the local people, sitting in the town hall. Their stupid, glum faces, lined up in rows. 'Everyone felt sad for her, and for your dad. Some people cried. But I didn't, because I knew the truth.'

She frowns at me, and I frown right back. This bit makes me angry.

'I knew that he used to hit you. I knew before anyone else, because I read about it in your diary . . . and why should he be allowed to forget what he did, when you have to carry it around with you everywhere? It's not fair. So I didn't feel sorry for him at all. He deserved to get sick.'

Beckett swivels round on the bed. 'I need . . . water . . .'

She reaches for a glass on the bedside table and gulps it dry. All of it, in one go.

'After your mum spoke, there was tea and chocolate biscuits, and I ended up talking to Kai. We'd never met before because he went to Mothdale Primary, and he was kind of a loner at secondary school . . . but I'd seen him around town. So when he told me he'd read all your books, I let him in on my secret. That I wasn't there to see Diane . . . I was there to see you.' Beckett puts her head in her hands. A strange groan comes out of her. 'Of course, I knew you wouldn't be there. You'd never come home for a town meeting in your life. But I'd *hoped*, so hard. I'd hoped and hoped that maybe, this time, it would be different.

'After that, me and Kai, we started hanging out every day. We turned into boyfriend and girlfriend, sort of by accident, because we were together all the time. It was like a book club, you know? Except we didn't just talk about your books. We talked about how we were going to track you down.'

'N-no, no, no . . .' Beckett's drunken voice is muffled by her hands. 'No, please . . .'

'You were very, very difficult to find, weren't you? You didn't do any events, or social media, and we were getting impatient, so we realised, if we wanted to see you, we'd have to bring you home.'

She drops her hands from her face. She's turned white. 'What?'

I feel myself smiling again. This is the best part.

'Leanne, you're scaring m—'

'Deciding to kill Harold was easy.'

Beckett lets out a whimper. This will be difficult for her to hear, but she needs to know. Everything I did, I did for her.

'Your father was evil, and he had it coming. But actually *doing* it, that was risky. We had to be smart and secret and sneaky. Luckily, the police in Heaviport are useless – my mum's been stealing from the same four shops for years and she's never even been cautioned – so I told Kai that as long as he was very, very careful, he could get away with it.'

Beckett starts to breathe fast, like she's having a panic attack. She'll be all right, though, once the shock wears off. 'S'can't be true. I won't . . . you're lying to me.'

I grab her arm, hard, and squeeze it. 'I would never lie to you, Beckett Ryan. Do you understand?'

She tries to pull away, but I won't let go.

I won't ever let go.

'Kai became friends with your mum, which didn't take long, because he was very charming . . . even you have to admit that. He started helping her with shopping, and jobs around the house, and looking after Harold after the carers went home. I stayed away, obviously, because she'd have recognised me and that would've ruined everything. And besides, if it all went wrong, I couldn't afford to end up in prison, could I? Because I need to be around, for as long as I can. For you.'

Beckett tries to get up, off the bed, but her legs don't work. Tears grow in her eyes. 'Stop. I can't take it . . .'

'Your dad was getting very weak. Diane was exhausted from caring for him, so Kai used to send her to bed early, to get rested, and then he'd stay up with Harold in the dark, whispering in his ear. Telling him things, horrible things, to confuse him. Telling him he was a child-beater and he was going to hell, and the devil was going to peel him apart with his hot and thin fingers and wear his skin like a long, pretty dress, and dance about, and laugh and laugh and breathe his stinking devil's breath. And your dad got worse. Everyone said he was deteriorating, and he was. Kai was driving him mad, scaring him to death. Giving him what he deserved. And then, after weeks of it, he couldn't take it anymore, and he had a stroke. He was gone.'

Beckett's eyes are wet and shiny. She shakes her head at me. 'Stop talking. Please . . . stop talking . . .'

'Clever, wasn't it? Clever, clever.' I let go of her arm. This time, she doesn't try to leave. 'But it wasn't enough.'

'Please—'

'Harold dying wasn't going to bring you home, was it? You hated him for what he did, so why would you travel all that way just for his funeral? One parent wasn't enough.'

A horrible sound bursts out of Beckett's mouth. Tears tumble down her cheeks. 'Mumma . . .'

'She had to go too, just like every toxic person in your life. I had to make all of them go away.'

She's crying, now. Really crying. I'm dying to comfort her, to hold her close, and I will.

But, first, I'm finishing my story.

'Kai was the most toxic of all. He wanted you for himself, and I knew it from the start. You weren't supposed to fall for him; he was only meant to bring you home, not steal you away from me. So I got rid of him too.'

'You're *lying*,' she spits, through her sobs. 'There was a land-slide. I *saw* it.'

'When I got your messages, I ran to the cliffside and found him hanging off the edge, after the ground had fallen. He was bawling his eyes out, so pa*thetic*. He wanted me to save him, but why would I? He was in my way, always acting like he loved you more than I did, when I was there before him, years before. I loved you first.' I think of his white knuckles gripping the rock face, bones showing under the skin, and it makes me feel alive. 'So I stamped on his fingers. I stamped on them hard, hard hard *hard*, and off he went, into the sea.

'I was going to keep it a secret, at first. I wasn't sure you'd understand. But then I found out what he did to you, when we were little. That there really was someone hiding in your bedroom at night.'

That was when I realised Kai was the one who made the draw-ings in Beckett's diary. All this time, I thought she did them herself.

But it was him.

'I knew then that I'd done the right thing, and one day I would tell you about it. About how I'd saved you, how I killed the monster under the bed.' My voice starts to shake with excitement. 'How I killed *all the monsters.*'

Beckett's gone a strange colour. Milky green, like a bar of soap.

'And now, it's just us. You, me . . . and the baby.' I reach for her stomach, my heart surging with love. 'We can raise it together.'

'I feel sick.' She stands up, too fast, and her eyes roll back in her head. 'I think I'm going to f . . . faint . . .'

'It's OK, Beckett, it's just the wine, and the hormones. The baby is taking your blood. You're sharing your blood with the baby now.'

Her hands try to grip me, but she's too feeble. 'N . . . Lea— pl . . .'

'You need rest, OK? Sleep, now. I'll take care of you.' I guide her down, on to my lap, until she's lying on her side, arms sticking out. Wrists floppy. 'I'll never leave you, not like everyone else. I'm your best friend. I've always been your best friend.'

I bend over so I can see her beautiful, pale face, resting on my thigh. Her eyes finally close and her breathing slows down, and I watch her fade away into dreamland, running my fingers through her hair, like she's a doll.

My perfect, porcelain doll.

'Just go to sleep, Beckett Diane Ryan. I'll be watching you.'

ACKNOWLEDGEMENTS

Thanks go to my wife, Pip, who will find this book altogether too creepy and may wish to hide it in the freezer.

To my agent, Ed Wilson, for his tenacity, canine-themed trousers and nose for a negroni. To my editor, Kasim Mohammed, for championing this story from the get-go, and to the whole fantastic team at Amazon – Laura, Sadie, Jenni and everyone working behind the scenes. You're all a joy to work with and you've made me a better writer.

To my family, for your unwavering love and support (sorry for all the swearing, Mum . . . the characters made me do it).

To George, for saying 'I think you should write a novel' ('I think you should win the lottery' would be a helpful next suggestion, if you're asking). And to The Lightyears, because the story of my life would be very different without you boys.

To Justine and the gang at Byte The Book, for relentlessly championing writers.

To the late John Howlett, the first 'proper' novelist to read my work. Thanks for taking the time, John. You probably never knew how much your words of encouragement meant to me.

Finally, to Jerry Owens, Jane Watret, Maureen Lenehan and Professor David Punter. Great teachers rarely get enough thanks, and each one of you has been an inspiration.

ABOUT THE AUTHOR

Photo © 2019, Tim Easton

Kit Duffield writes chilling psychological thrillers with gripping plots and killer twists. Sitting somewhere between Gillian Flynn and Shirley Jackson, his stories are inspired by our fears, obsessions and the things we see in the dark.

Find out more at kitduffield.com. Follow Kit on Instagram at @kitduffield.

Follow the Author on Amazon

If you enjoyed this book, follow Kit Duffield on Amazon to be notified when the author releases a new book!

To do this, please follow these instructions:

Desktop:

1) Search for the author's name on Amazon or in the Amazon App.
2) Click on the author's name to arrive on their Amazon page.
3) Click the 'Follow' button.

Mobile and Tablet:

1) Search for the author's name on Amazon or in the Amazon App.
2) Click on one of the author's books.
3) Click on the author's name to arrive on their Amazon page.
4) Click the 'Follow' button.

Kindle eReader and Kindle App:

If you enjoyed this book on a Kindle eReader or in the Kindle App, you will find the author 'Follow' button after the last page.